To: Helm
I'd like to introduce
you to the Shepherds.
Have fun

Bud Fussell

Also from Second Wind Publishing
Novels by Bud Fussell

Scoundrel

www.secondwindpublishing.com

Shepherds

By

Bud Fussell

Cut Above Books
Published by Second Wind Publishing, LLC.
Kernersville

Cut Above Books
Second Wind Publishing, LLC
931-B South Main Street, Box 145
Kernersville, NC 27284

First Cut Above Books edition published March 2013.

Cut Above Books, Running Angel, and all production design are trademarks of Second Wind Publishing, used under license.

For information regarding bulk purchases of this book, digital purchase and special discounts, please contact the publisher at www.secondwindpublishing.com

Cover design by Tracy Beltran

Manufactured in the United States of America
ISBN 978-1-938101-38-0

CHAPTER ONE

As David turned through the big brick entrance to the headquarters of Shepherd Apparel Group, he glanced at Jesse. "Well Dad, today's a big day for us. Are you sure you're ready for it?"

"Yep, I'm ready. I've been grooming you for this most of your life, and I think now is the time. You're going to do great."

"This has been my dream for a long time, Dad. I'm not going to let you down."

"I know you won't. I have complete confidence in you."

"Well, here we are. Dad, do you want to meet in your office or mine?"

"Let's meet in yours."

"Okay. I'll tell Ruby to get everyone together. Let's say fifteen minutes. Is that okay?"

"Perfect"

David went in his office to get ready for the meeting he and Jesse were going to have with their key people, and Jesse walked down the hall to his office. He wanted to get a special something to take to the meeting.

When everyone was present, David told his secretary, Ruby, to hold all their calls, and to please close the door.

Jesse started the meeting. "Folks, you're probably wondering why we are having a meeting on Friday instead of our regular meeting day on Monday. Well, you will still have your regular staff meeting Monday, but today is a special day, and I didn't want to wait."

"I started this company nearly forty years ago, and after a really bleak beginning, we have managed, with God's help and blessings, to grow into a major force in the apparel industry. David hadn't been born when we started. He came along a few years later and as soon as he was old enough, he started working here. He did the usual floor-sweeping and things like that until I felt he was ready for a little more advanced job. I believe I'm right when I say he started by running a bar-tacker. He ran several different machines, worked in cutting and other departments until he went away to college. After graduation he came in full-time, and has been here ever since. Over the last fifteen years I have come to rely on his work ethic, knowledge, and judgment when it comes to making business decisions."

"David, stand up. Folks, the reason for this meeting is to tell you that I am announcing my retirement and turning the reins of the company over to David. He is now the new President and CEO of Shepherd Apparel."

The group applauded.

"Several years ago, on a trip to Ireland, I bought this shepherd's staff, and it has sort of become a symbol of our company. David, I'm presenting the staff to you, and hope you treasure it the way I have. Congratulations, son. I love you, and I'm very proud of you. Now, do you have anything you want to say to your people?"

"I sure do," and David began addressing the group. He was a fine specimen of a man. At 6'1", his blond hair emphasized his tan, handsome face. The broad shoulders and small waist made his store-bought clothes look as if they had been tailored especially for his 37 year old frame. "I have worked with all but a couple of you for several years now, and I don't recall ever having any problem with anyone, and don't expect any problems in the future. You're all key to the success of this company, and with what I envision Shepherd Apparel becoming, you are sure enough going to be keys."

"I have been doing a lot of research, as well as corresponding with a lot of people, and Dad doesn't even know this, but if things work out the way I hope, Shepherd Apparel will soon become an international company."

"I have been in frequent touch with a man in Munich, Germany, and I think Germany may be the first country we go into. This man--"

Ruby knocked and opened the door. "I'm sorry Mr. Shepherd, but there's a man on the phone that I think you need to speak with. I told him I wasn't supposed to interrupt you, but he said some disturbing things, and I believe you should take the call. You might want to take it on my phone."

David went to the outer office and picked up the phone. "Hello, this is David Shepherd."

On the other end, "Is this Donny Shepherd's old man?"

"Yes, I'm Don's dad. What can I do for you?"

"This is the only warning you're gonna get, Shepherd. You'd better get a handle on little Donny, or he's gonna wind up with a broken kneecap or worse."

"Who is this? What do you mean broken kneecap? What are you talking about?"

"Your boy is messing with something that he's not supposed to. He's taking money outa my pocket, and if you don't stop him, I will. Got that?"

"I got it, but I don't know what you're talking about. He's just a high school boy. What's he done to take money from you?"

"Being just a boy is why I'm giving you a heads up. Ever hear of numbers, Shepherd?"

"Yeah, I think so."

"Well, little Donny has been running numbers in my area and taking several hundred dollars a week outa my pocket. As I said, this is your only warning. If I catch him back on the street, remember, you were warned." Click. The caller hung up.

Upset over the call, David went back into his office and told the group something had come up, and he would fill them in on the international plans later. As they were filing out, he said, "Dad, can you wait a minute?"

He told Jesse about the call. "Do you know anything about numbers, Dad?"

"As a matter of fact I do. I used to bet a few dollars from time to time. You have to be real careful, though. Most of the time, the game is operated by organized crime, and those people don't mess around with you. Do you remember hearing about that guy over in North Chattanooga a couple years ago that got killed? You know, the guy that ran that bar-b-que place out on Dayton Boulevard. It was said that he was killed because he crossed the mob. I don't know, but I do know you don't fool around with those people. If Don is involved in running numbers in some way, you had better do what you have to do to get him out of it."

"What does a numbers runner do anyway?"

"A numbers game is like a daily lottery. One version works like this: you pick one of one-thousand three digit numbers, and pay your local numbers runner one dollar to enter your bet. Each day, one three digit number is chosen at random and pays off $600.00. Normally, the runner gets ten percent. It can mount up in a hurry, depending on where you do most of your collecting. I have heard of people playing a one dollar bet every day for years. The numbers racket is a well-entrenched illegal gambling operation in most large cities, and I'm a little surprised at one here in Chattanooga."

"It all makes sense to me now. I couldn't understand why Don quit playing sports. You know, Dad, he might could have gotten a scholarship to college in baseball, but he can't play ball and run numbers at the same time. I guess the quick cash meant more to him than a scholarship. I'm really disappointed in him."

"I'm going to call the school and have them dismiss him at lunchtime and tell him to come straight here. I want to get him before he has a chance to get back out on the street. Better yet, I think I'll go to school and pick him up."

David called the school and later, when he got there, Don was waiting on him. Don favored his dad in both facial features and height. His 16 year old physique hadn't filled out yet, so he looked slender. He was a good athlete, but failed to play sports because of his outside activities. His mom, Judith, died three years ago of ovarian cancer, and David had tried overly hard to be both a mom and dad.

"Hey Pop. What's up?"

"A lot is up Don. I'm going to wait 'til we get to the office to talk to you. I'll tell you this – I'm very upset right now."

Don didn't know what to think about that so he just sat silently until they reached Shepherd Apparel. When they arrived, they got out of the car and walked silently into the lobby. When he passed Ruby, he smiled and said "Hi Rube. How's it goin'?"

"I'm just fine Don. Thank you."

David went into the office first and sat down at his desk. "Close the door, Don and sit down."

"What's wrong, Pop? I don't like the way you are right now."

"I'm going to tell you what's wrong. How long have you been running numbers, Don?"

"Running what?"

"Don't give me that innocent look. You know exactly what I'm talking about. I got a call this morning; a very disturbing call."

"Who from, Pop?"

"He didn't give me his name, but he knows who you are, and gave me what he called my only warning. He said you were taking hundreds of dollars out of his pocket, and if he sees you back on the street, he will break your kneecaps or maybe worse. How long have you been doing this, son?"

"I first did it last summer between my sophomore and junior year. It didn't seem like it would hurt anything, and I could make some good money."

"Is that why you quit football and baseball?"

"Yes sir."

"You know you could have possibly been in line for a baseball scholarship."

"Yes sir."

"Well, was the money worth losing the scholarship?"

"I thought it was."

"Well, you're stupid, Don. Give me your car keys."

"Pop, please don't take my keys. I promise I'll be good. Please don't take 'em."

"I'm going to keep them until I'm satisfied you're not going back to the street. This should help teach you a lesson, and it might keep you from getting killed. That's my main concern. At this point, I'm not sure you're smart enough to figure that out. Hand me your keys."

"Okay. Here they are."

"Now, Don, I'm going to increase your hours in the cutting department. This will help keep you out of trouble, and give you some extra money at the same time. I don't know what you've been making running numbers. I'm sure it was more than spreading cloth, but at least this is an honest way to do it. You've got a future here, Son. Don't mess it up."

"Now promise me you won't run anymore numbers. It would kill me if you went out there and something happened to you."

"I promise, Pop."

"Here are your keys. When we leave this afternoon, we'll go by the school and pick up your car, but I want the keys back when we get home."

"Okay."

"C'mon, let's go out to the cutting department. I want to tell Bud Weddle about your increased hours, and have him set up a regular routine for you after school."

"You're serious about this, aren't you Pop?"

"You're right about that. I may just be saving your life for you."

After they had their meeting with Bud Weddle, David went back to the building that housed the offices, and walked down the hall to Jesse's office. "Are you feeling any regrets Dad?"

"None at all. I've been looking forward to this day for quite a while. Did you get things squared away with Don?"

"I hope so. When I told him about that guy threatening to break his kneecaps or even worse, I think he realized that a seventeen year old is no match for those people. You never know about Don, though. He's such a free spirit I'll have to keep a pretty tight leash on him. You can never tell what hairbrained scheme he might come up with."

"It sounds like you've got things pretty well under control. Now, maybe I can catch some fish. It's been hard living on the lake and not having time to get out and do some fishing. I'm even anxious for today to end so I can get started on my retirement."

"That's good, Dad. Since you won't be here after today, you won't mind if I take over your office, will you?"

"I figured you would. Most of my stuff is already out, so move in whenever you're ready."

"Thanks. Since today's Friday, I may just use the weekend to do it. I'll get Don to help me. I don't want to take away from work time to move. I'm anxious to get started with our international expansion."

"Sometime you're going to have to tell me what you're planning. It sounds interesting."

"I will, Dad. I think you'll be impressed, and if I'm right, it will make Shepherd Apparel a lot of money. Since I didn't get to finish explaining the plan to the key people today, I'll be doing it at the staff meeting Monday. Would you like to sit in?"

"I'll let you know. I may be too busy doing nothing."

CHAPTER TWO

Monday morning was a beautiful, crisp, fall day. David was later than usual getting to the office since he had to take Don to school, but he was excited to get started as the new CEO. He was anxious to talk to his key people at the staff meeting, and explain his ideas about going international with Shepherd Apparel.

"Ruby, have you seen or heard from my dad this morning?"

"No, I haven't."

"Well, I guess he meant what he said. He's probably too busy doing nothing to come in today. Bless his heart."

In a few minutes the staff began to arrive for the meeting, and when the last of them were there, they all went into the conference room and closed the door behind them. The Monday meetings have always been relaxed and informal. Even though David was in charge and at the head of the large conference table, he sat down while he talked.

"Good morning, gang. First, I want to apologize for the interruption at Friday's meeting, but it couldn't be helped. Now that I've gotten that out of the way, let's look at what's important today. When we finish dealing with the scheduling, cutting, sewing, and all the regular stuff, I want to finish explaining what I started Friday about going international."

The meeting lasted for about thirty minutes, and then the floor went to David. "Before I do anything else, I want to make an announcement. All of you were here Friday when Dad gave me his shepherd's staff. The staff was very important to Dad, and I was really touched by his passing it on to me. I decided over the weekend to use the staff as our new company logo. Starting immediately, as we enter new Shepherd Apparel orders into production, the staff will be embroidered on every garment that carries our brand. We will also change our letterhead and invoices to show the new logo."

"Now, as I started to tell you Friday, I've been corresponding with a man in Munich, Germany about the possibility of opening an office there. Here's how serious I am about it. I've invited this man here, and hopefully we can work out something."

"This is a young man who just about owns the Dirndl market in Germany and Austria. His name is Ulrich Steen, and he is a manufacturers representative covering not only the majority of Europe, but he is planning to go into the middle-eastern countries as well. He sells other types of clothing in addition to dirndls, and I think we will be very lucky if we can hook up with him. Everybody raise their hand if you know what a Dirndl is. Joe, are you the only one?"

"Listen and learn. The dirndl is a female dress consisting of a top and blouse, wide skirt, and a colorful apron. Originally the dirndl was the working dress of female servants. In the late 1800's Kaiser Franz Joseph made it fashionable. The upper classes adopted the dirndl as a modern dress and wore it on their summer holidays. Today the wearing of the dirndl is generally regarded as a sign of national pride; in material, color and shape it is increasingly subject to modern influences."

"Does anybody have any questions? Yes, Joe."

"If we hook up with this man, will we be manufacturing stuff in Europe?"

"No, I intend to produce everything we sell in the U.S.. Next question-- Sam."

"If we open an office in Munich, how will that work?"

"I don't have all the details worked out yet, but if we do open an office over there, Ulrich will probably be in charge of it. I'll have to spend a lot of time with him to see how effective he would be as an executive, but so far, in our conversations, I'm impressed. You've got to remember, too, that he speaks German, and we don't."

"I think our main problem is going to be gearing up for a lot of increased production. It's possible that we will have to open an additional plant, and that will be a big job. We already have property where we can build a plant, but getting it built, buying equipment, trying to find enough people who want to work, and a host of other things will keep us really busy for a while."

"Anybody else have a question or comment? Yes, Tom."

"If we build a new plant, will we be making anything other than dirndls?"

"Oh yes, in fact, dirndls will probably be a very small or zero percentage of our production. Ulrich tells me that Europe is wide open for American type sportswear, and this is the area that interests me most. High quality women's sleepwear and lingerie is another strong possibility."

"Ulrich should be here within the next few weeks, and all of you will have a chance to pick his brain. He speaks very good English."

Ruby opens the door and says, "You have an overseas call from Mr. Ulrich Steen."

"Speak of the devil. Excuse me while I take this." David goes to his office to take the call. "Ulrich, how are you?"

"Very well, Mr. Shepherd. I hope you're doing well."

"Yes indeed, What can I do for you today?"

"If you will recall, you invited me to come to your place, so we can discuss the possibility of working together."

"I did indeed. Are you wanting to come?"

"Very much so. I looked into airlines, and can get a flight from Munich to Atlanta to Chattanooga on Wednesday. Would that fit into your schedule? Also, if you don't mind, I would like to bring my wife with me. Her name is Bathilda."

"Of course you can come Wednesday, and your wife is certainly welcome. Do you have your tickets already?"

"No, I wanted to talk to you first. I'll get them when we hang up."

"Great. Wire or call my secretary, Ruby, when you get your

tickets, and give her the arrival time, and I'll meet you at the airport. I'll get you a hotel, too. How long will you be staying?"

"We'll stay until Sunday. I need to get back for a presentation in Salzburg on Tuesday."

"Fine, I'm looking forward to meeting you and Bathilda. See ya Wednesday."

David went back to the conference room, and told the group about Ulrich's upcoming visit. He was glad he was coming, but it came so suddenly, he was going to have to really work to get ready. Everyone there seemed excited, and could sense some awesome things in the future for Shepherd Apparel.

As the meeting broke up, David called out, "Bud Weddle, wait up a minute, will you?"

"Sounds like we're going to be busy doesn't it, Boss?"

"Yeah, it does. What I wanted, Bud, is to remind you that Don will be coming in after school today to work for you. Don't give him any slack on anything that you need him to do. If whatever it is needs to be done a certain way, make sure he does it that way. He's a charmer, and will have you doing his job for him if you don't watch out. If he gives you the least amount of trouble, I want to know about it. Don't worry about making him mad; I want to know about it. Okay? He's going to be your responsibility while he's in the cutting room. Do we understand each other?"

"Yes sir. I'll take care of it."

"Good."

On the way back to his office, David stopped at Ruby's desk. "Call Eddie Randolph and have him come to my office."

When Eddie got there David said, "Eddie, I've got a job for you."

"Yes sir, Mr. Shepherd. Anything you want."

"Eddie, I took Don's car keys away from him, so he won't have any wheels for a while. What I want you to do is every afternoon, take the van, go pick him up at school, and bring him here. You know where he goes to school don't you?"

"Yes sir. Ashland High, right?"

"Right. Plan on doing this every day until I tell you to stop, okay?"

"Okay."

Tuesday was spent scurrying around making sure everything was clean and in good order. David enlisted Ruby's help getting his new office arranged and decorated just the way he wanted it. He spent all Monday afternoon and most of Tuesday getting ready for Ulrich's visit on Wednesday, and was satisfied when he left the office at the end of the day that he was prepared.

David met the plane himself. The big board showed flight 342 from Atlanta would be on time at 4:10, and that was just ten minutes away. Since he had not seen Ulrich, he made a sign to hold in front of him that said STEEN.

As the people came through the gate, David tried to guess which one was Ulrich. He shouldn't have had any problem since Ulrich's wife was with him. He pictured her as a short, dumpy, peasant type woman. In a minute he saw them just as they saw him. He shook hands with Ulrich, and then with Bathilda when Ulrich introduced them. Ulrich looked younger than he expected, and Bathilda was beautiful.

Ulrich was about 5'10", and had a good build. His brown hair was expertly cut, and he looked great in his clothes.

Bathilda was tall; maybe a little taller than Ulrich. She had long, black hair that was tied in a ponytail, and she was gorgeous in her designer outfit. Most women would die for a figure like hers, and her teeth were very white and pretty. Ulrich did well when he found her. So much for short and dumpy.

"There's a nice Holiday Inn not too far from our office," David said, "and that's where I made your reservations. Why don't we go there and get you checked in, and give you a chance to rest before we go eat. Does that sound all right?"

"That sounds good, David. We've been up and going for a long time today, and maybe a little rest will help us both."

"Do you think you will feel like going to get something to eat later? We don't have to if you'd rather not. The restaurant at the motel might be good, if you would rather stay in tonight."

"No, no, we want to experience everything we can while we're here. Going out to eat will be good."

"Good. Why don't I pick you up at seven o'clock? And oh yeah – I have a friend named Margaret that I'd like to bring if that's all right with you. Bathilda, I think you and Margaret will like each other."

Bathilda said, "By all means, bring her. I'm anxious to meet her."

"Good. It's a plan, then. Here we are at your home for the next few days. Let's go get you checked in, and I'll leave you guys alone for a while."

David checked them in, and had already pre-arranged for their bill to be sent to Shepherd Apparel. He signed the registration form and went with Ulrich to the car to get Bathilda and their luggage. All three of them grabbed a hand full of items and got everything to their room in one trip. David said goodbye and left for home to freshen up.

When he got home he called Margaret. He had talked to her earlier about the possibility of eating with them, and she was all set to go. Her house was about fifteen minutes from the Holiday Inn, so David said he would pick her up at 6:45.

In honor of his German guests, David took them to Fehn's, a restaurant established years ago by Mr. Joe Fehn, a German national. The restaurant was widely known for their fried chicken coated with corn flakes. When Mr. Fehn saw them, he came over to their table, and David introduced him to Ulrich and Bathilda. When Mr. Fehn found out they were German, the English language went out the window for several minutes. It was entertaining to sit there and listen to a three-way German conversation. The whole time they were talking, David could hardly keep his eyes off Bathilda. She was so pretty. In a few minutes the waitress brought the food, and Mr. Fehn excused himself, and he told David and his guests how happy he was to see them.

Dinner was delicious. David had a hamburger steak, and the others had the famous fried chicken. Bathilda and Ulrich had never had anything like that and thought it was wonderful. Business wasn't discussed while they ate; rather that time was used to eat and get better acquainted.

Ulrich told David and Margaret, "Most of my friends call me Urey."

And Bathilda interjected, "And I go by Thil."

"Okay, it's Urey and Thil then," David said. "That's good to know. It's a lot easier to say, too."

After a round of macaroon pie for Urey and Thil and banana cream pie for Margaret and David, the quartet sat for a long time talking about some of the differences in the customs of their nationalities.

Finally, David asked Urey to tell him about himself. He wanted to know something of his past, and what he hoped to accomplish in the future, and how did he think Shepherd Apparel would fit into his plans.

Urey began. "First of all, I am thirty one years old. I graduated from a private school in Munich at the age of seventeen and then graduated from the University of Bonn when I was twenty years old. The University is where I learned to speak English. I returned home to Munich after graduation and began working in an apparel manufacturing company. My goal was to be a sales executive, and after a year inside the factory and office, I had the opportunity to move into sales. The company I was with made dirndls, and I was fortunate to be very successful. After another year I decided to form my own sales agency, and I've done extremely well. There are four of us now, and we cover almost the entire continent of Europe, with the exception of East Germany."

"One of my burning desires is to be able to expand my business to the Middle East, and especially to Israel to try and help the Jewish people in any way I can."

"I don't know if you're aware that Munich was the spiritual capital of the Nazi movement, and I'm very sorry to say that my father was a well-known, cruel, Nazi SS officer. His name was Colonel Hans Steen. He played a large part in the cruelty and death of many Jews, and I am deeply ashamed of what he did. I feel a constant burden of guilt that makes me feel that I have to help the Jews in order to ease my conscience. I know I didn't play a part in their suffering, but I still feel guilty."

"Where's your father now?" David asked.

"He's dead. When the allies were getting ready to launch V E Day, the Third Reich knew it was coming, so Chancellor Hitler and several of his senior SS officers took their own lives. I was twelve years old at the time."

"Where's your mother?"

"She lives with my sister in Munich. Ever since the end of the war, she has suffered from extreme paranoia. She is constantly afraid that someone is out to get her because of my father's deeds. Until I went away to the University, the three of us lived with my uncle."

"David, now that you know this about me, do you understand why I feel so burdened?"

"Have you ever tried to get help?"

"No, I don't think I have a problem. I just have a desire to help the people my father mistreated. It doesn't interfere with my life or work in any way."

"That's very interesting, Urey. I'd like to hear more, later, if you're willing to share your story with me."

"Listen." David said, "I know you all must be tired, and we can continue this conversation tomorrow. Is that all right with you?"

Urey said it was okay with him, so they got up to leave. When they got to the register and David tried to pay the bill, the cashier said, "Thank you, sir, but this has already been taken care of."

"Did Mr. Fehn do this?"

"Yes sir."

"Is he still here?"

"No sir. He's already gone."

"Okay. I'll catch him later. Tell him I said thank you."

They walked through the parking lot to the car; then drove to the hotel where Urey and Thil were staying. They said goodnight, and David told Urey he would pick him up at eight o'clock tomorrow morning. Margaret told Thil she would call in the morning, and they would get together for lunch and an afternoon of shopping. As they drove away, David turned to get one more glimpse of Thil.

***

Urey was waiting outside the Holiday Inn when David got there at eight o'clock.

"Good morning, Urey."

"Good morning."

"Have you had breakfast?"

"Yes, I ate early."

The two men made small talk while David drove to Shepherd Apparel. When they got there, David led Urey first to Ruby's desk, where he introduced him to his secretary. Then, he took him down the hall, and introduced him to several of the key people in the firm. Other keys were located in other areas and other buildings, and they would get to them later.

Finally, they got to David's office, and sat down to talk. Ruby poured each of them a cup of coffee and left the office, shutting the door behind her.

"Well, Urey, have you thought much about what we have been talking about, about working together in a joint venture?"

"Yes. That's about all I have thought about. That's the reason I have come here now instead of later."

"That's good. Let me tell you a little bit about Shepherd Apparel and the vision I have for the company."

"Without going into company history, I'll start with today, since this is my first week as President and CEO. Urey, up until now we have been one-hundred percent domestic, meaning all our business has been and is conducted within the borders of the United States. The reason I contacted you is because I want to go international, and with your coverage of Europe, I feel you can help us."

"I know you're called the *dirndl king*, but I want you to use your influence and sales ability to introduce highly styled, top-quality, women's sportswear to the countries you cover. This is what I want immediately, but down the road I envision Shepherd Apparel getting into ladies' lingerie, a line of men's casual wear, children's wear, a line of jeans for the entire family, and even a line of outerwear for men, women and children."

"See this shepherd's staff? My dad gave this to me when he retired, and I've decided to make this our logo. Starting immediately, this logo will be embroidered on every piece of our brand that is shipped. I think this is a natural for Europe. Whatta you think?"

"I think that's very good."

"Do you think you can sell the kind of clothes I'm thinking about?"

"Without a doubt. There is a definite void in Europe for this kind of merchandise. When do think you can start shipping"

"It depends on what develops while you're here, and if we get together, how fast we can hire a designer to put a line together. Of course, sales are always booked for the next season, so you would probably book orders for a year from the time you get back to Germany. We have a few styles that we are currently making that could be booked for next season, but a full line will be a year away. If you're interested in getting on board with us, I think we can conquer the world of fashion. Whatta you think? Do you think we can make a big splash overseas?"

"I am sure we can. I can hardly wait to get home and get started. How will this work, David? Do you plan for me to be one of your salesmen or do you want my agency to work for you, or what?"

"Urey, I think what I would like to do is open a Shepherd Apparel office in Munich, and have you run it for me. I will pay you for that. In addition to your salary, I would like for your agency to handle most of the European sales, and of course, the agency would be paid a handsome commission. As Shepherd's leader in Germany, if you see the need for additional sales people, it will be up to you to hire them. How does that sound to you?"

"It sounds fine, David. What would you think, if after I get things rolling smoothly in Europe I branched out to Middle Eastern countries? There is a huge market in Egypt, Jordan, Israel and the other Mid-East countries. The Islamic women for the most part wear different type apparel over their regular clothes, so we would have to address that, but the women of Israel wear western style apparel, and that would be a good place to start."

"That may be a possibility down the road, Urey, but let's get Europe going first. C'mon, let me show you the Shepherd Apparel campus."

When they finished touring the facilities, David told Urey he wanted to treat him to a tradition in Chattanooga and most of the south. He wanted him to experience a sack-full of Krystal hamburgers for lunch. Urey couldn't seem to get enough of the little burgers. He started with three, and then ordered four more. He made David promise to bring him back before he left to go home. David said they needed to bring Thil, too.

The rest of Thursday and all Friday morning was spent planning and meeting with most of the key people, throwing out ideas, contacting designers, and other things that had to be done in advance of going international.

Friday afternoon was spent with David and Urey alone in David's office, getting down to a lot of specifics. Yesterday, David talked with one designer he liked, and she was to come see him on Monday. He hoped she would be the one he wanted. Getting a line designed had to come first before they could make samples, order fabric, book orders, or anything else.

David and Margaret took the visitors to the Town and Country for dinner, and this time they took Don with them. It was hard to tell which one had the hardest time keeping their eyes off Thil; David or Don. The meal was delicious as always, and they all had a good time.

David suggested that since they had accomplished nearly everything they had hoped to, they use Saturday as a free day. He would like to show them around, and experience some of the neat things the city had to offer. He also wanted to take Urey and Thil to the Krystal, Urey's new favorite place to eat.

After a fun day, they stopped at The Greystone for dinner, and David took his guests back to the Holiday Inn. They were scheduled to catch a Delta flight at eight forty-five Sunday morning to Atlanta connecting with a Lufthansa Air flight at eleven fifteen. They said their good-byes to Margaret and Don, and David said he would be there to pick them up at seven thirty in the morning. As they drove off, Don turned all the way around to watch Thil walk into the hotel. Smiling, David asked, "Whatta ya looking at, Don?" Don didn't reply.

The next morning David was at the hotel on time, and Urey and Thil were ready. The airport was not too far, so they had some time to spend together after they got checked in.

"Urey, I'm excited about what we are planning. How about you?"

"Yes, I'm very excited. I can hardly wait until it becomes a reality."

"Tell you what, Urey; I will probably need to come to Munich when I can. I will want to visit the new office, meet your people, and get ideas from them about the direction we want to go in the future. If I can get things done and work it out, I will try to get over there sometime next month."

"That will be good. We will look forward to your visit, won't we Thil?"

"Yes. We definitely will."

The speaker blared "Delta flight 364 is now ready to board at gate 5."

"Well, it's time for you guys to go. It's been a real pleasure spending time with you, and I look forward to working with you. Thil, it has been a real treat meeting you, and I guess I'll see you in Munich next month."

"I will look forward to it."

They all shook hands, and David gave Thil a kiss on the cheek. They said goodbye, and David walked to the parking lot to his car. He still had time to go home, get Don up and make it to Sunday School on time.

CHAPTER THREE

One year later

Don was on his best behavior from the time David took his car keys until school was out for the summer. Since he was so good and worked so hard in the cutting department, David gave his keys back as a reward. Don had missed his car, but his buddies saw to it that he wasn't too inconvenienced. They came to his aide by furnishing rides, double-dating in their cars, and sometimes even loaning him their cars without his dad knowing about it. Don was one of those charismatic individuals whose friends couldn't do enough for him.

Don, being Don, was about to go into another risky endeavor. The cutting department at Shepherd wasn't paying what he thought a high school senior needed, so he was laying the groundwork for something that would devastate his dad.

"Richard, This is Don. When can we get together and talk a little more about that idea we talked about yesterday?"

"Anytime you want to. How about after school tomorrow?"

"Sounds good. Why don't we meet at the Signal Drive-In?"

"Okay. See ya."

Chattanooga, like nearly all cities in the south, except for maybe Atlanta, did not have liquor-by-the-drink. That, and its geographical location made it a hot-bed for bootleggers. Chattanooga is located in the extreme southeastern part of the state of Tennessee, next to Georgia, Alabama, and North Carolina. Nearly every bootlegger in all these states had to travel through Hamilton County if they wanted to deliver their goods and the number of gallons was substantial.

Don's friend, Richard, was the son of a powerful state senator, Richard Powell. Senator Powell had the ambition and desire to become a United States Senator and was using his agenda against the bootleg liquor industry to help propel his status. He had already had several well-known bootleggers arrested and had put fear into the whole lot.

The old-time moonshiners couldn't figure out how word got to Powell that they were coming through a certain place at a certain time until they figured out there had to be a snitch somewhere. Moonshiners, like most all groups had a *grapevine* and one member of the *grapevine* would hear of activity getting ready to happen and would report it to the Senator.

Senator Powell's son, Richard, Jr., happened to overhear a conversation between his dad and the snitch one night and was dying to tell somebody about what he heard. He knew this man was a regular visitor to see his dad, but before overhearing that particular conversation, he had never paid any attention to the man.

He and Don were good buddies, and during lunch one day at school he told Don about what he overheard. Telling Don something like that was like pouring gasoline on a fire.

Don immediately saw the possibility of making some serious money.

At the drive-in the next day, Don told Richard, "You know, I've been doing a lot of thinking since you told me about that guy talking to your dad about bootleggers, and I think we can make some good money if you want to."

"How?"

"Didn't you say a guy you thought was a snitch on the bootleggers was a regular visitor to see your dad?"

"Yeah, a guy named Johnny. Why?"

"Look, if we can get the names of these guys hauling the liquor and can warn them for a price, there's no telling how much money we can make. They're all scared of your dad and since you're his son, they will know we're connected. We can ask so much for every gallon they bring through the county and threaten to go to your dad if they don't pay. That way, they're not only getting a heads up on where the danger is, but they get to deliver their stuff safely. Surely, that would be worth fifty cents a gallon to them if they want to stay in business."

"I don't know. Don. It sounds risky to me."

"Do you know of anything that doesn't carry a risk?"

"Well, no, but I don't want to involve my dad in anything that could hurt his reputation."

"This won't involve your dad. The only person that could get hurt in this would be the snitch, and who cares about a snitch?"

"Don, let's think about it some more. I'm just not sure I want to take the chance."

"Tell you what, Richard. Let's think about it overnight and decide what we'll do tomorrow. You wanna meet here at the same time?"

"Yeah, that'll be okay.

***

Shepherd Apparel Group is now known as Shepherd Global Apparel Group and business in Europe is beginning to flourish. Urey and his staff have been booking orders like crazy. He has added two additional sales people to cover some areas they were unable to cover previously. One of the new men was brought in to take up Urey's slack since he had to spend so much time doing Shepherd business rather than selling, himself.

At home, David has built a new 125,000 square foot plant and equipped it with the latest in cutting, sewing, and shipping equipment. He hired a fellow named Ed Henry, formerly with DuPont to be the new plant manager and Ed was doing a fine job, so far. Business was looking so good, David was already thinking about possibly needing to build yet another plant, especially if they got into the family outerwear business.

International postage was so expensive, Urey mailed orders

only once a week. Every Monday a box was delivered containing orders from the previous week along with other kinds of correspondence.

It looked like Shepherd Global had hit the jackpot when they took on Urey and David wanted to keep striking while the iron was hot. He had some ideas that he needed to spend time going over with Urey, so he called and told him to come to Chattanooga and to bring Thil if he wanted to.

Urey arrived in Chattanooga the following week and he and David began serious talks almost immediately. Margaret was called to entertain Thil and when business ended the four went out to eat. Don was busy doing his own thing, so they almost missed him, but when he found out Thil was there he did come by to get a glimpse of her and speak to her and Urey.

In the afternoon of the second day of their visit, David said, "Urey, we've talked about several things since you've been here, but here's the main reason I wanted you to come over here. I'm very happy with the way you have started out with our company, and I can see that you are going to continue to grow our business in Europe. You told me that your assistant, Gerhard, is looking after a lot of the day-to-day business, and that pleases me. Now hold on to your hat."

Urey, how would you feel about moving to Chattanooga? Here's why I asked; you told me before that you would like to go into the Mid-East, especially Israel, and I think we're ready to do that. I'm also ready to explore the possibility of going into Asia."

"I would like to promote you to Vice President of Global Operations and have you set up offices in London and Tel Aviv to start and other cities as we grow. I feel that in order to look after that large of an operation, you would need to live here near our headquarters. I know you're used to traveling a lot and this job will require even more travel than you're doing now, but we need you, Urey."

"If you decide to accept the offer, I'm open to the idea of promoting Gerhard to your position, if you think that would be a good move."

"I know this has to be a shock to you, and I don't expect your answer today, but I want you to think about it and talk it over with Thil and see what she thinks. I know of some beautiful homes that are for sale, and I'm sure we can find something you guys like. In fact, there's a real *honey* for sale next door to me. Talk it over tonight, and if you want to, we can ride around tomorrow and look at some of them."

Urey was speechless. It took several seconds after David finished talking before he finally said, "David, you've caught me totally by surprise. I don't know what to say except I'm flattered that you would consider me for such an important position, and I will certainly talk to my wife about it tonight. When do you have to have an answer?"

"As soon as possible"

"All right. David, would you mind if Thil and I just eat at the hotel by ourselves tonight? We need time to weigh different scenarios in order to make the decision. I'm inclined to tell you "yes" now, but I must consult my wife before I can give you a firm answer. Is that all right?"

"Yes, that's fine. Why don't we knock off now and let me take you to the hotel?"

"All right."

When they got to the hotel David said, "I'll see you in the morning at the regular time; eight o'clock, okay? Have a great evening."

"Good bye, David."

***

As usual Urey was waiting outside the hotel when David arrived. "Good morning. Urey"

"Good morning, David"

"Did you sleep well?"

"Yes, thank you, considering"

"Did you eat breakfast this morning?"

"No, Thil and I just had coffee."

"Why don't we stop by the Krystal and get some biscuits and take them to the office?"

"That would be good."

When they arrived at the office, Ruby poured coffee and the two men sat at the table and ate their biscuits. "Did you and Thil have a chance to talk about what we discussed yesterday?"

"Yes we did and after weighing all the pros and cons we could think of, we agree that we would like to accept your offer and move here."

"Wonderful. Did you also discuss when you would be able to move?"

"Yes. We think it will take the better part of a month before we can wind up our business in Germany. It might even take a little longer, but we can set a month as a goal."

"Excuse me for a second, Urey." David calls to the outer office, "Ruby, come in here please?"

"Yes sir. What can I do for you?"

"Urey and Thil are going to move from Munich to Chattanooga. Isn't that great? I want you to call whoever you need to call, probably the Immigration office, and find out what kind of paperwork has to be done in order for them to move."

"Okay, I'll find out. Urey, it'll be nice having you here."

"Thank you, Ruby."

"Urey, did you say anything to Thil about looking at houses?"

"Yes, and she's anxious to see what American houses are like."

"Okay then. Why don't you call her and see when she can be ready and we'll pick her up. We'll ride through some nice neighborhoods and see what's available, and if you see any you like, we'll call the realtor and ask to go through them."

"Ruby, please call Urey's room at the Holiday Inn and let Urey talk to Thil."

"Yes sir."

As they drove to the Holiday Inn, David asked, "What do

you think about promoting Gerhard to replace you?"

"I think he would be perfect for the job."

"Okay, then, we'll do it. When you get back to Munich, you can do that as your first official action as vice president. When you do it, call me. I'll want to talk to him."

They picked up Thil around ten-thirty and began their house-search. David stayed mainly in areas on or near the lake and others on the eastern side of the city. They saw several beautiful homes with *FOR SALE* signs, but narrowed them down to three. One of them was next door to David.

While they were at that house, David went into his and called the realtor. She was a member of Multiple Listings and could show them all three of the houses they liked. They agreed to meet at one of the houses at two o'clock and in the meantime they would grab a quick bite to eat.

The first two houses they looked at were very nice, but each one had something that either Thil or Urey didn't like. The third one was next door to where David lived and the couple immediately fell in love with it.

Thil commented, "The architecture here is so different from Germany. It's beautiful and warm; not like at our town."

The location was the main attraction. While not on Chickamauga Lake, it was on a private 78 acre lake, owned jointly by the residents of the neighborhood. It had a large level lot with large oak and hickory trees. The lawn was immaculate with plush Zoysia grass, beautiful flowers and manicured shrubbery.

The house was a huge rambling ranch built of wood and mountain stone. It was 3800 square feet consisting of four bedrooms and three baths. A huge den with a five-foot wood-burning fireplace with gas pipes to make lighting easy pretty much clinched the deal.

A large patio off the sliding doors of the den ran to the fence surrounding the forty foot pool. All this backed up to the edge of the lake. It was a show-place if there ever was one.

Urey and Thil were like two excited kids. They would talk

first to each other in German, and then to David, and then to the realtor, and then start over again. When their excitement died down a little, they decided to make an offer on the place, but didn't know what to do. They asked David, who in turn asked the real estate lady and the process began.

Money would not be a problem, so it was just a matter of getting everything done. The house was already vacant and could be occupied whenever they wanted it.

The real estate lady told Urey, "Mr. Steen, I appreciate your business. I'll get started with the paperwork the first thing in the morning. It will more than likely take two or three weeks to get the loan approved, the appraisal, and all the other things involved. How can I get in touch with you?"

Urey said I'll be in Germany. David, can she contact you?"

"Yeah. Just call me and I'll see that we get done whatever has to be done. Here's my business card. I can contact Urey when you're ready, but it's probably going to be a month before they can come back. Will that be all right?"

"That will be fine," she said.

They said goodbye to the realtor and walked over to David's house, where he poured a glass of wine for each of them to celebrate their move and the purchase of their house.

After the wine, David drove them back to their hotel. It had been a tiring and exciting day. He asked, "Would you guys like to go somewhere for dinner or would you rather just get something to eat here at the hotel?"

"David, would you mind if we just stayed in tonight? I think all the excitement we've had today has exhausted Thil. If you don't mind, we'll just stay here."

"That will be fine. I'm tired, too. Say, Urey, if we can get your plane reservations changed, could you possibly stay here for an extra day? With the big changes, there's an awful lot of planning that has to be done, and I think we need to get started. If you can stay, I'll try to get the tickets changed.

"We can stay if you want us to, but I'll have to call my office. I'm supposed to make a presentation in Austria,

Wednesday, and I'll have to get one of my partners to cover for me."

"Good."

CHAPTER FOUR

Moving across the world is no small task, but in the case of Thil and Urey, things were simplified because they decided to keep their place in Munich. Urey would use it as his base when in Europe and Thil would have a place to stay when she went back for visits. That made the move easier, but very expensive because of having to buy all new furniture in Chattanooga.

After David's decision to go global became a reality, his ideas for expansion seemed to have no bounds. "Ruby, would you tell Urey to come to my office, please?"

"You wanted to see me, David?"

"Yeah. I've been thinking about what you said a while back about wanting to go into Israel and other Mid-Eastern countries and I want us to explore that idea. First of all, where do you want to go first, Israel?"

"Yes, remember we talked one time about maybe setting up an office in Tel Aviv? I would really like to do that."

"The Israeli women wear western type clothing, don't they? They don't wear the long dresses and head-scarfs like the Muslim women, do they?"

"No. They wear clothes just like Thil and Margaret."

"Okay. We'll look into that as the first place we go when we move into the Mid-East. Before we do that, though, I want to get Europe saturated with Shepherd Apparel," David said. "How do we stand on getting the London office open?"

Urey said, "I have been negotiating with some people about an office and warehouse, and should know when I get back there in about two weeks. If all goes well, we should be able to start operations there in about a month or six weeks."

"Good. Now when you get that open and running, what are

your ideas about opening Tel Aviv?"

"Well, David, at this point I don't have any ideas other than I would like for us to go there. After we get London open, what if I go there and see what we need to do? I just feel that there is a large market in Israel."

"Okay, that sounds fine. Now what about some of the other middle eastern countries? Where do you want to open besides Israel?"

"I think the first place after Israel would be Egypt and then Jordan. The political situation in some of those countries right now is such that it would be risky to attempt any kind of a start-up in them."

"Let me ask you something, Urey. I know all those Arab countries are Muslim countries and I know the types of clothing the women wear over there. The Muslims are so strict about some things, I'm wondering if they're allowed to buy clothes made by a non-Muslim company. If they're allowed to buy from a company like ours, we could do some serious business. I don't know who makes their clothes now, but I would bet that whoever is making them is not nearly as large as we are and are probably more limited in what they can do in terms of style, quality and quantity. How about looking into that, will you?"

"I certainly will. David, I realize I have only been here for two weeks, but I think I need to get to London as soon as possible to try and finalize the deal on the office and warehouse I told you about. I'd like to leave Monday if that's all right."

"How long do you plan to be gone?"

"It depends on how things stand in London, and I need to go to Munich to be sure Gerhard is on the right track. I would say that I would be gone a minimum of two weeks."

"Okay. Tell Ruby to make reservations for you. Are you going to take Thil?"

"No. Not on this trip, but she'll be fine."

David said, "I'll keep a check on her, and I'll have

Margaret look in on her, too.

***

School was out for the summer and Don was using every spare minute he had trying to get his plan together to capture some of the bootleg liquor money coming through the county. His friend, Richard, was trying to back out of getting into the deal, fearing what it would do to his father if he got caught, but Don kept pushing him and was able to get Richard to get certain information; names, places, and other things Don felt he needed.

Richard would always try to be close-by when the informant would come to see his dad. The snitch would always come to their house because he didn't want to say anything on the telephone and he didn't seem to mind if Richard was around. Richard would write down the names of the bootleggers the guy mentioned and give them to Don. One night, the name of a man came up who could be considered as a kind of *godfather* and when Don got the name, he went about trying to find out how to find the man. Once he found out, he talked Richard into going with him, and they went to see the man. When he knocked on the man's door, his heart was beating up in his throat. His first impulse was to run, but he managed to act brave in front of Richard, who was paralyzed with fear, and stayed until the man came to the door.

The man's name was Horace Edwards and he seemed to be pretty nice. Don introduced himself and Richard and when he said Richard Powell, the man stiffened and asked, "Like Senator Powell?"

Richard said, "Yes sir, he's my dad."

"Well, what can I do for you boys?"

Then Don began to lay out his plan. "Well, Mr. Edwards, we have a proposition that we think you might like. It's something that can possibly keep you and your friends in business and can help Richard and me with our college funds"

"What are you talking about, kid?"

"First of all, Mr. Edwards, we know about the business you're in, and we know that you are considered sort of the leader in this area. We also know that you know Senator Powell has a vendetta against bootleg liquor. Now, here's the deal."

"You may or may not know that one of your fellow businessmen has turned into an informant and tells Richard's dad about a lot of the deliveries that are going to be made in the county. I'm sure you're aware that a lot more of your friends are being arrested than used to be. Well, that's because this man tells Sen. Powell what deliveries are going to be made before they happen."

"Now here's what we would like to do for you. We're just a couple of high school kids and nobody suspects us of anything, so we have a pretty free hand when it comes to being where we can overhear conversations. Whenever the snitch comes to Senator Powell, we can get the names of the people he mentions and pass them on to you, so you can have your friends postpone the delivery or take an alternate route. This will save their products, a lot of money, and maybe their freedom. Are you interested so far?"

"Keep talking. What are you wanting out of this?"

"Again, we're only a couple of high school boys and we don't need much, so we think that the very modest fee of fifty cents a gallon for all the liquor brought through Hamilton county would be fair. When you think of all that's being lost due to all the arrests, it's easy to see that fifty cents a gallon is nothing. What do you say?"

"It sounds mildly interesting, but I'll have to talk to some people. Come back at this time Saturday and we'll talk some more."

"Okay, we'll see you Saturday. Oh, by the way, we got your name from the snitch I told you about, if that makes any difference, and we have a list with several other names on it. Just so you know."

"See ya later, kid."

When they left, Richard said, "You know, he was a pretty nice man. I figured he'd be mean, but he wasn't."

The boys were pretty keyed up about the prospects of making a lot of money. They were optimistic, but they knew the deal was nowhere near done. Don kept thinking it was going to happen because the man didn't say no and invited them back to talk about it. He had to keep Richard on a positive note because without Richard's ability to get the information, nothing could happen. Richard was coming around a little more since he was realizing they could make a lot of money.

On Saturday morning, Don called Richard. "You remember we've got an appointment this afternoon?"

"Yeah, I know."

"Want me to pick you up?"

"Yeah, what time?"

"We're supposed to be there at three. I'll pick you up at two thirty, okay?"

"Okay."

When they drove up to Horace Edwards' house, Mr. Edwards was sitting in a rocker on the front porch. "You boys find a chair and sit down."

They each pulled up a chair and sat down as instructed. Don asked, "We're wondering if you've decided anything yet."

"Kid, I've got some real unhappy *friends*. They're unhappy that there's a snitch somewhere and they're unhappy that two high school kids have their names. They realize they're between a rock and a hard place and have no choice but to go along with your proposition. They're also unhappy about having to pay fifty cents a gallon for protection."

"Now here's how the deal is going to work. Some of my *friends* and I have let it be known that certain deliveries are going to be made, but the information is false. We want to see what your snitch reports to Senator Powell. When he reports and you get the information, come back and see me. If he reports the false information and you bring it to me, then we'll know we have a problem. At that time, we'll make a decision on what to do."

"That sounds fine, Mr. Edwards," Don said. If you have already put out the false information, the informant should be going to see Richard's dad at any time. When we get his information, can we just come on back out here and tell you?"

"Yeah, the sooner the better."

"Okay. We'll probably see you soon."

On Monday night, right after dinner, Senator Powell had a visitor. He and the man went into the den to talk and, as usual, he didn't close the door.

Richard stood just outside the door and heard everything they talked about. He wrote down names, locations, times, and other information about moonshine deliveries to be made later in the week. After the man left, he went up to his room and called Don. "Hey, Don"

"Hey"

"The dude was just here to see my dad. I wrote down a lot of stuff and we can go to Mr. Edwards' whenever you think."

"Great. I've got to work 'til three-thirty tomorrow afternoon, but I can go after that. You want me to pick you up?"

"Yeah, I guess. What time?"

"I'll see you at four tomorrow afternoon."

"Okay."

The boys arrived at Horace Edwards' around four-thirty on Tuesday afternoon. They sat on the porch again and when they showed Mr. Edwards what they had, he was livid. He said he couldn't believe that one of his associates would do something like that.

"Okay, guys, I guess I'm stuck. Now, here's how this thing will have to work. Do you know where the YMCA is downtown?"

"Yes sir."

"We agree to your price of fifty cents a gallon and we'll make one payment a week. You can pick up an envelope on each Saturday night in front of the Y, but you'll have to show your I.D. to our messenger before he will give it to you. Here is half of a *queen of hearts* playing card from a Las Vegas casino. This is your I.D.. Our messenger will have the other half. You must match the two halves of the card or there's no payday. Is that understood?"

"Yes sir. What time," Don asked.

"Seven o'clock."

"You boys keep the information coming and we'll take care of you each week."

"Yes sir. Thank you," Don said.

"Thank you," Richard chimed in.

As they rode back to town, they sang a duet of *"We're in the Money."* Don dropped Richard off at his house. "Keep your ears open, and I'll see you at school, Monday."

"Okay. See ya."

***

On Friday afternoon, David finished at the office around three-thirty and went home. Since the weather was warm, he changed into shorts and went out on the balcony to enjoy the fresh air and the view.

David's house was a large, two story colonial with five bedrooms and four and a half baths. Across the back of the house, on the second floor, a sixty foot balcony extended out eighteen feet giving an unobstructed view of the lake. This was his wife's favorite place when she was alive and the furniture, accessories, and decorating was unbelievable.

About two-hundred feet away, he saw Bathilda sitting by her pool, reading, so he decided to go over there. He buzzed the buzzer on the gate and when she saw him, she smiled and ran to unlock the gate. "Hi Thil. How're you doing."

"Fine, except I'm lonesome without Urey being here."

"That's one reason I came over. I talked to him earlier today, and he said he will more than likely be an extra week before he gets back. He settled on the lease for the office and warehouse in London, but he's having a hard time finding someone he's comfortable with to run the operation, and he can't leave there until he finds the right person. I know he has been gone for a week and a half already, but these things happen sometimes and Urey, being a responsible man, won't leave until he's satisfied it's okay to leave. He said to tell you that he will call you tomorrow."

Thil muttered something in German that David couldn't understand, but he could come pretty close to guessing what she said.

They then walked over to the pool and sat down in a couple of the comfortable chairs and talked about unimportant things until David asked, "What are you going to do for dinner?"

"I don't know. I haven't thought about it. After the news you just gave me about Urey, I'm not very hungry."

"I'll tell you what. Come on over to my house with me, and we'll finish that bottle of wine we opened when we toasted your moving here. I think there are a couple of glasses left and if there aren't I have another bottle. After a glass or two, you may be relaxed enough to want something to eat."

David took her by the hand, but before they got too far, Thil said, "Wait a minute, David. Let me go lock my front door. You go on, and I'll be there in a minute."

"Okay. I'll go pour the wine."

It was about ten minutes before she got there and David said, "I thought you got lost."

"No, I just wanted to freshen up a bit." She had changed clothes and brushed her hair and looked beautiful. She was such a natural beauty she would look good in a feed sack.

"Here's your wine."

"Thank you." As she reached over to take the glass from David's hand, she grabbed the glass and his hand together. She held on for several seconds as their eyes met. As they were moving slightly toward each other, Don appeared on the balcony, "Hi, Pop. Hi, Thil. What's cooking?"

Thil quickly took her hand away from David's and said, "Hello, Don."

David said, "Hi, son" and asked, "Did y'all get that order for Florida cut?"

"Yes sir. It's done."

"Good, we're late on that one. What are you going to do for dinner?"

"Some of us are gonna grab a bite and then go out to Lakeshore. Why?"

"I was just wondering. Thil and I might go get something and I thought you might like to go with us."

"I told the guys I'd go with them," Don said. "I'm going to pick Eddie up right now. Today's payday, you know?"

"I know. I'll see you later."

After Don left, David and Thil got back to their glasses of wine. David poured another glass and asked, "Would you like for me to order pizza and we'll just stay here and eat?"

"That sounds wonderful. Besides, this wine is starting to go to my head."

When the pizza came and they started eating, Thil said, "This is delicious. I must have been hungrier than I thought. Will you pour me another glass of wine?'

"Sure thing."

She got up and came over to the bar where David stood. She had a piece of pizza in one hand and her wine glass in the other. She held out the glass for David to fill and then stood there, face to face with him. Their faces were only inches apart. David's overwhelming desire was to kiss her, but his better judgment took over and the only thing he could think of was, "I don't need it, but I think I'll have one more piece of pizza."

David could see that with each sip of wine, Thil was getting more amorous, so he tried to talk about anything he could think of in order to get her mind off him. He tried talking about Urey and this helped most of all. About an hour later, Thil said, "David, I think I need to go home. I've enjoyed the evening."

"Me too. I'll walk you over there."

"No, No. The lights are all on, and I'll be all right." She kissed him on the cheek, and he walked her to the door. "I'll see you, David. If you're not too busy tomorrow afternoon, come over and sit by the pool with me."

"Maybe I will. We'll see."

CHAPTER FIVE

At the end of three weeks, Urey finally got home and he was really glad to see Thil. They were both used to him being gone a lot, but not for three solid weeks. He was going to be in Chattanooga for two weeks before leaving for Tel Aviv. He would likely be gone two weeks on that trip. Thil knew when they moved, that he would be gone quite a bit, but she didn't realize it would be that much.

Margaret had been a life-saver for Thil. Ever since their meeting when Urey and Thil came on their first visit, they had become friends. Margaret was lonely as was Thil, and doing things together was therapy for both of them. Her presence made Urey's absence a little more bearable.

Urey tried to explain that once he got the different branches established, he would be home more. She seemed to understand, but it was still hard for her.

"I have much to tell you, David. I hired two sales reps when I was in London plus a man named Liam McAlister to act as manager of the Shepherd office and warehouse. I feel sure he will be good, and I feel comfortable leaving him there by himself. I went to Munich while I was in Europe and was really pleased with the way Gerhard had taken over and was running things."

"Now that we have London up and running, the entire continent of Europe, except for East Germany, will soon be ours. I have confidence in both our managers and will be very surprised if our business doesn't mushroom within the next few months. I made sure I hired men who would let nothing stand in the way of their jobs. Now, I'm anxious for us to think about going into Israel and the Mid-East."

"Whoa. From what I read in the paper and see on TV, there's a lot of bad stuff going on over there. I saw just yesterday some guy in Israel blew himself up along with nine others. You sure don't want to get in the middle of that kind of stuff."

"David, what you read and see are isolated incidents. They get headlines in order to sell papers and get ratings. The country is not like that. It's a wonderful country full of wonderful people. The people I've met are warm and friendly and love their families just like the people here. I think if you let the terrorists keep you from doing business there, you're going to miss a huge opportunity. Israel is wide open for clothes such as we offer, and I can't stress enough how much we need to go there."

"Well, show me your research, and we'll see if we can make it work.

Urey convinced David that Shepherd Apparel is ready to start operating in Israel so they made plans to start the ball rolling. Urey would go to Tel Aviv and start looking for a building and personnel.

"David, what would you think if I made a quick trip to Cairo while I'm in the Mid-East? It's only a short hop from Tel Aviv and it could possibly pay big dividends in the future."

"Whatever you think, Urey. You're the one in charge of global operations. Do you know anything about Muslim clothing? If you don't, you'd better learn about it. We sure don't want to do anything that would violate Islamic laws, so just be sure you know what you're doing when you go over there. When are you planning to leave?"

"I was thinking about this on the way home from London and I thought then if you approved my plan, I would stay home two weeks and then leave. I hate to leave Thil any earlier after just getting back from a three week trip. I would like to leave a week from next Monday. Will that be all right?"

"Whatever you say."

Urey worked hard in his office for the next few days as

well as spending hours in the library. He wanted to get as much information as he could about Israel; its' customs and government and religion. He wanted to find out about Egypt as well. He knew Islam was their primary religion, but he didn't know anything about it, nor did he know anything about Egyptian culture. He wanted to learn as much as he could before he went over there. He thought if he could learn about those things, they might, in turn, help him learn about commerce in those countries.

The departure day for Urey's next trip came too soon for Thil. She took him to the airport and told him a tearful goodbye. His itinerary called for him to be gone two weeks, and she dreaded being alone for that long. She waited until he boarded and then went to the window and watched him take off.

As she drove back to her house, a feeling of utter loneliness consumed her. She was in a strange country and her husband had just left her to go to the other side of the world. Tears rolled down her face as she felt so sorry for herself. Arriving home, she pulled her Mercedes in the garage and just sat in it, crying for several minutes. When she finished crying, she went into the house and changed into a pair of shorts and halter top.

It was a beautiful early summer day, and she grabbed her book and went outside and sat by the pool. The sun and the pool made her feel better, and she soon got into her book. After fifteen or twenty minutes, her eyes got heavy, and it wasn't long until she was asleep.

Since it was Saturday afternoon, David was at home. He had worked that morning, but finished up around noon. After leaving the office, he went to the Red Food Store to buy groceries and then went home. After he ate lunch he went out on the balcony to get some sun. When he got out there, he looked over and saw Thil asleep by her pool. He decided to go over and they could keep each other company. He yelled, "Hey, Thil." She raised up and looked around. David yelled again. "Hey, Thil, unlock your gate, and I'll be over in a minute."

She got up and unlocked the gate and waited just inside until David got there. "Would you like to have a Coke or something?"

"No thanks. I just need some company and thought you might need some, too."

"You're very wise, David. I need company very much. Thank you for coming over."

They took seats in the comfortable chairs by the pool. "Was Urey's flight on time?"

"Yes. He should be well on his way now." He had to catch an El Al plane in Atlanta and I don't remember what time it was supposed to leave, but I know he must be in the air."

The two talked about Urey's job, and how much he loved it, Shepherd Apparel, and how it is growing since Urey came with them, and how she liked America since she got here."

When they started to run out of things to talk about, David asked, "How would you like for me to call Margaret and the three of us go somewhere to eat tonight?"

"That sounds wonderful."

"Okay then. I'll go call her right now. Is there anywhere in particular you'd like to go?"

"No. Surprise me."

"Okay, but you may be sorry. What time do you want to go?

"Is six-thirty all right?"

"Six-thirty it is." David went over to his house to call Margaret and set up their three-way dinner date.

Thil was at David's promptly at six-thirty and they left in his car to pick up Margaret. Nobody wanted to make the decision on where to eat, so David went to a surprise place. While they were eating, David made the remark that "who would believe that three attractive, lonely people would be eating meatloaf on Saturday night at the S & W Cafeteria?"

"Margaret laughed and said, "Leave it up to David Shepherd to do the unusual."

Thil said, "I love it here. The food is delicious."

When they finished, David asked, "Is there anywhere you girls would like to go?"

Nobody said anything, so David headed to Margaret's house and dropped her off. "I guess I'll see you at Church in the morning."."

"Okay, Good night."

On the way to David's, he said, "I bought a fresh supply of that good wine this afternoon. Would you like a glass before we end the evening?"

"Yes, that would be very nice."

When they reached David's and walked into the house, Don was in the den, dancing to the radio with a smile on his face from ear to ear. When he saw David and Thil, he grabbed Thil and danced around the room before Thil could break away from him. "Man, you're in a good mood tonight," David said.

"I know. It's been a good week."

"Are you staying home tonight?"

"No sir. I'm going to pick up Pee Wee. We're gonna go to the nine o'clock movie and I may spend the night with him."

"Be careful. See ya."

***

Don and Richard had their first meeting in front of the YMCA at seven o'clock, where they showed their half of the *queen of hearts* and picked up an envelope from a messenger. They hurried to the car and opened it, and their eyes got big when they saw a stack of one-hundred dollar bills. The bills totaled twenty two hundred dollars; eleven hundred for each of them. "Boy, whatta ya think about this now, Richard?"

"Man, I never dreamed it could be this much. Do you think it will be this much every week?"

"I don't know, but it could be. I'll tell you something, Richard. We've got to be very careful not to let the name of the snitch get out. If anybody finds out about him, the others will probably kill him and then they won't have to pay us. Something else bothers me, too."

"What?"

"You know, you hear nearly every-day about some group wanting to get liquor by the drink approved, and it looks like their movement is gaining strength. Once it's approved, people won't be buying moonshine like they are now, and our little business will end, so we need to make hay while the sun shines and be very careful with our money. Be sure you don't buy any extravagant things that will cause your parents to get suspicious."

"We're both under eighteen so we can't open a bank account and we need to find some place to hide all this money. Do you have any ideas?"

"Not right now, but I can probably find a place somewhere in our house or garage. Where are you going to hide yours?"

"I don't know yet, but I think I can find a place in my room somewhere. Since my mom died, Pop seldom comes in there. The only person, besides me, is the lady that cleans and she doesn't usually do anything but change my bed and vacuum and dust."

"Man, I can't believe this, can you?"

"Richard said, "No. I think I may have died and gone to heaven."

Don said, "I'm supposed to go to the movie with Pee Wee tonight and I just hope I don't act any different than I usually do. We need to go, Richard. I need to find a place to put this money before I pick Pee Wee up."

Don took Richard home and then hurried home, hoping his dad wouldn't be there when he got there. Sure enough, he wasn't, so Don took the money to his room where he found what he thought was a secure place to hide it. He then went downstairs and turned the radio on. The music matched his mood, and he couldn't help but get up and dance, and that's when his dad and Thil came in.

***

Don left and when he had time to get out of the driveway, David took a bottle of wine out of the refrigerator and a couple of glasses from the freezer. Thil sat in one of the plush leather chairs and David took a seat in the matching one next to hers. They talked about what a good afternoon and evening it had been and were looking forward to what the weather man said would be a duplicate tomorrow.

"David, would you mind if I ask you a personal question?"

Surprised, David said, "Of course not. What do you want to know?"

"I've been wondering ever since we met, what is your relationship with Margaret?"

"My relationship with Margaret? Purely friendship. Nothing more. Margaret and my wife were best friends and her husband was a good friend of mine. When my wife died she and Tom were there for me and did everything best friends could do. A year after my wife died, Tom had a fatal heart attack, and that left Margaret and me to take care of each other. She doesn't have any children and she's very lonely. Don is gone all the time so it's like I don't have any so we just keep each other company. So, now you know what my relationship is with Margaret."

"Thank you for telling me. I'm very fond of Margaret."

"Ready for a refill?"

"Not just yet. I have to go to the bathroom. I'll get one when I get back."

When she returned to the den, David had turned on some easy listening music and was standing at the bar, pouring himself a refill. He told her to get her glass and when she did, he filled it. They stood close to each other for a couple minutes, and at one point, when David said something amusing, Thil laughed, and put her hand on his and gently squeezed it. Then they took their seats in the leather chairs and enjoyed their second glass of wine.

For their second refill, they both got up and went to the counter where David got another bottle from the refrigerator and opened it. He poured each of them a glass while the glasses were sitting on the counter, and before she picked hers up, Thil threw her arms around David and kissed him. David kissed her back very passionately. David said, "Thil, we can't do this. We had better go sit back down."

They walked around the counter and this time, instead of sitting in the two chairs, they sat on the sofa, next to each other. David sat down first and then Thil sat next to him, close enough to lay her head on his shoulder. Neither of them said anything for a few minutes and then David said, "Thil honey, we can't do this. You're married, and I'm your husband's friend. We just can't betray him."

"Are you not attracted to me, David?"

"It's not that I don't want to. You're the most desirable woman I know, but it just wouldn't be right." And with that she turned toward him, put her right leg over his, and straddled his lap. Lifting his chin, she kissed him, tenderly. She continued kissing him so passionately he couldn't resist any longer, and they headed to the bedroom.

After a couple hours of feverish passion, they got up and got dressed. Thil wanted to stay all night, but David was afraid Don might decide to come home, so he made her go home.

"Will I see you tomorrow", she asked.

"You definitely will. I'll be home from Church between twelve thirty and one o'clock and I'll see you then. You want to have a sandwich together?"

"That would be nice. I'll see you tomorrow." She gave him a quick kiss on the lips and said, "Good night and thank you, David."

David stood at the door and watched her until he was sure she was safely inside her house, then he turned off the lights and went upstairs to his bedroom. He straightened up his bed and took a shower before he turned in for the night. He went to sleep thinking about the experience he had just had.

As he sat in Church the next morning, he couldn't help but think about Thil and their night together. He knew what they did was wrong and he felt no small amount of guilt, but at the same time, he could hardly wait to get home so he could see her again.

When David pulled into the garage, he got out of the car and walked around to see if Thil was by the pool and sure enough, she was. He hollered across the fence and told her he would be over after he changed clothes.

"Okay. I'll unlock the gate."

He put on a pair of shorts and a tee-shirt and ran down the stairs. He walked through the gate to her pool and she wasn't there. He looked around and didn't see her, but heard her say seductively, "David, here I am." She had stepped inside the door to the house and motioned for him. When he reached her, she threw her arms around him and gave him a big kiss.

"Boy, that was a great hello."

"I missed you, David."

"Well, we can spend the whole afternoon together. Last night we said we would have a sandwich together. Do you still want to?"

"Yes I do and I've already made lunch. I'm going to give you German food. Does that sound good to you?

"It sounds wonderful. I'm hungry."

"All right then. Let's eat."

They took the food to a table near the pool, and since they were having German food, it was only natural they have beer. It was a very enjoyable lunch, and after they finished, David helped clean up, and then they found the comfortable chairs by the pool.

During a break in the conversation, Thil asked, "David, can I come back to your house tonight?"

"I don't know, honey. It depends on where Don will be. I'll have to try to get up with him to see what his plans are."

"If I can't come over there, maybe you can come here. Would you like to do that?"

"I'd love to, but this is Urey's house and I would'nt feel right coming into his home to be with his wife. It's bad enough that we're together, period."

"Try to figure out something, David, because I want to be with you. Where is Don this afternoon?"

"I don't know. Tell you what. I'll go over to the house and try to find where he is and where he's gonna be. I'll be back in a few minutes. Better still, go with me."

The two went to David's and went out on the balcony while David got the rolodex and started looking for numbers of Don's friends. He started with Pee Wee since that was where he was supposed to have spent the night last night, and after two or three calls, he found him. Don said he and some of his buddies were going out to eat dinner and then to a movie. He would be home after the movie; somewhere around nine-thirty.

David went to the balcony and sat down next to Thil. "Don won't be home until after nine o'clock tonight, so we can be together all afternoon."

"Good." She put her arms around him, but David said, "Let's go inside. While this place is fairly private, you can never tell who might be watching."

David's bedroom was actually a suite with a sitting room that had two chairs and a loveseat. When the weather was too cold or rainy to use the balcony, the sitting area off the bedroom was where David and his wife used to sit. It was cozy and they chose the loveseat. David tried to pace himself, but Thil was all over him. He asked, "How about a glass of wine?"

"No, thank you," and she kissed him again.

David could see there was no use putting things off, so they got up and went to the bed where they stayed most of the afternoon.

When they got dressed and went out on the balcony, David tried to enter into a serious conversation with Thil.

"Thil, you know what we're doing is wrong don't you?" Thil didn't answer. She just looked at him and smiled. "I'm serious, Thil. You're married and not only married, but married to my friend and employee. This would crush Urey if he knew. What are we going to do about it?"

"David, I know we are wrong, but I have needs that Urey can't help."

"What do you mean?"

"Urey would kill me if he knew I told you this. Urey and I love each other very much, but when we go to bed, he has a hard time."

"You mean he's impotent?"

"Most of the time. Do you remember him telling you how guilty he feels about the deeds his father did?

"Yeah, when we were at Fehn's."

"Well, his guilt complex has carried over to his sex life. It has caused him to have very high blood pressure and depression. He went to a doctor in Germany about his impotence and the doctor said that was probably the cause. That is one reason he is so anxious to help the Jewish people. He thinks if he can help them enough to ease his conscience, then he might correct his blood pressure and depression and in turn, help his other problem. I don't know if this is correct or not, but I do know we seldom make love, so you see why I need you so badly?"

"Yeah, I see. I had no idea."

"David, please don't push me away."

"I won't. Are you hungry?"

"A little. Do you know what would be good?"

"What?"

"Some Krystal hamburgers."

"That does sound good, doesn't it? I'll get my car keys."

CHAPTER SIX

The following week was a *crusher* at work. Equipment was still coming in for the new plant, and David hardly had time to turn around. He was going to the office around six thirty and not getting home, most nights until after seven. Thil would call, but he was so tired he went to bed early and didn't see her except for Wednesday night, and he sent her home early that night.

Don was also staying home more than usual, and that made their rendezvous' more difficult. David promised her when they were together Wednesday night, that he would make time for her on the weekend, and she seemed to understand.

"I can hardly wait," she said.

"Me either."

Late Friday afternoon, Don went to his dad's office. "Pop, I know this is short notice, but Richard and Pee Wee and a couple other guys are going to Daytona Beach, Sunday, and want me to go with them. Do you think I could go?"

"This really is short notice. Did you talk to Bud Weddle about it?"

"Yes sir. He said we're in pretty good shape unless some large, extra rush orders come in. He thinks it would be all right for me to go if you give your okay. Whatta you think?"

"Well, if Bud thinks it's okay, I guess you can do it."

"Thanks Pop. I'll spend the night at Richard's Saturday night and we'll leave early Sunday."

"Am I going to get to see you at all this weekend?"

"I'm gonna be home tonight. Wanna eat out?"

"Yeah, that sounds good. Say, Urey's still out of town. Why don't we invite Thil to eat with us?"

"It's okay with me. Where are we going to eat?'

"You pick it. I'm so glad to be able to spend time with you, I don't care. Just pick a place that has something besides hamburgers."

"Let's go to Fehn's. I like their fried chicken."

"Fehn's it is. I'll call Thil to see if she wants to go."

They had an enjoyable evening, and David felt good getting to spend some time with Don. After they left the restaurant, Don said he needed to go by somebody's house to pick up some clothes he had left there, which he wanted to take to Florida, so David went straight home so Don could get his car.

Thil walked into the house with David and he offered her a pleasant surprise. "I know you heard Don talking about his trip to Florida next week, didn't you?"

"Yes, it sounds like a lot of fun."

"Thil, how would you like to go to the mountains for a few days? We could run up to Gatlinburg Sunday and stay two or three days."

"Gatlinburg? It sounds German. I'd love to go."

"Okay. I'll go to the office in the morning and line out instructions for everybody while I'm gone. Why don't you come by around ten and we'll try to call Urey to be sure he isn't coming home early. We wouldn't want that, would we? He's scheduled to be back Friday, I think."

In Gatlinburg, they stayed in a beautiful hotel that backed up to a thick forest. Between the hotel and forest a beautiful brook flowed over the mountain stones, making a rippling sound that only a mountain stream can make. Sitting on the balcony, looking at the trees and listening to the brook, a very romantic atmosphere was created.

"Let's go inside," Thil said. Closing the door behind them, they embraced and she pulled David down to the bed.

The couple spent the next three days in the mountains and returned home on Wednesday afternoon. "David, this has been the best time of my life. Thank you."

"I enjoyed it, too, "David said. "Look, let's eat in tonight and have one more night together, and then I've got to get to work tomorrow. Urey will be back day after tomorrow and you've got to get ready for him. What's the first thing you're gonna do when he gets back?"

"I don't know. It will depend on him."

***

Urey got home on Friday and after resting up over the weekend, he went to the office Monday morning. After he looked at his mail, he got Ruby to pour him some coffee and he headed to David's office. "Hi, David, long time, no see."

"I know. It's good to have you back. Did you have a good trip?"

"Yes sir. Very good."

"Profitable?"

"It should prove to be. I was able to lay the groundwork for Shepherd Global to open an office and warehouse in Tel Aviv Yafo whenever you're ready to move."

"What do you mean Tel Aviv Yafo?"

"That's the official name of Tel Aviv now. The city merged with another city and they added Yafo to the Tel Aviv name."

"Oh. What do you think about the prospects of doing business over there?"

"I feel it's an excellent opportunity. Israel is growing and the city of Tel Aviv is doubling in size every few years. Tel Aviv is an industrial mecca and their economy is very strong. The type clothing we furnish is a natural for Israel, and I think the sooner we get there, the better."

"Urey, you're in charge of the overseas business, and you've done well so far, so I'm inclined to go along with what you recommend. Did you get to Egypt?"

"No sir. I ran out of time. I got so involved in Israel, I felt I needed to get back. I still want to go, but maybe I should wait 'til we get things moving in Israel. David, I didn't take any time away from Shepherd Global, but I accidentally stumbled upon a charity that I think I want to get involved with. It helps the victims of the Germans in World War II."

"It sounds to me like you have a lot of things hanging over there. When do you plan to go back?"

"Well sir, I normally like to stay at home with my wife for at least two weeks between trips, but I think this is so important, I would like to leave Sunday if that meets with your approval. I talked it over with Thil, and she realizes how important it is, especially the charity I told you about.

"How does she feel about your leaving again so soon?"

"Actually, she urged me to go ahead and leave Sunday. Will that be all right with you, David?"

David, seeing Thil in his mind, said, "Yes, of course, if you think you need to. Do I need to go with you?"

"No sir. I don't think so right now. Maybe on a future trip you should, but this time there will be very little going on except a lot of back-breaking work, getting the office and warehouse set up. Thank you, anyway."

"How long do you plan to be gone?"

"It's hard to say, David. I think it will probably take me at least two weeks to find and set up an office, and if you will give your permission, I would like to take a week of my vacation to devote to the charity I mentioned. That is important to me. I guess to better answer your question, we should plan on three weeks, for sure, and four weeks, maybe. Is that too long?"

"Not if you produce volume."

"I will do that, Boss. Now, I had better go to my office and start getting things done to prepare for my trip."

***

This trip to the airport wasn't nearly as devastating to Thil as the last time she took Urey, when he was going to Israel. While she loved Urey, and in one way, hated to see him leave; another way, she could hardly wait to see David. She hadn't seen him in more than a week.

When she got home from the airport, she called him. "Hi. Guess what?"

"What?"

"Urey's gone and I'm all by myself. What are you doing?"

"Well, I'm sitting in here talking to Don about his day at work. He just got home."

"Can I see you?"

"Maybe. Let me see what Don's going to do and I'll call you or if you're going to be by the pool, I'll come over in a little while. I should know before I come."

Don left a few minutes after he got home and would be gone until around midnight, opening the door for his dad and Thil to take up where they left off ten days ago.

In a little while, David glanced over at the pool next door and Thil was lying on a chaise lounge in a white two-piece bathing suit. The suit, contrasted with her deep tan, long shapely legs, and coal-black hair, said, *Come on over big boy.* No words were necessary.

Opening the gate, which Thil had unlocked, David approached her. Hearing his foot-steps, she turned over and said, "Hi."

"Hi."

"This sun's hot. Would you like to have a beer?"

"Yeah. That sounds good. It is hot out here."

Thil got up and went into the house and came back out carrying two Michelobs. David took one and took a sip. "Boy, that hits the spot."

As they sat, enjoying their beers, Thil said, "Do you realize we haven't been together in about two weeks?"

"Actually, it's only been ten days."

"Well it seems like two weeks or even longer."

"Honey, Urey was here. Didn't that matter?"

"No. The warmest thing I got from Urey was a kiss."

"Didn't he try?"

"Yes, but he couldn't do anything. I believe he's getting

worse."

"Maybe you two need to get away for a few days and go somewhere that's romantic. At Urey's age, it's a shame he's in such a fix. I hate to think who you would be with if I wasn't around. When Urey gets back, why don't you see if you can get him to go to a doctor?"

"I don't know. I'll think about it."

They each had one more beer and Thil said, "Let's go to your house. You want to?"

When they got to David's bedroom, David stopped to lock the door, and when he turned around, Thil was already out of her bathing suit and turning the bed down. He undressed and got in bed, and Thil acted as if she hadn't been with a man for a really long time. They stayed in bed for a couple hours and for the last thirty or forty-five minutes, David seemed to have his mind somewhere else. "What's wrong, David?"

"Thil, we need to talk. How about going to your house and get out of your bathing suit into some clothes and come back. We'll go get something to eat if you want to. If you would rather fix a sandwich and eat here or at your house, we can do that, but I want us to talk, okay?"

"What about, David?"

"Let's wait 'til we get dressed, and we'll talk."

"You're scaring me. Tell me."

"We'll talk later, okay?"

"Okay. You come to my house, and I'll fix the sandwiches."

"All right, I'll be over in a few minutes."

When David got to Thil's, she was almost finished making Rueben sandwiches. "In Germany we always make these with homemade bread, but since I don't have any, deli bread will have to do."

"They look delicious. Can I help you do anything?"

"No. Everything's ready. Let's take it outside and eat by the pool. Will you carry the chips? I'll come back and get the beer."

As they ate, Thil's curiosity got the best of her and she asked, "What do you want to talk about, David?"

David's mouth was full and he had to chew and swallow before he could answer. "Thil, do you ever feel guilty about what we're doing?"

"No. Why?"

"Well, I don't think I'm ready to stop, but I really feel that we should slow down. We're acting like a pair of over-sexed teenagers."

"Don't you like being with me?"

"You bet I do. You're the most sensual woman I've ever seen, but that's not the problem. The first thing is that you're married and you're married to my friend. The second thing is I am CEO of a large company with more than two thousand employees. Most of those employees are just plain, good, Church-going people and that's what I'm supposed to be. What if some of those people saw you and me together and they figured out what was going on? It would deeply disappoint them, not to mention that they would tell everybody, and my entire company would lose respect for me. Thirdly, I would hate for Don to know what we're doing. He sees us together, and I don't think he has reason to be suspicious, but he's not stupid. He'll soon figure it out. He's still naïve enough to think a married woman should not mess around on her husband."

"What are you trying to say, David? I love you."

"That's another thing. You're not supposed to love me. You're supposed to love Urey."

"Does this mean you don't want to see me anymore?"

"No, honey. We shouldn't see each other anymore, but I'm too crazy about you not to see you. You said you love me. Love is a powerful word, and if our situation was different, I would tell you I love you, too, but with Urey in your life, I can't tell you that. All I'm saying is we need to slow down and be careful. There's a lot at stake. Do you understand what I mean?"

"Yes, but I still love you. When can I be with you again?"

"Tomorrow starts a new week, and I'm going to be really busy. We're starting some operations in our new plant, and there are always problems when you first start, so I don't know when. I'll have to call you."

"You will call, won't you?"

"I sure will; in fact, I'll call you every day. It's just that I don't know when we can see each other. Shepherd Global has gotten so big since Urey started with us, I'm going to have to hire an assistant if I'm going to have any time of my own at all. Don't worry, darling. We'll get together, just not as often as before. Are you sure you understand?"

"Yes, David, but I don't have to like it."

"Atta girl. Now let's clean up our mess, so we can get back out here and enjoy the sunset."

***

Two Months Later

School had started and the Saturday night meetings at the "Y" were still being held, but Don and Richard were having to be really careful to avoid suspicion since many school activities took place there. Each week the two were splitting anywhere from two to three thousand dollars, and so far, each boy had socked away around fifteen thousand dollars.

Every time the boys would go to Horace Edwards' house, Horace would try to pressure them into revealing who the snitch was, but there was no way they would give out that information. It had gotten to where Horace liked the boys and they liked him, and each trip had become very relaxed, but Don and Richard remained on guard every time they went there.

***

Urey had been spending a great amount of time overseas.

Gerhard had settled into running the entire European operation and that freed Urey to spend most of his time in the Mid-East. He had spent some time in Egypt and had done some preliminary legwork there, but ninety percent of his time was spent in Israel.

When in Israel, every spare minute was spent with the charity to help WWII victims. That was taking time away from being at home with his wife, and while Thil didn't care that much, David did. Urey continued to show increases in Shepherd's business and David couldn't argue with that, but he felt that when Urey wasn't involved with Shepherd business, he needed to be home.

David had told Thil to call him at the office anytime if it was important, but not to call otherwise. One afternoon, Ruby buzzed David. "Mr. Shepherd, Bathilda Steen in on line one for you."

"Hello."

"David, can you talk?"

"Yes. What is it?"

"Are you sure nobody's listening?"

"I'm sure. What's up?"

"David, I'm pregnant."

"You're what?"

"I'm pregnant."

"Well, congratulations. Have you called Urey yet?"

"No. David, I'm almost sure the baby is yours."

"Why do you think that?"

"Because you're the only one I've been with during the time period when I conceived."

"Are you sure?"

"Yes, I'm sure. I need to see you."

"Okay. Let me finish up a couple things, and I'll be there in about thirty minutes."

When he got to Thil's and rang the bell, she opened the door almost immediately and threw her arms around him, bawling. After he got her calmed down, he asked, "Are you sure you're pregnant?"

"Yes"

"Did you go to the doctor?"

"Yes, I went today. I missed last month, but that had happened before, so I didn't think too much about it, but when I missed this month, I went to the doctor and he confirmed what I had thought."

"And you're sure it's not Urey's?"

"Yes. It's yours."

"Okay. Here's what we're going to do, Sweetheart. When Urey comes home next week, I'm going send the two of you on vacation to someplace that's very romantic. While you're gone, you will need to do everything you can do to seduce him. He won't be able to resist you and after you have made love with each other, a little later, you can tell him you're pregnant. Naturally, he'll think the baby is his, and everything will be fine. Don't you think that will work?"

"I don't know. What if he can't do anything?"

"Surely he can. I think I'll send you on a cruise. How romantic is that? If he can't do anything there, then something is definitely wrong with him. I think it'll work."

"All right, but if it doesn't, I hope you can think of something else."

"That'll work."

CHAPTER SEVEN

Urey was exhausted when he got home the following week and didn't want to do anything his first day except lie around the pool and sleep. Thil was the ever-attentive seductress, but it was all for nothing. "I'm sorry, Thil, but I just don't have enough energy to do anything but rest today. Maybe tomorrow will be better."

On his second day home, he went to the office and caught up on some of his paperwork and had lunch with David. At lunch they talked about all that was going on with regards to Shepherd Global in Europe and the Mid-East. Urey was very enthusiastic about all that was happening and told David, he was anxious to get back, but he would have to be extra careful because things were starting to heat up in Israel.

"Maybe you should stay home until things cool down."

"No, David. I need to get back. I'll be safe, I assure you.."

After a few minutes discussing business, David sprung a surprise on Urey. "Urey, I don't know if I've told you before, but I want you to know that I appreciate what you're doing for our company. You stay gone more than anyone should have to and never complain about it. You have apparently hired the right people to run the different offices because all of them are doing good business. I want to do something for you and Thil to show my appreciation. I mentioned Thil because she is making sacrifices as well by having to stay home alone while you travel. Urey, I'm giving you and Thil a two-week South American cruise. You will occupy the honeymoon suite on board and every need and wish will be taken care of. Not only is everything taken care of, I'm going to give you a thousand dollars cash, spending money."

"David, I don't know what to say. As an employer you have already done much more for us than was required of you. I know I'm gone much of the time, but thanks to you and Margaret, I don't have to worry about Thil. She has told me how much the three of you are together and I should thank Margaret."

David thought, *I hope he doesn't try to see Margaret. She won't know what he's talking about.*

Urey continued. "I know many commercial travelers who can't do their job as well as they need to because of worrying about having to leave their wives and families at home. I don't have to worry about that because I know Thil is being well taken care of."

You have no idea how well.

"I can't express to you my gratitude for what you are offering to do for us, but I must respectfully decline your offer. David, I have so much going on right now in Tel Aviv that I feel I must get back there as soon as possible. I make it a practice never to take time for pleasure when there's important work to be done. This is what I require of my people and it would not be right for me to violate it. Thank you, my friend, but no thank you."

"I can't believe you're turning down an offer like this. This is a once in a lifetime offer. I want you to think about it before you make your final decision."

"All right, I'll think about it, but I'm sure my answer will be the same."

When they finished lunch, they returned to the office where each went to their respective offices.

The next day they went to the same place for lunch. After they sat down and ordered, David asked Urey if he had thought about the cruise offer. "Yes, I did think about it, but as I told you yesterday, I feel that I must get back to my responsibilities in Israel."

"Did you talk to Thil about it?"

"No. This must be my decision."

"I was afraid you were going to refuse the offer, so I've come up with Plan B. Urey, I'm just trying to show you my appreciation and I understand that you feel your responsibilities, so here's a different offer."

"Maybe the two-week time period for the cruise was too long and the reason for your refusal, so listen to this. There is an island in South Georgia named Jekyll Island. It has a very nice beach, excellent hotels, good restaurants, and other amenities to make a perfect vacation. Why don't you and Thil pack your bags and let me send you down there for one-week? It'll make a new man out of you."

"David, again I can't express my gratitude enough, but I must say no. I know it's hard for you to understand, but I could not relax and enjoy something, knowing I should be somewhere else. Maybe, sometime, when things start running smoothly overseas, you will consider making your very generous offer again. Speaking of overseas, would you mind if I leave Thursday to go back?"

"Urey, that only gives you four days at home."

"I know, but I need to get back."

"Did you tell Thil you're leaving?"

"I told her I was thinking about it."

"What did she say?"

"I think she has gotten used to it. She said to do whatever I wanted to do."

"Well, you have my permission to leave, but I think you're making a mistake.

***

The El Al plane touched down at Ben Gurion International airport and Urey de-planed and went to the baggage claim area. From there, he took a taxi to his hotel. On the ride to the hotel, the cab driver told him about a suicide bomber blowing himself and three other people up the day before. He said a heightened terrorist alert had been issued and the general population was on edge.

Conflict between the Arabs and Jews had been going on for thousands of years, so this was not something new, but anytime a fanatic that looks just like everyone else blows himself and others up in public, it's cause for concern. While Urey kept his eyes open for anything that looked unusual around him, he wasn't overly concerned.

Ramat Gan was the suburb where the Shepherd office and warehouse was to be located. Only a few miles from downtown Tel Aviv, the pace was slower and the rent lower, but containing just about every convenience found downtown. The hotel where Urey stayed was on that side of Tel Aviv, so his twenty minute commute was simple. Most of the time, he took a city bus to work.

Since it was Friday, Sabbath began at sundown and he didn't have time to do much work, so he took a cab to the office of the charity with which he had been working. Just being in the presence of those people and giving them a kind word or anything else he could do for them greatly reduced the guilt he was carrying. Some of the people didn't trust him because he was German and some recognized the name Steen. Those who knew who Urey's father was would not have anything to do with him, but others welcomed his kindness toward them and forgave him, even if he was German.

***

As David turned into his driveway after leaving work Friday afternoon, Thil met him. "Hi."

"Hi," he answered. "What's up?"

"Nothing, really. I just wanted to see you."

"I'm glad to see you, too. Wanna come in?"

"Yes. I'd like that."

They walked through the kitchen into the den and David asked, "How about a glass of wine while I go upstairs and change clothes?"

"That sounds good. Where's Don?"

"Gone to a football game."

"Since you won't be eating with him, why don't you come to my house for some bratwurst?"

"I love bratwurst. It's a deal. Sit here and drink your wine, and I'll be back down in a few minutes and have a glass with you,"

"Okay. Hurry."

The weather was still warm so David was going to change into shorts. He took his clothes off, but before putting on the shorts he went to the bathroom. When he opened the door to come out, Thil was standing there with her wine and a glass for him. "Why don't we have our wine up here?"

It had been nearly two weeks since they had been together and David was in no mood to turn her away. "Okay, but let me get some clothes on."

"No, no, that's not necessary. Let me just slip out of mine, then we'll be even."

"Whatever you say." She came to David and they kissed as she undressed. They were next to the bed and just fell over into it.

When they finally got ready to get up, David said, smiling, "What about that bratwurst? I'm starved."

"You silly thing. All right come, I'll give you bratwurst, but I warn you. I might bring you back here for more wine when we finish."

"Well, let's have some bratwurst and see what happens."

Thil and David saw each other on Saturday and Sunday afternoon. David had still not been able to find a suitable assistant at the office and he was spending, on the average, twelve hours a day at work. That didn't leave time for much of anything else, except sleeping. He did manage to call Thil every day to check on her.

A couple days, she and Margaret got together and did things. They both liked to shop, so they probably spent a great deal of time at Eastgate shopping center buying no-telling what. Margaret had been kind of suspicious about Thil and David because she used to see David every day or two, and for a while after Thil and Urey moved, she would see Thil pretty often. Now, she hardly ever saw either one. She did spot them together one time and that set her to thinking that maybe something was going on.

It was almost seven when David got away from the office Friday. It had been a long day and he was beat. He got in his car and drove straight home, intending to shower and go to bed early. Thil had been watching for him from her window and when he pulled into the driveway, she was there by the time he got out of the car. "Hi. I missed you."

"I missed you, too."

"Can I see you tonight?"

"Honey, you can see me, but at the risk of sounding like Urey, I'm too tired to do anything."

"That's all right. I just want to be with you."

"Okay. Come on in and have a glass of wine. I'm going upstairs to shower and change clothes, but I can't do like last Friday, okay?"

"All right. I'll wait in the den for you."

When he finished and went downstairs, Thil had poured a glass of wine for him. He sat down and hadn't taken more than two or three sips before he was sound asleep. Thil stayed for a long time just to be with him and finally went home around ten o'clock.

After a good night's rest, David had a lazy day on Saturday. He had a late breakfast and called Thil to tell her he was going to come to her house and sit by the pool and would she please unlock the gate?

When he got there, the gate was unlocked, but Thil was nowhere to be seen so he pulled up his usual chair and sat down. After about an hour, he heard a car in the driveway and turned to see Thil's Mercedes pulling in. She had been to the store to buy groceries. He got up and they unloaded the bags together. Then he went back and sat down. After a little while, she came out, and they spent the rest of the day together.

On Sunday, after David went to Church, he called to see if she would like to go somewhere to eat. She did, and afterwards, they spent the rest of the day together.

On Monday, David had to get back to the grind. He did find time to call her, but only talked a minute. He was so busy. Tuesday was very busy as well and he didn't leave the office until almost eight o'clock.

At nine-fifteen Wednesday morning, Ruby went to David's office and said,"Thil Steen is on the phone and she sounds upset."

"Hi Thil. What's up?"

"David, Urey's dead."

"He's what?"

"Someone blew up the bus he was riding and killed twenty one people. What do I do, David?"

"Sit tight. I'll be right there."

David stopped by Ruby's desk and told her what had happened and told her to get on the intercom and tell all their employees. He said he would be with Thil if anybody needed him.

Thil was crying when David walked in the door. She ran to him and put her arms around him. "I'm so sorry, Thil. Can you tell me what happened?"

"A man from the State Department called and asked if I was Mrs. Ulrich Steen. When I said I was, he told me there had been an incident in Tel Aviv, Israel." He said, "Mrs. Steen, my name is Charles Hall with the United States State Department. I regret having to inform you that your husband was killed at six p.m. last night in Tel Aviv, Israel by a suicide bomber while riding a public transportation bus. As we get more information, we will be in touch with you. Again, I'm sorry. Good bye."

"That's all I know, David."

"Where are you going to have them take his body?"

"I'm going to have it taken to Munich. Will you go there

with me, David?"

"Of course I will."

"Are you going to try to get there to make the arrangements or do you have someone there that can do it?'

"His mother is still alive and he has a sister. He also has an uncle. I doubt if his mother can do much, but his sister may be able to make the arrangements. If she can't, then I'm going to call Gerhard Lehman at the Shepherd office. I'm sure he wouldn't mind. He and Urey were close."

"When do you think it will be?"

"I don't have any idea. I have to wait until the State Department calls and tells me when they will deliver the body. I'm going to call his mother and sister today and I will probably call Gerhard as well."

"That's a good idea."

"Would you like to come to my office and call from the company telephone? It will save you a good deal of money, and my secretary can help you place the calls."

"Yes I would like to do that."

"We'll go to the office when you're ready. I think Munich is six hours ahead of us so it's late afternoon over there right now. If you want to reach them today, I suggest we go to the office pretty soon."

"Let me freshen up, and change clothes, and I'll be ready. Thank you for helping me, David."

"Next to Don and my Dad, you're the most important person in my life. I would never dream of not helping you. This is probably the wrong time to say this, Thil, but I love you."

She put her arms around him and said, "Thank you."

Making overseas calls had become *old hat* to Ruby. She had been calling Urey and Gerhard every week since he came with Shepherd Global, so she knew how to do it. She placed the first call to Urey's mother and as usual, the operator had to place the call, and then when the connection was finally completed, the operator called back to say the call was ready. After what seemed to be forever, the phone finally rang, and the call had gone through. Giselle, Urey's sister answered, and Thil said in German, " Hello, Giselle, it's Thil. How are you?"

Also, in German, "I'm fine."

"Giselle, is Mother Steen there? I need to talk to her."

"Thil, the doctor sedated her and she's in bed. Can I help you?"

"Giselle, I have some very bad news. Urey was in Israel and was killed by a suicide bomber."

Giselle let out a scream and began sobbing. "When did this happen?"

"Last night. I only found out this morning. Giselle, I want to bring him to Munich to be buried. Can you help with the arrangements?"

"I don't know, Thil. I'm so tied down with Mother, and she's unable to do anything. I just don't know. Is there no one else you can call?"

"I didn't call anyone else, Giselle. You're his sister so I just naturally thought you would want to be the one, but don't worry about it. I'll find someone else. Do you want me to call you when we have the arrangements made, or do you think you will be too busy to come to your brother's funeral?"

"Yes, I want to know when it is. You seem angry, Thil. Please don't be angry with me."

"Good-bye Giselle," and she slammed the telephone down.

"Ruby, would you mind placing a call to Gerhard Lehman? He's at the Shepherd office in Munich."

The call to Gerhard went a little smoother than the last one. It was only a very few minutes before the operator called saying they were connected. Again, in German, "Hello Gerhard. This is Thil Steen."

"Hello, Thil. How are you?"

"I'm not very well today, Gerhard. I'm calling to tell you that Urey was killed last night in Israel."

"Oh no. What happened?"

"He was on a bus and a suicide bomber blew them up."

"That's terrible. Are you bringing him here or to America

to be buried?"

"I want to send him to Munich since that's his home. Gerhard, would you please help with the arrangements? It's hard for me to do it being all the way over here, and I can't leave until the State Department calls and tells me when I can get the body."

"Of course I'll help. Urey was my best friend and I love you, Thil. Are you going to have a burial or will he be cremated?"

"I haven't had time to think about that. What do you suggest?"

"Since he didn't go to Church, I wouldn't have a funeral. A graveside service might be good, but if it were me, I think I would have him cremated."

"Will you look into having that done, please?"

"Yes. I'll take care of it."

Thank you Gerhard. I'll call you when I hear from the State Department. Oh yes. Gerhard will you please call the other fellows in the agency and tell them?"

"I certainly will."

"And another thing, Gerhard. When I come to Munich, David Shepherd is coming with me, and I think he will want to meet with you and the other guys."

"Good. We'll be looking forward to seeing him. Thil, I'm terribly sorry about Urey and don't worry about the arrangements. I'll take care of everything."

"Thank you, Gerhard. Good-bye."

"Good-bye. Thil. I love you."

"Oh, I nearly forgot. Gerhard, I'm going to give the telephone to Ruby. Will you please give her the name and address of the funeral home"

"Yes, I will." Ruby took down all the information and gave it to her.

While Thil was talking to Gerhard, David called Margaret, explaining the situation, and asked her to please stay in touch with Thil. He told her he would stay with her the rest of the day, but he had to work the next day and hated for her to be by herself all day."

Margaret said how sorry she was and told David she would go to Thil's the next morning and stay as long as she was needed.

When Ruby finished talking to Gerhard, David asked Thil, "Do you need to talk to anyone else? How about your family?"

"I don't have any. Didn't I tell you that?"

"No, I don't think you did. Do you want to go back home now?"

"Yes, please."

"Do you feel like eating any lunch?"

"No, thank you. I'm not hungry."

"Come on then. I'll take you home. Ruby, I'm going to take Thil home, and I don't know if I'll be back today or not. If you need to reach me, call Thil's house."

"Okay. Thil, I'm real sorry about Urey. If I can do anything for you, please let me know."

"I will, Ruby. Thank you."

CHAPTER EIGHT

Business at Shepherd Global was at its highest level, ever, and David was absolutely *slammed*. He simply had to find someone to assist him. He decided it would probably be better to promote someone from within the company rather than to look outside. Already, there was a group of key people on whom he depended, so he would try to decide which one of them would make a good assistant.

With the death of Urey, it was likely that he would have to start traveling a lot more. He hoped that Gerhard might be able to move into managing the entire Global operation. Israel was on the verge of opening up, and Urey had done a lot of work there, but with the political situation the way it was, there might be a delay. Still, David was sure he would have to spend more time in Europe. The Mid-East might have to wait. He would have a better feel of the situation after he met with the sales team after Urey's funeral.

A light seemed to come on in David's brain while he ate lunch. *Why didn't I think of this before now? Tom Ratcliff is the one to move up. I'll talk to him when I get back to the office.*

As David passed Ruby's desk on the way to his office, "Ruby, would you please tell Tom Ratcliff to come to my office?"

When Tom came in, David said, "Hi, Tom. Have a seat." Tom waited for David to talk. "Tom, I guess you heard about Urey."

"Yes sir. That's terrible."

"Yes, it is. This is why I called you. Tom, I need help. As you know, our business has mushroomed since we went international. Urey was looking after most of the international part, but now that he's gone, it looks like I'm going to have to take over that part, at least until I can get someone else to take it over. Urey's wife is going to have him cremated and buried in Germany, and I'm going over there with her."

"While I'm there, I'm going to meet with our European sales staff and hopefully get things smoothed out, but I'm sure I will be spending a lot more time overseas and that brings me to you."

"You started working here when you were in college, didn't you?"

"Yes. I started working in the shipping department when I was a sophomore at U.C. and then worked in different departments until I graduated. After I graduated, your dad said I would make a good salesman and put me in the sales department and here I am."

"Well, I would like to put you in another department; in fact, I want to put you in all the departments. Tom, I hope you will accept my offer to make you my assistant. With the job, you will be given the title of Vice-President and your responsibilities will be to run the entire company when I'm away and to help me run it when I'm here. Naturally, a pay increase accompanies all that. Whatta ya say?"

"Wow!! I don't know what to say. I have loved Shepherd Apparel ever since I came here and now this. Wow!! To answer your question, yes, sir, I accept and promise I will do my best to make you proud of the job I do. Wow!"

"Okay, then, it's a deal. Try to get everything wrapped up in your office this afternoon if you can and come in here when you arrive in the morning. I will be going to Germany in a few days and will need to outline some things for you to do while I'm gone."

"Do you know how long you'll be gone?"

"Not at this point. Maybe a week."

"I'll stay in touch and will try to be where you can reach me if you have to."

"David, I don't know how to thank you. I won't let you down."

"I know you won't. Listen, why don't you go call my Dad? He always liked you and I think he would be tickled about your promotion."

"That's a good idea. I'll do that."

***

Friday was another *crusher,* and David wished he had brought Tom in a long time ago. Thankfully, Tom sort of knew what was going on, so it wasn't as if he were a dead weight around his neck. David was trying to anticipate the following week since he felt Thil would find out about Urey over the weekend, and would have to leave.

Normally, the office was closed on Saturday, but with everything that was going on, he, Tom, and Ruby came in for half a day. David was right about Thil getting a call. The State Department called around nine o'clock Saturday morning and said they would ship Urey's body to the funeral home in Munich where Thil wanted it to go. They told her it would arrive on Sunday. Thil called David immediately and told him what they said.

"Do you need to call Gerhard? If you do, you can come here to the office. Ruby's here, and she can help you."

"Thank you, David. I would like to do that. Could I come now?"

"Yeah. When you get here, ring the buzzer, and someone will let you in. See you in a few minutes."

When Thil got there, Tom let her in, and they went to David's office. David told Ruby to please make a call to Gerhard and said Thil would have to help with the address and number since it was late Saturday in Munich.

While Ruby was placing the call, David was getting *antsy.* "Are you wanting to leave today or tomorrow, Thil?"

"If we can get a flight today, I would like to go today, but if we can't, tomorrow will do."

"Okay, when Ruby gets through there, I'll have her call the airline."

After so long, Ruby finally reached Gerhard and handed the phone to Thil. While Thil was talking to Gerhard, David told Ruby to call and get reservations for two on a Lufthansa flight to Munich. "We'll let Shepherd pay for Thil's ticket on this one, Ruby."

"Mr. Shepherd, there's a flight that leaves at six-fifteen tonight. The next one leaves at seven-forty-five tomorrow morning. Which one do you want?"

David interrupted Thil's phone conversation and told her about the two flights. "How about it, Thil? It's going to be hard for me to get the one tonight, but I will if I have to. Do you think we can catch the one in the morning just as well?"

"Whichever is best for you, David."

"Ruby, book two on the seven forty five and Ruby, make them first class."

She gave him one of those looks out of the corner of her eye but did what she was told.

Thil left and David told her he would come over to her house when he got home. It was getting close to noon, and Tom and Ruby were ready to leave for the weekend. David apologized to Tom for leaving him hanging, but assured him he felt he could do the job. "I'll tell you what I'm going to do, Tom. I'm going to call Dad and explain everything that has happened and ask him to help you if you call him. I'm sure he will be glad to help. After all, he did your job for forty years."

"That'll be great."

Ruby and Tom left, but before David did, he packed a briefcase with stuff he might need when he met with Gerhard and the others after Urey's ceremony. When he finally got everything, he called home to try to catch Don before he took off. When Don answered, David told him to not leave until he got there.

Don was outside, doing something on his car when David

drove up. "Hi Pop. What's up?"

"Remember me telling you that I'm going to Germany with Thil? Well, we're catching a plane early in the morning, and you will have to take us to the airport. Be sure you get in early enough tonight to be able to get up at five-thirty in the morning. Our plane leaves at seven- forty-five. We still have to get our tickets, so we'll need to be at the airport by about six-thirty. We'll have to leave here a little after six."

"Okay, Pop. No problem."

"Don, where do you want to stay while I'm gone, with your Granddad?"

"Pop, I'm almost eighteen years old. I'll just stay here."

"I'd rather you stay with someone. How about Margaret?"

"No, Pop. Let me stay here. I'll be all right."

"Don, if I agree to let you stay here, you have to promise that you won't have any people in here."

"I promise. I won't have anybody here."

"All right, but I'm going to ask a couple people to check on you and if they tell me you've had people in or had a party or anything like that, I'll take your car keys when I get back. Is that understood?"

"Okay, Pop. I promise."

Don thought, *I might not even go out tonight. After I make my pick-up at the "Y", I think I'll just come home and stay. That should impress Pop.*

David walked over to Thil's and Margaret had just gotten there. "Hi ladies."

They both spoke and Margaret said, "I understand you're going on a trip."

"Yeah. I've never been to Germany. I'm just sorry it has to be under these circumstances, but I'll have a good guide. By the way, Margaret, I agreed to let Don stay at home by himself. If you have a chance, would you mind checking on him a time or two. I told him he couldn't have any people in, and if I found out he did, then I would take his car keys.

"I'll be glad to. Do you think he would go out and eat with

me if I asked him?"

"He might. You can never tell about Don."

"Thil, do you need anything right now? If not, I'm gonna take off. I've got to go to the grocery store and buy something for Don to eat while I'm gone, and then I've got to run a couple more errands."

"I don't need anything, David. Thank you."

"If I don't see you again today, be ready to leave at six-fifteen in the morning."

"Okay, David."

"See ya, Margaret."

"Bye, David."

***

The flight from Chattanooga to Atlanta took only twenty minutes. They left Chattanooga on Delta but had to catch a Lufthansa flight from Atlanta to Munich. Lufthansa had just started flying the new 747's and it was really something. The first class section was unbelievable and David and Thil were like two kids.

After the plane had leveled off at thirty six thousand feet, it wasn't long until they were served lunch. While they were eating, David told Thil, "You know something, honey, with everything there was to do, I forgot to make a hotel reservation."

"You don't need to make a reservation. I want you to stay with me."

"Do you think that would be right?"

"Why not? My apartment has plenty of room for two people."

"What will people say if I stay with you?"

"What people? Urey's mother wouldn't understand, and I don't care about his sister. His uncle might not even be there, and Gerhard certainly won't care. I don't care what they say, anyway. I want you to stay with me.""Okay. Whatever you say."

After the delicious lunch was over and their trays picked up, David had the stewardess hand him a pillow, and he laid back for a nap. Soon, Thil did the same. That would help pass the time on the ten hour flight.

CHAPTER NINE

The plane landed at eight-twenty and as they were leaving the plane and walking toward the terminal, Thil shouted, "Gerhard" and ran to him and threw her arms around him. "How did you know we would be on this flight?"

"There are only a few flights from Atlanta, so I called the airline and asked if your names were on the passenger lists and when I asked about this one, they said your names were there."

"Gerhard, this is David."

"Hello David. I feel as if I know you. It's good to meet you."

"Good to meet you, too, Gerhard.

After they got their bags, Gerhard said, "I have my car. Where do I take you?"

"Thil said, "We're going to my place. I have plenty of room, so David is going to stay there with me."

"That's good. You don't need to be alone."

On the way to Thil's, Gerhard said, "The funeral home called, and Urey's body came in too late to do anything today. They said the cremation would not be finished until tomorrow afternoon and wanted to know what kind of service you want. I told them I would have to let them know."

"David and I talked about this on the plane and I think we should just have something simple right before the ashes are put into the mausoleum. Maybe a prayer and a few remarks by Father Wilhelm. Father Wilhelm was only a slight acquaintance of Urey's, but he was the only priest Thil knew. Will you call and tell them that?"

"Yes, I'll take care of it."

"Thank you,"

Gerhard pulled up in front of a beautiful apartment building and said, "We're here."

Thil said, "This is where Urey and I lived before we went to America."

"It looks really nice," David said.

Gerhard helped unload the bags and carried Thil's upstairs for her to her apartment. When she unlocked the door, and they got inside, she asked Gerhard to come in, but he said he needed to go, and that he would come tell her the next day when the funeral home called him. He kissed Thil on the cheek and shook David's hand and said, "Sleep well. You should rest tomorrow. It may be late before we know anything. I'll come over the minute I hear. Good night."

"Good night, Gerhard. Thank you for meeting us."

"You're welcome."

Just as soon as Gerhard left, Thil walked over to David and put her arms around him, "Thank you for being here with me. I don't know what I would do without you."

"I'm glad I can be here. I'm tired. Are you?"

"Yes. I'm about ready for bed."

"Where do you want me to sleep?"

She walked to a bedroom and said, "You can sleep here."

"Okay. Thank you. If you don't mind, I think I'll turn in."

"I am, too."

David thought he was in the spare room, but in a few minutes Thil came in and slipped into bed beside him. "Surprised?"

"A little," he said.

She turned toward him and put her arms around him. "I love you, David."

"I love you, too. Thil, we're both too tired tonight, but tomorrow or sometime soon, we need to have a long talk."

"What about?"

"Lots of things. You just lost your husband and you're pregnant by someone who's not your husband. Don't you think these are things that need to be discussed?"

"Yes. I guess they do."

"Well, let's try to get a good night's rest, and maybe we can talk about it tomorrow. Good night." David turned over to go to sleep, but Thil had other ideas, and she won.

Since the apartment had been empty, there was nothing to eat in the pantry, so when they got up the next morning, they couldn't even have coffee. "Are there any places close, where we could get some coffee?"

"Yes, about a block away. Do you want us to go, or would you like for me to go get some and bring it back?"

"I don't care. Are you hungry?"

"No, not this early. Why don't I go get coffee and bring it back?"

"That sounds good. Bring back two or three cups for each of us."

"All right. I'll get dressed."

Thil disappeared, and when she came out of the bedroom, she was wearing white pants with a navy polka-dot top and had put her hair into a ponytail. She looked amazing. "I'll be back as soon as I can."

"Be careful. If you pass any men on the way, they may kidnap you, you look so good. Maybe I should go with you."

"You're silly. Nobody would have me."

"I would."

"You're the only one who counts. I'll be back in a few minutes."

While Thil went to get the coffee, David went into the bathroom to shave and shower. She returned just as he was finishing getting dressed.

Thil brought three cups for David and two for herself. She also bought a newspaper, but didn't realize until she got back to the apartment that David couldn't read it. They laughed about that.

As they drank their coffee, Thil told David about her growing up and living in Bonn. "I am too young to remember much about the war, but I remember how hard it was on nearly

81

everyone. I am an only child and my father was killed when I was eight years old. I remember how hard my mother worked to try to feed us and how she insisted I study hard and do well in school. I devoted myself to doing well in school and it paid off. I was given a scholarship to the University of Bonn, and that's where I met Urey. He was a senior, and I was a freshman."

"We dated a few times while he was still at the University; then, he came back to Munich after graduation. He got a job in Munich, and I didn't see him for a long time. Then, more than a year later, he called me and said he was in Bonn and would like to see me. We went out and after that, every time he would go to Bonn, we would see each other."

"When I was a senior, my mother died, and Urey just happened to come to Bonn that very day. When he found out about mother, he came to see me, and you can't imagine how much he helped me get through that terrible time. We continued to date whenever he was in Bonn, and after I graduated, we got married, and I came to Munich with him."

"We lived in a small flat for the first couple of years, and then when he began to be successful, we moved here. This is what you call in America a condominium. We own this apartment."

"Oh, I see. It's very nice, Thil. Have you had time to think about what you're going to do with it? Do you think you might sell it?"

"I don't know yet."

There was a knock on the door, and it was Gerhard. "The funeral home called and everything will be ready around four this afternoon. Do you want to have the service then or wait until tomorrow?"

"What do you think, David?"

"I think it would be best if you wait until tomorrow. That will give you time to get in touch with Urey's family and any friends you might want to invite."

"That's a good idea. That's what we'll do. Gerhard, would

you please tell the funeral home to deliver the ashes to the mausoleum and set the service up for ten o'clock. They should work out the details with Father Wilhelm."

"Gerhard," David said, "why don't you take us to the Shepherd office, and Thil can use the telephone there. Also, we probably need to rent a car. Is there a rental place other than the airport?"

"David, my wife and I have an extra automobile, and I will be happy for you to use it."

"Are you sure?"

"Yes, it's just sitting there. I'll tell my wife to bring it to the office."

"Well, if you're sure. That will be a big help. Thank you."

The three of them got in Gerhard's car and rode to the Shepherd office. When they got close, David noticed the sign out front that said *SHEPHERD GLOBAL APPAREL GROUP*. He couldn't read anything except *SHEPHERD*, but he knew what the other words said. It gave him a sense of pride and he asked Gerhard to take a picture of it sometime and send it to him.

As soon as they got inside, Gerhard called his wife, Daniele and told her to bring their extra car. Thil would be using it. Next, he led Thil to a desk where there was a telephone and directory. While she was calling a few friends and relatives of Urey's, David and Gerhard sat and talked in Gerhard's office. "Have you told your sales staff that I would like to meet them while I'm here?"

"Yes, they're just waiting to hear from me, telling them when."

"Since the funeral is tomorrow, there may not be enough time, so why don't you set it up for Wednesday morning? That way, while we're meeting, Thil can visit friends, or whatever she wants to do, and we will fly back on Thursday. Do we need more than one day? If we do, we can go back Friday."

"David, if you're in no rush to leave, why don't you plan to leave Friday? With the loss of Urey, there is an awful lot to learn and understand, and I think it would benefit you as well as us."

"Okay. We'll get a flight Friday."

"Gerhard, while we're waiting on Thil to get through, I want to ask you something. Would you be interested in taking Urey's place with Shepherd Global? I thought about this all the way across the Atlantic, and I think you would be the natural successor to Urey."

"Would I have to move to America?"

"I haven't thought about that. Would that be a problem for you?"

"It would. My wife and I both have large families, and it would be very hard to move that far away from them. If I could stay in Munich and travel out of here, I don't see any problem. I would love to have Urey's job, but I don't think we would want to move to America."

Gerhard's wife came in, so David and Gerhard ended their conversation, but before they stopped talking completely, David said, "Gerhard, when the others are here Wednesday, we might not have a chance to talk about this, so what about you and I getting together after the service tomorrow?"

"That would work just fine. Let's plan on it."

"David, this is my wife, Daniele. Daniele, this is David Shepherd. I'm sure you know who he is."

"I certainly do. It's so nice to meet you, Mr. Shepherd."

"Please, call me David."

"All right, David. It was really nice of you to come here with Thil. I'm sure she needs support right now."

"I wouldn't have thought of not coming. I thought the world of Urey, and I'm crazy about Thil. I'll help her any way I can."

Thil finished with her calls and came in the room and was surprised to see Daniele. When they saw each other, they squealed and hugged each other. For David, it was amusing to hear their ninety-mile-an-hour conversation in German. When they ended their conversation, Thil told David they should go.

David agreed.

David told Gerhard and Daniele, "It was a genuine pleasure meeting the two of you and I look forward to seeing you again, tomorrow." He shook hands with both of them.

Thil kissed each of them on the cheek and said good-bye.

On the way to Thil's apartment, they stopped at a food market and picked up a few things to have for breakfast the next morning. They bought coffee and some different kinds of strudel. Thil said they could have coffee and a strudel for breakfast and would eat out at lunch. Maybe, some of her friends would join them after the service.

When they left the market, Thil asked, "Are you hungry?"

"I'm starved. We missed breakfast, remember?"

"Let's go get a sandwich. Want to?"

"Yeah, that sounds good. You'll have to order for me."

"I will. I'm going to order something you've never had. It will be a surprise."

"Okay. I trust you."

David had no idea what he was eating, but he enjoyed it. He asked Thil what it was, but couldn't understand what she told him. After lunch, they went back to Thil's apartment and took a nap.

Thil woke up first, and her moving around woke David. They had bought some wine at the market, and Thil asked David if he wanted some. He said he did, and they sat out on the balcony drinking it together.

"Thil, did Urey have any insurance, or do you have insurance in Germany?"

"Yes. He had insurance, but I don't know how much. All our papers are in our house in America."

"But you're sure he had some."

"Yes, I know he did."

"We'll need to find that policy when we get back. Do you think it is for enough to take care of you for life?"

"I don't know, David. Maybe."

"Well, whatever it's for, I don't want you to worry about

your baby. Since I'm the father, I will take care of it, financially, and hope I can be a part of its life."

"David, I want you to always be a part of our lives. I love you and I know the baby will, too."

"Here's how I think you should work this, Thil. Since no one knows you're pregnant except you, your doctor, and me, I think you should just let people assume the baby is Urey's. People will want to help you since they will believe the baby's daddy is dead, and they will have a high opinion of you. If they knew you were pregnant by someone else, your reputation would be shot, but I'll be right there to take care of you, so let them keep thinking Urey is the father. What do you think about that?"

"I think you have a good idea, David. I'll do that. Do you promise you will be there for me?"

"You couldn't drive me away. How about another glass of wine?"

"Coming up, wise sir."

They talked until dinner time, then, Thil took David to a nice restaurant where, again, he didn't know what he was eating, but liked it.

When they got back to the apartment, they watched television until bedtime and then turned in. This time they went straight to sleep.

***

At the mausoleum, Tuesday morning, there was a small group. Urey's sister and uncle were there, but his mother wasn't. Thil figured she was too sedated to attend. Urey's business partners and their wives were there along with three of Thil's friends and their husbands.

At ten o'clock sharp, Father Wilhelm stood in front and spoke. He didn't have a great deal to say because Urey didn't attend Church and barely knew the priest. He talked about some of the things Urey's friends had told him about Urey and how good a man he was. He talked about the tragedy that caused his death and then asked everyone to bow their heads while he said a prayer. He then walked over and shook Thil's hand, Urey's sister's hand and his uncle's and that was it. Someone from the funeral home placed the urn containing Urey's ashes in an open space in the wall and everyone consoled Thil.

Thil appeared to be sad because she loved Urey. Even though their relationship was not very physical, he was a good man and meant so much to her. She made a special effort to try and comfort Urey's sister, but his sister was so self-absorbed, it was as if she didn't realize what was going on. They talked for a couple minutes, and Giselle said she had to get home to her mother.

In a few minutes it seemed that nothing had happened. Everyone was talking about normal things and some said they had to go. They all hugged Thil as they left. Pretty soon there were only eight besides Thil and David. Someone said it was too late for breakfast and too early for lunch, so why didn't they go to a place they knew for brunch? The group consisted of Urey's business partners and their wives.

"David, would you like to do that?"

"Sure. That sounds good."

They formed a small caravan and drove to a restaurant that served some of the best food David had ever tasted. Everyone ate until they couldn't eat any more.

As they broke up and started to leave, David asked Gerhard, "Can we still get together today?"

"Yes, anytime you wish."

"Why don't you have Daniele go home with Thil, and you and I can go to the office, now. It shouldn't take too long. I just want to talk to you away from the others."

"All right, let me tell Daniele."

"I guess I had better tell Thil, too."

At the office, David picked up where he left off the day before. "Have you thought about what we talked about yesterday?"

"Yes, I did, David, and I also talked to Daniele about it. We both like everything about the offer except moving to America. Daniele even considered that because she would be close to Thil, but then had to consider the costs of leaving our families. If you will consider letting me continue to live in Munich, I'll gladly accept the job left by Urey."

"Ever since we talked yesterday, I've been thinking about that, and I think maybe we can make it work without your moving, but you'll have to travel to Chattanooga fairly often. I know you can do the job because you have already been doing a big part of it, but there's much more that you don't know. Before you will be able to really grasp what the job entails, I think it will be necessary for you to come to Chattanooga to see how we do things."

"I will be glad to do that," Gerhard said.

"Now, Urey had been spending a great deal of time in the Mid-East and had the Tel Aviv office almost ready to open when he got killed. Where do you stand on traveling over there?"

"David, I'll travel anywhere in the world as long as I can come back here to my home."

"All right. Let's say you step into Urey's job and start traveling constantly, who would we have here to manage things?"

"Do you remember which one Bruno Meyer was at the restaurant?"

"Yeah, he was the serious one."

"He is serious, but he's an outstanding salesman and a very astute businessman. If you're asking me for a recommendation, Bruno would be the one."

"Can he speak English?"

"A little. He'll have to work on that."

"How about his wife? Do you think she would stand for the long hours and extensive travel involved in the job?"

"Yes sir. He's already doing that. He's the leading rep in

our group and has been traveling constantly for years. This job might even cut down on some of his travel."

The two talked for another hour or so, and David asked Gerhard to take him to Thil's. They were to meet with the others the next morning, and he would announce Gerhard's promotion and talk to Bruno."

***

Early Wednesday morning, Thil drove David to the office. Gerhard was already there as was Marlene, the office secretary. Gerhard introduced her to David and she said in English, "I'm very happy to meet you, Mr. Shepherd."

"Oh, you speak English," he said.

"I'm trying to learn your language."

"Well, you're doing very well. Keep it up."

In a few minutes, Ludwig Rolf, Heinrich Schmidt, Bruno Meyer, and Franz Wagner showed up, and Gerhard started the meeting, speaking in German. The first thing he did was re-introduce David. "I know all of you met David yesterday as a friend of Thil's. This morning I want you to recognize him as the CEO of Shepherd Global Apparel Group. David will do most of the talking and since there is a language barrier, I will act as translator. My English is not that great, but maybe we can get through. David, I give you the floor."

"Fellows, I've been planning to come to Munich with Urey to meet you guys for several months, but I didn't know my being here would be under these circumstances. I think we all know what a void Urey's death has created, but as the saying goes, *"life must go on."* Urey was instrumental in Shepherd's expansion, and I want us to build on that. When I first met him, he convinced me that you people are the best in the business, and after seeing what has happened with our company, I know he was right. The first thing I want to do this morning is announce Urey's replacement. After much thought and much conversation with this gentleman, I want to present the new

Director of Global Operations, Gerhard Lehman."

"Gerhard and I have agreed that he will not have to move to Chattanooga. He will be going to Chattanooga for some training, but will make his headquarters here. I will be coming here fairly often and between the two of us and you guys, we will see that Shepherd Global continues to grow."

Everyone applauded.

David spent the rest of the morning discussing the future of Shepherd Global and what he expected from each of the men. After a while, Gerhard said to David, "It's lunchtime. Would you rather we go out and get lunch or would you rather we order something brought in?"

"Why don't we just order something?"

"Okay. Marlene, will you take everyone's order and call it in. David, do you know what you want?"

David, trying to act like he knew what he was doing said, "I'll have a Rueben sandwich,"

"What do you want with it?"

That threw him. "Oh, just anything."

With a slight smile, Gerhard told Marlene to order chips with David's Rueben.

Stretching their legs while they waited on their lunch, David told Gerhard to bring Bruno into his office. He wanted to talk to him. In a minute, the three of them were alone and David closed the door. "Bruno, I wanted to talk to you to see if you would be interested in moving into Gerhard's job. It's a pretty big job, but I think you can do it."

"David, I'm honored to be considered. Yes. I would like to have the job."

"Great. If we don't have time to talk this afternoon, we can meet here in the morning and go over the duties and other things involved. I think one of the first things you should do is learn to speak English fluently. There are a lot of companies with which we do business whose people can't speak German."

"I will do that, Mr. Shepherd."

"Please, call me David."

The sandwiches came, and David thought his Rueben was the best he had ever tasted. Two of the others also had Rueben's, but David didn't have any idea what the others were eating. When he finished and while some of the others were still eating, he stood up and resumed what he was saying before they broke for lunch. In a couple minutes, he paused. "When I first started talking to you this morning, I announced the promotion of Gerhard. Now that we're starting after lunch, I want to announce the promotion of Bruno Meyer. Bruno will step into Gerhard's job."

A couple clapped, and they all made positive comments. The meeting continued for the next two hours before David announced that he was finished and asked for any comments or suggestions. There were none, so he dismissed the group except for Gerhard and Bruno.

Before he sat down with them, he told Gerhard to tell Marlene to have his and Thil's plane tickets changed to Friday. He said to tell her to call Ruby at his office when she found out the arrival time in Chattanooga and have Ruby tell his son to pick them up at the airport.

He got back to Bruno and Gerhard and for about an hour tried to outline what he expected from Bruno. He emphasized to him that he should listen to what Gerhard told him because Gerhard had been doing the job and knew almost everything there was to know about it. He finished up, and told Gerhard he was ready to leave. He shook hands with Bruno and told him he would be back soon and smiling, said, "I may give you an English test when I come back." He looked over at Marlene and she was smiling. "Don't laugh, Marlene. I might give you one, too."

"Yes, sir. I'll be happy to take it." She frowned a little before smiling again and said, "Mr. Shepherd, your flight leaves Munich at ten-twenty Friday morning and arrives in Chattanooga at four-ten Friday afternoon. Is that all right?"

"That's perfect. Thank you."

"Gerhard, can you take me to Thil's?"

"I surely can. Are you ready?"

"Yes, I'm ready. Marlene, it was a pleasure meeting you. I'll be back in a couple months, and I'll see you then.

On the way, David told Gerhard to come and get him the next day if he needed him for anything. He reminded him that they wouldn't be leaving until Friday. Gerhard said he would, but hoped he wouldn't have to. He thought both of them needed to rest.

When they got to Thil's, David walked in, and Thil was asleep on the sofa. He tip-toed over to her and kissed her on the forehead. She opened her eyes and put her arms around his neck before he could get away. She pulled him close and they kissed. "Did you have a good day?" she asked.

"Yeah. It was a good day. We accomplished a lot. Was your day good?"

"Yes. It was very good."

"Well, I'm through working unless Gerhard needs me for something, and we're not going home until Friday, so we have the whole day together, tomorrow."

"That is good. I'll take you around and show you some of the sights of Munich. Would you like that?"

"Yes I would, but I'd be happy just being with you."

The next day was like a vacation. They went where they wanted to, when they wanted to, and did whatever they wanted to. Thil was educating David on the lives and customs of Munchners. She showed him sights of which he had seen pictures but never dreamed he would actually see. He was continually amused just listening to the people talk. Sometimes he would try to guess what they were saying, but knew he was wrong every time.

On Thursday afternoon, he had Thil take him by the Shepherd office. He had forgotten to arrange for a trip to the airport the next day, and he hoped Gerhard could take them. "I'll be glad to take you. I'll pick you up at eight o'clock. Is that all right?"

"That's great. See you then."

CHAPTER TEN

It was a brisk, sunny morning when the plane took off and the city of Munich was beautiful. Pretty soon they were at their cruising altitude and Thil and David sat in their seats holding hands. "Honey, are you glad this is all over?"

"Yes I am. If it hadn't been for you being with me, I don't know what I would have done. David, I want to be with you all the time."

He looked at her, but didn't say anything.

They talked about how strange Urey's sister was and how nice all the others were who attended the funeral.

"Do you remember meeting Andrea?"

"Yes."

"She was my very best friend. It was so good to see her again."

"Why don't you invite some of your friends to Chattanooga sometime?"

"Do you think I could?"

"Why not? It would be just like what we're doing right now."

"Thil, I've been thinking about your apartment. You know, now that Urey's gone, I'm going to have to come to Munich fairly often, and of course, I'll need somewhere to stay. Your apartment would be ideal for that. If you decide you are going to sell it, maybe I can buy it, or if you decide to keep it, I'll be glad to rent it. And oh yeah, you can come with me when I come. That way, you can see Andrea and your other friends three or four times a year."

"That sounds wonderful, David. Why don't I just keep the apartment and you and I will both have a place to stay when we come back. I don't want to come back without you."

"Not even to see Andrea?"

"Not even to see Andrea. I'm serious. I don't want to come back without you; in fact, I don't want to do anything without you. I love you so very much."

"I love you, too, honey. Why don't we try to get some rest? It's going to be a very long flight"

Thil raised the arm rest and laid her head on David's shoulder. "Night night."

Pretty soon the stewardess asked him if he wanted anything. He asked if they had any English language magazines, and surprisingly, they had several. He picked out a Sports Illustrated and looked at it until his eyes got heavy. It was only a few minutes until he was asleep.

At noon, a stewardess asked if they wanted lunch. Of course, they said yes, and she brought them a great club sandwich with chips, salad, and Jello. They both ordered a Coke.

When they had finished their lunch, Thil had to go to the rest room. When she returned to her seat, David took her hand in his and said, "Thil, this may be a bad time for this, especially since you buried your husband only three days ago, but I've been thinking about this ever since the minute I found out Urey was dead. You say you love me and you know I love you, so would you consider marrying me?"

"Would I consider marrying you? David, I've been praying you would ask me. Yes, Yes, Yes! I'll marry you."

"Wonderful. Now ours will be different than most couples to start with. We need to keep our engagement quiet until I can talk to Don and my dad. I think we should go to Ringgold or Jasper or somewhere like that to get married because of your pregnancy. We still want people to think the baby is Urey's, so until you start showing, we just won't mention we're married; then, after you are really showing, we'll announce our marriage. People will still assume the baby is Urey's, and that will make us heroes because of what we did for the baby. Does that make sense to you?"

"I will have to tell Don and Dad what's going on so you can move into my house with me. We may have to tell Margaret, too. We'll tell them you're pregnant, but we won't tell any of them that the baby is not Urey's. We may never tell anybody that."

"I have some things that I have to take care of when we get home, so it will be a few days before we can get married, okay?"

"What kind of things?"

"Thil, for most of my life God had played a major role in everything I did until we met. I don't believe either one of us intended for what happened to happen, but it did. We both had serious physical needs and we let them get in the way of what was right. If you will remember, I asked you if you felt guilty about what we were doing. That was because I was feeling guilty. I still feel guilty, especially about the baby, but Thil, God is a forgiving God, and I feel the need to go and talk to my pastor about it. He's a straight-up guy that I can confide in and he will give me good advice. I want to talk to him before we get married, but since this is the weekend, I won't be able to see him until Monday."

"You're not going to change your mind are you?"

"Absolutely not. I just want to start our marriage, knowing I have been forgiven."

"Another thing, Thil. I have never stopped going to Church, and after we're married, I would like for you to start going with me."

"What do I have to do?"

"Just go and hear about God and His Son, Jesus. Then if you believe and decide to ask Jesus into your heart, you will be saved and go to Heaven when you die, otherwise you will go to Hell. Do you believe in God, Thil?"

"I don't know. I've heard of Him, I think."

"Well, when we're married, you'll have a chance to learn all about Him. Is what I'm telling you making any sense at all?"

"The wedding part does, but the other is kind of confusing. The wedding part is what I'm interested in, anyway. Let's just stay with that for right now."

"Okay, Love, we'll do that.

"David, you have never told me about your wife. What was she like?"

"Judith was a fine woman. We were high school sweethearts, and we had the typical teen age romance. I was a good athlete and she was a cheerleader. Everybody assumed we would someday get married, and we did. We had one son, Don, and he was truly, the apple of her eye. She could not get enough of Don, nor he, his mother. Then one day she felt really bad and went to the doctor. They ran a series of tests and found she had ovarian cancer. She only lived a few months after that. Don was fourteen at the time, and I have been trying hard to make up for the loss of his mother, but I'm afraid I've fallen way short. Maybe, if she were still here, he wouldn't be constantly getting into trouble."

"Until you, I have not been with a woman since Judith, so you see how special you are to me? All the other women I have met have fallen short of the ideals I wanted until I met you, and you have exceeded everything I ever hoped for. If we both live to be a hundred, I believe our marriage will be the best ever."

"You're wonderful, David. I can't wait to be Mrs. David Shepherd. Bathilda Shepherd – how does that sound?"

"I think it sounds great."

The rest of the trip to Atlanta was spent talking about their lives after they got married. Thil's house would have to be sold. Urey's car was newer than hers, so she would keep it and sell hers'. They would file the insurance claim and do a thousand other things when they got back. Talking about all that had to be done seemed to tire them out, so they took a nap.

It wasn't long until dinner was served, and it was so good, they both ate like they hadn't eaten in days. Their first class meal consisted of a New York Strip, baked potato, salad, rolls, and red velvet cake. A bottomless wine glass was included.

As soon as they finished dinner, they could feel the nose of the plane start pointing downward, so they knew they were approaching Atlanta. When they arrived in Atlanta, they almost had to run in order to get to the Delta gate in time to catch their connecting flight to Chattanooga. They made it with time to spare because their flight was going to be thirty minutes late taking off. Finally, they took off and twenty minutes later landed in Chattanooga at four-fifty.

Don was there to pick them up, and seemed glad to see them. He put his arm around his dad's shoulder and kissed Thil on the cheek. "Have a good flight?"

"Yes, it was wonderful," Thil said.

"Don, you ought to see Munich. It's really something."

"I'd like to."

I'm going to be going back pretty often, so maybe I can take you sometime."

"Great."

On the way home, Don asked what they were planning to do for dinner. "There's not much to eat at home because I ate just about everything. You're going to have to go to the store, Pop."

"That figures. I don't know about Thil, but I'm not very hungry. We had a big meal on the plane just about three hours ago, and I can probably get by with just a snack of some kind."

"You can come to my house. I have some bratwurst and other things if you would like to have something like that. Don would you like to come over for some bratwurst?"

"Naw, not really. I've got a date, and we'll probably just go to Signal Drive-In or somewhere and grab a bite. We're going to the Tivoli, and we might wait 'til later to eat."

"All right, but if you change your mind, come over."

"Thanks, Thil."

When they got home, Don carried Thil's luggage to her house. He went into his house without David seeing him and went up to his room. In a few minutes, David called for him and when they came together, "Don, what are your plans tomorrow?"

"I don't know, Pop. Why?"

"I've got something very important to talk to you about, and I want you to set aside some time for me."

"Okay. When do you want to give me the talk?"

"I'm not going to give you a talk. I'm going to talk to you. There's a difference. I will be at the office in the morning. How about we go to the Krystal for lunch and we'll talk there."

"Sounds good, Pop. Just let me know when."

"Okay. I'll call you before I leave the office."

Don rummaged through the kitchen for something to snack on, then, went to his room, got ready and left for his date. David immediately called Thil and went over there.

Walking into her bedroom, "What are you doing, unpacking?"

"Yes, I want to get the suitcase put up."

"I told Don I want to talk to him tomorrow. We're going to meet for lunch and I'll tell him about us then."

"What do you think he will say?"

"It's hard to tell about Don. He likes you a lot, but if he thinks I'm trying to replace his mother with you, he might put up some resistance. I'll just have to pick my words carefully. Don't worry about it. It will all work out."

"I'm not worried about it because I know you can make anything work out. When will you talk to your dad?"

"I'm going to call him tonight to let him know I'm back, and I think I'll see if I can go over Sunday. While I'm there, I'll talk to him."

"Do you still think you will tell Margaret?"

"She has always been such a good and trusted friend, don't you think I should?"

"You probably should. David, will you stay with me tonight?"

"I don't think I should, at least until after I have talked to Don, but I will stay until late. Don won't get home until about midnight, so we have that much time. You'll probably want to go to bed before that anyway, and I'll stay and tuck you in."

He winked and Thil smiled.

David spent the rest of the weekend working, talking to Don, buying groceries, and seeing his dad.

"He was very pleasantly surprised when he talked to Don by the way Don backed him up on his and Thil's plans to get married. David thought he must be tired of living in a house without a mother. Even though Thil was not that much older than Don, she would still be a mother figure and Don liked her. David thought that talking to him would be the hardest part of this, but he was fooled. He was all for it. His dad was happy for him as well, so the only other person he needed to talk to was Margaret, and he didn't have to be in a hurry for that.

On Monday, David went to see his pastor, Rev. Nathan Fowler. He explained his relationship with Thil to the pastor and told him what he was planning. The pastor reaffirmed what he already knew; that God was a forgiving God and prayed with him. He didn't really tell him anything new, but it helped David just to talk with him.

He returned to his office to finish up a few things and called Thil. "I'll be there in a few minutes. Have a glass of wine poured when I get there. We're going to celebrate."

"Celebrate what?"

"I'll tell you when I get there. Love ya. Bye."

When he walked into Thil's house, she had the wine poured like he told her. He picked up his glass and said, "Here's a toast to happiness. Everyone I've talked to has been happy about our plans and wished us happiness, so here's to happiness."

They sipped their wine and talked about the excitement in their lives. As their glasses emptied, "Thil said, "I have something to toast, too."

"What?" David asked."

"I got a telephone call today."

"From whom?"

"Don."

David's heart sank. "What did he want?"

"He called me to tell me how happy he was that I'm marrying his dad. He said if you loved me, he was sure he would love me, too. I was thrilled about the call."

"Wow!! That calls for another glass."

They drank another glass and David said, "I think we should go eat. Let me see if Don wants to go with us."

He called his house but got the answering machine. He told Don if he got the message in the next few minutes, he and Thil would be at The Greystone and to come join them. If not, he would see him later.

On the way to the restaurant, Thil said, "You never did say what we were going to celebrate when you came home from the office."

"I didn't, did I? Well, I thought our getting married was reason enough to celebrate, What do you think?"

"I think it is, but we haven't gotten married yet."

"We will this week if you want to. I've been thinking that it would be better if we go down to Ringgold and get a Justice of the Peace to perform the ceremony."

"Why go to Ringgold?"

"Because it's in Georgia. If we get married in Chattanooga, our names will be in the paper after we get our marriage license, but Georgia doesn't put that information in the Chattanooga paper."

"Oh, I see."

"Would you like to marry me this week?"

"I'll marry you anytime, David."

"How about this? Thanksgiving is Thursday. Since this is going to be a secret, we won't be able to take a honeymoon, so why don't we go to Ringgold, Wednesday, and then we can at least have a long weekend. You liked that place where we went in Gatlinburg and we could go there if you'd like to."

"That sounds wonderful, David. I can hardly wait."

"Okay then. It's a date."

***

Thil suggested they ask Don to go to Ringgold with them, and when they asked, he was really happy that they wanted to include him. The three rode to the Justice of the Peace together, and then they dropped Don off, at home, on their way back through Chattanooga.

On their way to Gatlinburg, they were like typical newlyweds. Holding hands, David getting kissed on the cheek, giggling at things that weren't even funny, and just acting silly in general.

The hotel and surroundings were every bit as romantic and peaceful as they remembered from the time they were there before, except this time it was cold. The trees in the woods had lost most of their leaves, but watching the babbling brook was mesmerizing after a long workout in bed. David built a fire in the fireplace and they sat on a loveseat with their arms around each other, enjoying the fire and talking about how they looked forward to their future together.

"Do you think Don will be uncomfortable when I move into your bed?"

"I don't think so, but if he is, he'll get over it. This younger generation is definitely more liberal than I was at their age."

"Are you hungry, David?"

"I sure am. Where would you like to eat, and what kind of food would you like to have?"

"It doesn't matter, but I'm hungry. Let's get ready and go, so we can get back. I'm anxious to spend a romantic evening with my new husband."

"That kind of talk will get you in trouble." Patting her on the belly, he said, "In fact, it looks like it already has," then he leaned over and kissed her.

The next three days were incredible. It was as if they had never been together before. David attributed part of it to his not feeling guilty about being with Thil. Whatever the reason, they made the most of their time together.

Sunday afternoon came too soon, but they had to leave and get back to Chattanooga. When they got home, Thil went to her house and picked up a few things she would need, but she would wait until the next morning to start moving most of her belongings.

Things were surprisingly relaxed between her and Don when she changed into her pajamas and robe. It was almost as if there was nothing new; that everything was as it had always been. She and David were both grateful for that.

The newlyweds couldn't have been happier for the next few months. David was working very hard and every other month making a trip to London and Munich. Thil went with him to Munich, once, but they felt that in her condition, she shouldn't travel that far, so she spent her time trying to make their home perfect for her husband and stepson.

As the time for the baby approached, Thil got more uncomfortable. She had gained quite a bit of weight and didn't feel well. It was almost time, and she was ready to get it over with.

CHAPTER ELEVEN

On the way to the hospital, David reminded Thil, "Honey, when they come in and ask questions about the family in order to make out a birth certificate, be sure you remember to tell them the baby's father was Urey and the baby's last name is Steen."

"Are you still sure this is what you want to do?"

"Yes. It's important for both our reputations. In a few weeks or months, I'll officially adopt it and then it will be a Shepherd."

"Okay, David. You know best."

David sat in the waiting room alone wondering if he was going to be the father of a boy or a girl. He watched three other expectant fathers, and he didn't want to behave the way two of them did. They were so nervous, they acted silly. The remaining dad remained quiet and behaved the way David thought a grown man should. Occasionally the phone would ring, and someone on the other end would update one of them about his wife.

Pretty soon they called one of the silly men and told him he was a father and he left the waiting room. It wasn't long before the other silly acting man was called, leaving David in the room with the quiet one. David thought he would go over and introduce himself to the man, but before he could do it, Don walked in. "How's she doing, Pop?"

"I guess she's doing okay. I haven't heard anything in a while." No sooner had he said that, than they called him."Mr. Shepherd, you have a fine baby boy. Please meet the doctor and your son in the hall outside the nursery."

"C'mon Don. It's a boy."

When they arrived where they were told to come, the doctor and a nurse carrying the baby was just getting there. The doctor congratulated David, and the nurse pulled the blanket down just a little so he could see his face. They talked for maybe thirty seconds, and the baby was taken away. That was the last time David would be able to see the baby outside the nursery until he took him and Thil home.

Hospital rules would not let anyone near newborns except doctors, nurses, and the mothers. Fathers were only allowed to see their sons or daughters through the glass of the nursery and could only see their wives for a short time during visiting hours. Since Thil had just given birth, visitation was relaxed a little. David was allowed to be with her until they moved her into a regular room; then, he would have to start visiting at the regular visiting hours.

**

Shepherd Global was wide open. They were constantly hiring for both the office and the plant. The day after Thil gave birth to their baby, David was interviewing a man for a possible sales representative job. In the midst of the interview Ruby interrupted. "Dr. Roger Crane is on line one for you."

"Hello."

"Hello, Mr. Shepherd, this is Roger Crane. I wonder if it would be possible for you to meet me at the hospital?"

"Of course I can. Would two o'clock work?"

"Mr. Shepherd, I really need to see you as soon as possible. Could you come now? I'll meet you at the nursery."

"I'll be there in twenty minutes."

"Gary, we had a baby yesterday, and that was the doctor wanting to see me immediately. I'm sorry, but I've got to go. Can you come back tomorrow?" Without waiting for an answer, he ran out of the office and got in his car.

When he got to the nursery, the doctor was inside with the babies and it looked as if he was with his baby. He tapped on the window and when Dr. Crane saw him, he came out. "Good morning," he said to David. "Let's go down to your wife's room, and I'll talk to you both together."

When they got to Thil's room, David leaned over and kissed her and told her, "Dr. Crane wants to talk to us."

A frightened look came on her face. "What about?"

"Mrs. Shepherd, I'm afraid I have disturbing news. When examining your baby, we found that he has a very bad illness."

"What kind of illness?" David asked.

"It's called Pediatric Leukodystrophies."

"How bad is it?"

"It's bad. I'm afraid it's always fatal. It is a very rare disease. Not much is yet understood about this condition. The disease affects infants and young children. The brain of the afflicted child lacks myelin. This is a fatty coating that covers the cells of the brain and helps to insulate much like an insulated electric wire. Without myelin, sluggish electric signals occur between neutrons. This deficiency causes multiple sclerosis. A child diagnosed with this condition may live for a year or less. I'm terribly sorry."

Neither of them understood what the doctor had said, and asked, "Doctor, what do we do?"

"The Pediatric Department will meet with you and show you how to care for him and give you a list of instructions."

"When do you think we can take him home?"

"That's hard to say. With this condition, he will have to remain in Intensive Care for several more weeks. He will be closely monitored, and we will just have to take one day at a time. Keep in mind that researchers are working hard to find cures for these diseases and who knows, they might find one for this any day now."

"Thank you, Doctor."

"I'm sorry."

After the doctor left, Thil went to pieces. David picked up the phone and called his office. "Ruby, I won't be back today. The baby's sick. I'll let you know later about tomorrow." Then he sat on the edge of the bed and consoled Thil. Thoughts of his office ran through his mind and he thought, *Man, am I glad I've got Tom there to take over. Things would really be a mess without him.*

Right before lunch, someone came in to get information for the birth certificate. Thil was so distraught, David furnished the information. He gave the baby's name as Robert Jeffrey Steen and the father's name Ulrich Ludwig Steen. Afterwards, he felt guilty and determined to call his lawyer and have adoption papers drawn up immediately.

A nurse came in and told him visiting hours were over until that night, but he refused to leave. He explained to her about the baby and said he would not leave his wife. He figured she would call security, but no one came. David stayed with Thil until almost ten o'clock. She had just about worn herself out, crying, and he asked a nurse to give her something to make her sleep. After she took the pill and was getting drowsy, he decided to go home. He leaned over her bed and kissed her. "Sleep tight and I'll see you in the morning."

"Okay. I love you."

"Love you, too."

The next morning, David phoned his company's lawyer and set the wheels in motion to legally adopt little Bobby. He was now ready for him to have his last name. He told the attorney to expedite it and have it done immediately.

Thil and David were able to see the baby two or three times a day, but weren't allowed to hold him. He just laid there with all kinds of tubes in him and Thil, especially, was so sad. The hospital released her after four days, and David took her home.

After she went home, she made at least two trips a day to the nursery, even though there was nothing she could do. David would try to go at least once a day.

While eating lunch one day, David felt like he needed to talk to his pastor, so when he finished he drove to his Church, taking a chance on finding him. Luckily, he was there. The Church secretary ushered him into the pastor's office. "Hi,

Nathan."

"Hi David. How are you?"

"Fine."

"How's Thil and the baby?"

"Thil's fine, but there's no change in the baby."

"I'm sorry. What can I do for you today?"

"Nathan, I'm just trying to do anything I can do that might convince God to spare the baby. I know it was conceived in a sinful way, but Nathan, that's not the baby's fault. I've asked God for forgiveness, and I don't know what else to do. Do you have any suggestions?"

"David, many times the one who does the sinning is not necessarily the one who has to pay for the sin. Sometimes, someone else pays for it. You say you've asked God to forgive you; well, if you were sincere, I'm sure He has forgiven you, but someone will still have to pay for the sin. I don't know this for sure, David, but it's possible that the baby is going to have to pay for it. I know that's hard to hear, but that's the way God works. I wish I had the answer, but I don't. Let's continue to pray and trust that He will give you and Thil the strength to deal with the situation. David, let's pray right now."

Nathan and David prayed together, then, David went back to the office, hoping the prayer had done some good.

Ruby collared him as he walked in. "David, your attorney called and said to tell you the matter you called him about had been taken care of."

"Thank you, Ruby."

Three weeks went by. One morning Dr. Crane called David at his office and said he and his wife needed to come to the nursery. David called Thil and told her to get ready and he would pick her up in just a few minutes. They had to go to the hospital. She was a nervous wreck when he got there and feared the worst.

They hurried to the nursery and met Dr. Crane. "Good morning, Mrs. Shepherd, Mr. Shepherd. I'm sorry to have to tell you this, but your son passed away this morning. I'm so very sorry, but I can assure you that little Bobby is much better off now than if he had lived. There's no cure for that disease and not only would he be in a vegetative state, but the two of you would no longer have a life of your own. The disease is not hereditary, and both of you are young, so there's time for you to have other healthy children. Again, I'm very sorry."

The doctor led them to a desk down the hall, manned by a nurse who asked which funeral home they wanted to use. David told her and he and Thil left.

Surprisingly, they both seemed to be somewhat relieved on their way home. They knew the doctor was right because they had already talked about it, but it was still hard to realize they had lost a child.

"Thil, honey, we're going to do like Dr. Crane said: we're going to have more children and we'll get started creating one whenever you're ready."

A slight smile came on Thil's face. "Well, let's don't do it today."

***

The funeral was only a graveside service, attended by David's father and son. Margaret and several employees of Shepherd Global were there and Rev. Nathan Fowler officiated. It was a very simple service and that's the way David wanted it. He was glad he had thought to take care of the adoption when he did. Now, the baby's grave marker will have the name *Infant Robert J. Shepherd* instead of *Infant Robert J. Steen.*

As David had predicted, he and Thil were looked upon as heroes. She, for losing a husband while pregnant and he, for stepping up and marrying her to give her husband's son a family. He hoped now that it was over, everything from this point forward would be new.

"Honey, would you like to go somewhere for a few days?"

"Where do you want to go?"

"I'm thinking about Jekyll Island. I tried once to send you and Urey down there, but he didn't want to go. He wanted to go back to Israel, instead.

"He never told me."

"I think you would love it. There are nice hotels, pretty beaches, and good restaurants. We could drive down in the morning and stay four or five days and do absolutely nothing. Whatta ya say?"

"All right. If you want to go, I do, too."

"We'll need to go to the store and buy some food for Don. That rascal can sure eat."

"I know."

"I'm going to take you home and then go by the office. There are some things I need to go over with Tom before we leave. Could you please go to the store and get the groceries?"

"Yes, I'll go. Is there anything special you want me to get?"

"You know what kind of stuff Don eats. Just get some different things, and if he runs out, he can go get his own."

Six-thirty found them on I-75. David wanted to beat the rush-hour traffic, so they left early. They drove to Cartersville before they stopped for breakfast at the Cracker Barrel and then it was clear sailing to Jekyll Island. If they got hungry for lunch, they could find a place in Savannah or Brunswick, but they both agreed that the big breakfast would probably last them until dinner.

When they got to Jekyll Island, they checked into a really nice hotel and looked forward to relaxing for a few days.

***

All of a sudden, there was trouble in Don's paradise. He called Richard. "Richard, you haven't called."

"I know. Johnny W. didn't show."

"I wonder why."

"This is the first week he's missed. There must be

something wrong."

"You know, if he doesn't come by tonight, we may have a problem, Richard."

"What will we do?"

"I guess we'll just have to go to Horace Edwards' and tell him."

"What do you think he'll say?"

"What can he say, except we won't get paid this week."

"I hope that don't happen."

"Me too. Tell you what. If he doesn't show by suppertime, call me and we'll try to figure out something."

The extortion program the boys have been pulling on the bootleg whiskey business for the last several months has been running too smoothly. It was bound to hit a snag somewhere and the informant failing to show up at Senator Powell's, just might be the snag they hoped would not happen. At seven o'clock, Richard called back. "Don, he still hasn't come, and Dad and Mom are going out to eat, so he must not be coming. What are we going to do?"

"Let's go up to Horace Edwards' and tell him. I'll pick you up."

"Okay."

When they pulled up to the Edwards' house, Horace saw them and met them on the porch. "Hi boys. What are you up to?"

Don started, "Well, Mr. Edwards, the informant didn't show up at Senator Powell's this week, so we don't have anything to tell you."

"That right?"

"Yes sir. If he happens to come tomorrow or Sunday, we'll come back with the information, okay?"

"Boys, I've gotten to where I like you both, but this is the end of the line for your little scheme. There will be no more payments and I strongly advise you to keep your mouths shut. Several of my associates still don't like the fact that they have had to pay you for every gallon coming through the county, and there's no telling what they might do if they were to hear that you had been talking to people. Do you understand what I'm saying?"

"Yes sir. Can I ask what has happened?"

"Let's just say that me and my boys are no longer in business."

"But Mr. Edw-"

Before Don could say anything else, Horace said,"That's all I'm going to say about it. I don't want you coming here again, understand?"

"Yes sir." The boys walked down the steps, got into the car and left.

Richard asked, "You think they found out about Johnny W.?"

"They must have. Whatever happened, it looks like we're out of business."

"What are we going to do for money?"

"I guess I'll keep working at Shepherd Global. At least I make a little. But Richard, we've got quite a bit put back, so it's not like we're broke. I just hate for it to end."

"Me too. I guess I'll try to find some kind of job to last until I start college. Do you think your Dad's company would hire me?"

"I don't know. Why don't you come by and fill out an application?"

"I may do it."

When they arrived at Richard's, Don let him out and then went home.

That night the phone rang and Don answered. It was Richard. "Have you seen today's paper?"

"No, why?"

"Do you have a paper?"

"Yeah."

"Well, look on page three. It says they found a body up at Wolftever Creek identified as fifty-four year old John Watson. Don, that's got to be Johnny W."

"Sure sounds like it. Richard, we may be lucky to be alive. We had better be really careful about where we go and who we talk to. I don't want to wind up in Wolftever Creek."

"Me neither. I'll talk to you later."

Don was at home alone and he made sure all the doors and windows were locked. He re-read the newspaper article and serious paranoia set in. He went upstairs and locked himself in his room where nobody could see him. He didn't own a gun, so he took a butcher knife from the kitchen upstairs with him.

CHAPTER TWELVE

The weather had been perfect for the couple's vacation. At times, their baby's passing brought sadness, but for the most part, the get-away was just what they needed. "Thil, honey, I hate for this to end, don't you?"

"I sure do. I can't believe Urey turned down your offer to send us down here."

"I can't either, but I hope you've enjoyed being here with me."

"You're the perfect companion, David. I've enjoyed every minute."

"We'll make it a point to take more of these trips. I intend for us to enjoy life. Now that Tom Ratcliff is taking much of my work-load off of me, things are going to be better. You know what I've been thinking about?"

"What?"

"Shepherd Global has gotten so big and my travel is so spread out, I think I'm going to buy an airplane. It only makes sense to me and I can take you with me sometimes. How would you like to fool around at thirty-thousand feet, going six-hundred miles an hour?"

Laughing, Thil said, "You're crazy. That would be a new experience, though."

"Well, let's plan on doing that. After we get home, I'm going to start looking for a plane. I've got to go to Munich in about three weeks, and maybe I can have the plane by then. Do you want to go with me?"

"Yes. I could see Andrea and some of my other friends. David, it's exciting being married to you."

"Thank you. It's exciting being married to you, too."

After David decided to buy a plane, he was in a hurry to get one. It was late afternoon when they got home, so he would have to wait until the next day to start looking. The next morning he called a friend at the airport who had once worked for Grumman Aircraft. He thought his friend could tell him how and where to start looking, and he was referred to an aircraft broker.

"Hello, Mr. Mosier, my name is David Shepherd and I'm interested in buying an airplane."

"Good. What are you looking for?"

"I really don't know. If I get one, it will have to be large enough to make frequent flights to Europe and the Middle East, and it would be good to have a bedroom."

"We have listings for several nice planes, but from what you're telling me, we need to look for something that's been customized."

David said, "And oh yeah, I would like for it to be able to fly non-stop from Chattanooga to Munich. Do you have anything with that kind of range?"

"We may have. Mr. Shepherd, can I call you back in a little while. We've got a lot of planes listed, but they're scattered all over the world, and it's going to take some time to locate just what you're looking for. If you'll give me your number, I'll try to get back to you before lunch. Is that all right?"

"Yes, and when you call me back, you'll be able to answer questions about the plane, won't you?"

"Absolutely. We're one of the largest aircraft brokers in the world and each staff member is highly trained and an expert in all phases of aircraft technology."

"Great. I hope you can find what I'm looking for."

"I'll get back to you. Thank you for giving us a chance to work with you, Mr. Shepherd."

Work had piled up during the time David was gone, and he was really behind, but he had a hard time getting his mind on it for thinking about the airplane. Thankfully, Tom had been there to do some of it or else he would have really been in a *pickle.*

David sent for Tom, and they went over all that had been going on, actually, since the baby was born. Tom had been trained well and did an outstanding job, and David made sure he let him know how much he appreciated him. After Tom went back to his office, David called for Ruby to come in. "Ruby, it's good to be back."

"It's good to have you back. Did you have a good trip?"

"It was perfect. We didn't do much of anything except lie on the beach, but it seemed to take Thil's mind off the baby and that's why we went. Tell me what's been going on at Shepherd Global."

"Those men you have in Germany are amazing. I think they must have everybody in Europe wearing Shepherd clothing. Oh yeah, I wish you had been here the other day when I called Gerhard. During the call I spoke with Bruno. I wish I had a recording of that conversation. I couldn't understand him, and he couldn't understand me, and we both got tickled. Finally, Gerhard rescued us. That Bruno needs to learn English."

"He's working on it."

"Have you gotten on to Don about something?"

"No. Why?"

"Nothing, really, but ever since you and Thil left, it seems like he has been here constantly. Always before, when the bell rang at quitting time, he was one of the first ones out, but lately he has been staying until we close the office. I just thought maybe you two had been into it."

"I wonder if he's in some kind of trouble. Maybe I'll have a talk with him."

The phone rang and Ruby picked it up at David's desk. "A Ted Mosier is on the phone for you."

"We'll talk more later, Ruby. Hello, Mr. Mosier, this is David."

"Mr. Shepherd, I may have good news. I have located a Boeing 707 that has been customized just the way you want. It has a full galley, or kitchen in laymen's terms plus a private bedroom. It has sleeping berths for an additional six, and its appointments are impeccable. The airplane was owned by a famous rock star, who upgraded to a larger plane. Mr. Shepherd, this airplane is in perfect condition and ready to take off whenever you are ready. There is one inconvenience, I'm afraid. The airplane is in London."

"Ted, can I call you Ted? Please call me David. Ted, what a coincidence. I'm scheduled to go to London and Munich in three weeks. I was going to Munich first, but maybe I can reverse things and go to London first. If I could move it up a week, would that work for you?"

"Yes sir, it would. You just let me know when and where you'll be, and I'll have someone pick you up and take you to the plane."

"Can someone take us up? My wife will be with me."

"David, as you know, it costs a lot to operate an airplane, especially one the size of a 707, and we don't test-fly like you would if you wanted to test-drive a Pontiac, but if, when you see it, you are definitely interested in it, we will certainly take you up for a test flight."

"Fine, I'll get back to you when I get my schedule set. Ted, is this the only thing you have that's appointed the way I want it?"

"Yes sir. As I told you, we have many planes available, but this is the only one with a full bedroom."

"What color is it?"

"I was going to talk to you about that. The rock star who owned it had it painted with all kinds of psychedelic colors. If you buy it, you will probably want to repaint it."

"Can I get some help on that?"

"What kind of help?"

"Some help with the cost of getting it painted. I'm sure painters won't do it for free."

"Let's see what you think of the plane, then, we'll talk about all the other things. Can we do that?"

"Yeah, I guess so. If I can, I'll call you tomorrow."

"Great. I look forward to hearing from you. Good-bye."

The afternoon went smoothly. David got the stack of papers down to a reasonable height, so it didn't look as bad. He had Ruby place calls to Liam in London and Gerhard in Munich to see if it would mess things up if he reversed his itinerary and move his visit up a week. He told them he would get back to them.

"Hi Thil. Are you fixing dinner or would you like to go out?"

"I'd love to go out. I didn't get to the grocery market and there's not much here."

"Good. I'll find Don and we'll take him with us. He probably hasn't had a good meal in a while."

They let Don pick where they would eat and he chose Fehn's. He and Thil liked their fried chicken and David always picked the hamburger steak. When Thil and Mr. Fehn got together, it was always amusing to listen to their conversation in German. As Mr. Fehn was leaving the table, he turned to David, "You didn't get what we said about you, did you?"

"No I didn't. What did you say?"

"Ask your wife."

"What did you all say about me?"

"I'm not going to tell you."

"All right, but you'll pay for it."

"Ha ha. I'm scared."

"You'd better be. Just wait."

During all the fun, Don just sat in his seat, depressed. "What's wrong, Son?"

"Nothing."

"It doesn't look like nothing. What's wrong?"

"I said nothing."

"Okay."

David had had a busy day, and he was tired, so he didn't ask if anybody wanted to do anything else. He just drove straight home, went upstairs and changed clothes to get comfortable.

***

Don went to his room when they got home and closed his door, Thil and David went out on the balcony, and in a little while, Don went to the door and said, "Pop, can I talk to you in my room for a minute?"

"You can," and he got up and went with him to his room.

"Pop, I didn't want to say anything about this, but I think I have to. You're gonna be mad at me, and I don't blame you. Pop, I'm scared. I think my life may be in danger."

"What have you done, Don?"

"I don't know how to tell you, Pop, but Richard and I have been pulling a con on a group of bootleggers."

"Youuu've what?'

"We've been taking money from moonshiners."

"How much are you talking about?"

"Richard and I each have thirty-two thousand dollars."

"What?"

"Thirty-two thousand dollars."

"What did you do to get this, son?"

"Well, you know how bad Richard's dad hates the bootleg whiskey business. Well, there was a guy who started coming to the Powell's to see Richard's dad and one time Richard overheard them talking. Pop, this guy was a bootlegger, himself, but he turned into a snitch. He would tell Senator Powell when and where loads of whiskey would be coming through the county, and Senator Powell would tell the police and they would arrest them."

"This was happening all the time, so Richard and I came up with a plan. We found out who one of the head men was in the whiskey business and went to see him. We told him we knew there was a snitch, and we could help them. He wanted to see if we knew what we were talking about, so they put out some false information. When the guy gave that to Richard's dad and we gave it to our man, we had a deal."

"We told him we wanted fifty cents a gallon for every gallon coming through Hamilton County and they agreed to it as long as we fed them the information. He gave us half of a playing card, which he called our I.D.. Every Saturday night we would meet someone in front of the "Y" and put our card up to his; then, they would give us an envelope with money in it. Every week, Richard and I split about two thousand to twenty-five hundred dollars until last week."

"The snitch didn't show up at the Powell's, so Richard and I went to the man's house we had been dealing with to tell him that. He apparently already knew it and told us there would be no more payments, then that same day, it was in the paper that a man was found murdered at Wolftever Creek. That was the snitch, Pop."

"Before we left the man's house, he told us to keep our mouths shut and that several of his associates were mad because they had been having to pay us."

"Pop, I'm scared to death."

"Don, do you know what they call something like this?"

"No. What?"

"It's called extortion, and it's a bad thing. Does Richard's dad know about this?"

"I don't know."

"Well, I'm going to call him right now. What's his number?" Don gave it to him. "Hello, Senator. David Shepherd. How're you?"

"I'm well, thank you. How're you?"

"Fine, thank you. Listen, has Richard told you anything about this deal he and my son, Don have been doing?"

"No, he hasn't said a thing. Is it something I should know about?"

"Yes it is. Richard, would you mind if Don and I come to your house right now?"

He paused a few seconds, then said, "Of course. Come on."

When they got to the Powell's, the Senator called Richard and they all went in the Senator's office. "What's this all about,

David?"

"I would like for Richard or Don to tell you. I'll fill in anything they leave out."

Richard began, and both he and Don told the story. The Senator was flabbergasted. "I've never heard of anything so outlandish. It's a wonder both of you aren't dead. Who is this man you dealt with? I need to know." But the boys wouldn't tell.

David asked, "Richard, what do think we should do?"

"I don't know, David. This whole thing is so unbelievable, at this point, I don't know what to do."

The Senator told the boys, "Boys you need to watch your step for a while. If you go somewhere, be sure there are plenty of people around you. Don't go anywhere unless others are around. That includes dates. If you have a date, see that there are plenty of people there. I don't know if anybody is after you or not, but if they are, chances are they won't do anything in front of other people. Let's just hope there aren't any hotheads out there."

"Do you think we need to get the police involved?" David asked.

"Not at this point. They extorted an illegal business, so I don't know if that's technically a crime or not. Let me think about this. Do either one of you boys have anything else to tell us?"

They both said, "No."

"David, thank you for coming over and sharing this. I just hope we don't have a problem on our hands."

"Good night, Senator."

"Good night."

On the way home, David asked, "Are you glad this is all over?"

"I guess, but I hate to not get that money anymore."

"I'll bet and do you know what you're going to do with that thirty-two thousand dollars you have?"

"I may buy a car now that I don't have to hide it anymore."

"No, no. You're going to put it in the bank where it will draw interest, and then you're going to take it and pay against your tuition at U.C. next year."

"That's not fair, Pop. I made that money, so I should be able to spend it the way I want to."

"Not fair? I make the money I get, but I have to spend it on your food, your clothes, a place for you to live, and just about everything else you have. Is that fair? Is it fair that I have to take my money and spend it on your education when you have thirty-two thousand dollars? Tell me about fair, Don."

"I guess you're right, Pop, but can I keep some of it?"

"I'll tell you what. You can keep two thousand dollars, but the rest goes in the bank."

They pulled into the garage but didn't get out right away. David was still talking. "Don, I don't know what to make of you. Your Granddad and I have worked hard to build a nice business; one that I had hoped you would step into one day, but Son, as bad as it hurts to say it, I question whether or not you have enough integrity to operate a company with a spotless reputation like Shepherd Apparel. First, you were mixed up in the numbers racket until you were threatened with bad things, and now this thing with the illegal whiskey trade. I'm baffled."

"You're gonna be going to college next year and you're supposed to be a man when you go to college. Have you even thought about what you want to do when you graduate? Do you want to come into Shepherd Apparel, or do you want to do something else? It's time you started thinking about it. Let's go into the house. We'll talk more later."

***

Don's escapades were wearing heavily on David's mind when he went to work the next morning, but his spirits were soon lifted by an unexpected phone call. "David, there's a Ted Mosier on line one for you."

"Thanks. Hello, Ted. Good morning."

"Good morning, David. I'm very excited this morning. I received a call from our London office, and they have just taken in a beautiful DC-8 that is appointed the way you want. The airplane formerly belonged to an Arab Sheik who wanted a larger plane. It just so happens this plane is in London at the same location as the 707 you're going to see. London faxed me a picture of the DC-8 and it's very nice. I think you will want to see it."

"I sure will. Ted, I haven't finalized the change to my schedule yet, but I should have it done later today and I'll call you. This sounds really nice. It sounds nicer than the psychedelic one."

"Don't judge a book by its cover, David. The 707 is a great plane. A fresh coat of paint will make it look like new."

"I wonder what the interior looks like."

"Of the 707?"

"Yeah. If the outside is psychedelic, there's no telling what the inside looks like."

"You would think that, but the exterior is strictly for his fans. This entertainer likes the finer things, and the interior is very plush with neutral colors."

"Well, let me get to work, Ted. I'll try to give you a call right after lunch."

"All right. Have a good morning. Goodbye."

After calling Gerhard in Munich and Liam in London, David was able to finalize moving his trip up a week. He called Ted to set up the appointments to see the two airplanes. He was so excited; he had to call Thil and tell her. "You're going with me, aren't you?"

"Yes, and I can hardly wait."

"Why don't you come down here and call Andrea. You can use the company phone, and Ruby will help you with your call."

CHAPTER THIRTEEN

Two Weeks Later

The British Airways plane was a little late leaving Atlanta, but the pilot said they would try to make up the time en route. They had a good tailwind which helped. Thil and David were imagining what the planes were going to look like. She would look at a group of seats and say, "I think I would like a swivel chair there or a sofa would look nice over here. David, do you have tables and lamps on an airplane?"

David didn't know, but he went along with her imagination. They would know tomorrow after they saw the two airplanes.

"I'll bet the Sheik's plane is the nicest," she said. "Which one do you think will be the nicest?"

Kidding, David said," I want the one with the psychedelic colors on the outside."

"You know you don't want that one."

"Yeah, that's the one I want."

They kidded back and forth until the stewardess came to offer lunch. After lunch, they got quiet and soon were asleep.

Time passed quickly. It didn't seem long until they landed at Heathrow Airport in London. They claimed their luggage and caught a cab to the Airport Hilton where they checked in. David's appointment wasn't until the next day, so they had plenty of time to kill.

It had been several weeks since Thil gave birth, and her sensuality had come back with a vengeance. No sooner had they put their suitcases on the racks than she was all over

David. They fooled around until dinnertime and then ordered room service. After they ate, they both put their pajamas on and lay in bed watching television until they went to sleep, which wasn't long.

The next morning, the airplane broker sent a car to pick them up. Since they were staying near the airport, it didn't take but a few minutes to get where they were going. As soon as they turned into the area where the planes were, the 707 with the psychedelic paint job was the first one they saw. If there was ever such a thing as tasteful psychedelic, that was it. It was loud, but something about it made you like it. A beautiful white plane was parked next to it and Thil hoped that was the Sheik's plane.

The lights and ventilation system had been turned on to give the feeling of current activity. Having been on what was considered a very nice plane the day before, they were absolutely blown away when they stepped inside the rock star's 707. It was like Ted had told David. A book shouldn't be judged by its cover. Everything inside was plush and very tastefully decorated. The galley had everything needed to cook a full course meal and the bedroom contained a queen-size bed with its own bathroom. Thil couldn't understand why anyone would ever give up a plane like that.

"What was the name of the rock star who owned this," David asked.

"I'm sorry, but we're not permitted to divulge his name. That was a condition for his consummation of the sale of his new airplane."

"Is his new plane painted like this?"

"I don't know, but I presume so."

Next, they went to the Sheik's plane, and again, they were overwhelmed by the luxurious appointments inside. It was clearly owned by someone who had never experienced anything but wealth. Even the most common, unimportant things like the bathroom faucets were gold plated. David sat in one of the swivel, easy-chairs and mired up. He thought, *It's almost sinful to have this much luxury.*

"What do you think, Thil? Which one do you like best?"

"I like both of them. Which one do you like?"

David asked the agent, "Are these planes priced the same?"

"No sir. This one is two-hundred thousand dollars higher than the first one. It is also one year newer."

"Who do I negotiate with, you or Ted Mosier?"

"You should contact Mr. Mosier."

"Okay. I'll call him when I get back to the states. He told me that if I was truly interested in buying one of the planes, I could get a test flight. Can you handle that?"

"Yes sir, but it will take a little while to assemble a crew. Would early this afternoon work for you?"

"Yes. That'll work."

"Which one do you want to test?"

"I want to ride in both of them, so I can choose which one rides the best."

"Very well. I'll send a car for you at one o'clock. Is that all right?"

"Perfect."

Thil, David, and a team of three crew members took off around one-forty five in the rock star's 707. It was wonderful. The weather couldn't have been better for flying. They had never imagined anything like it. One thing David was concerned about was the engine noise and the 707 turned out to be reasonably quiet, and he liked that. They flew for about thirty minutes before landing.

Next, after the flight crew got everything ready, they took off in the sheik's DC-8. David thought, *"Man, this is something. This is twice as nice as the 707 and much quieter. I'm going to see if I can work something out on this baby."* He inspected everything about the plane much more closely. He went to the flight deck and talked with the crew and got their opinions about which plane flew the best and asked about a hundred questions. They stayed in the air forty-five minutes before landing.

"Which one do you like the best, now, Thil?"

"I like this one."

"Me too."

When they got inside, he gave the broker the numbers where he would be for the next week and said if he didn't hear from Ted before he got home, he would call him then. He said he would be in London until the next afternoon and then, in Munich until Tuesday. They thanked the fellow and the car took them back to the Hilton. The day was almost gone and it was too late to go to the office, so David called Liam and told him he would be there first thing in the morning.

They were getting ready for bed when the phone rang. It was Ted Mosier. "David, how did you like the two airplanes?"

"I liked them a lot, especially the Sheik's, but I don't like the extra two-hundred thousand bucks."

"How about the 707?"

"I liked it, too, except for the paint job."

"Can we make a deal on one of them?"

"I don't know, Ted. What kind of deal will you do on the DC-8?"

"David, if you will make a commitment today, I'll reduce the price one-hundred thousand dollars."

"What about the 707? Will you have it painted?

"I can't do that, David, but I'll tell you what I will do. I'll share the paint cost with you."

"That's no deal. I tell you, Ted, let me think about 'em for a few days, and I'll call you next Wednesday when I get home."

"We may not have them next Wednesday. David."

"Well, if you don't there'll be more coming on the market later. I'm in no rush. I'll call you Wednesday."

"Okay, David. Good bye."

David thought about the two airplanes all through the night and couldn't get the DC-8 out of his mind. *Chattanooga has probably never seen an airplane as nice as that one,* he thought.

Around three o'clock the next afternoon, while David was

at Liam's office, the phone rang, and it was Ted. "David, I talked to my manager, and he said we could come down another fifty thousand dollars on the DC-8. Will that make it attractive enough to you to deal?"

"Ted, I don't know. I wasn't expecting your call and I haven't had time to think any more about it. I'm really busy this afternoon, and I'm going to Munich in the morning. I gave you my Munich number. Why don't you give me a call at that number around four, Munich time tomorrow?"

"I'll do that, David. Goodbye."

"Ted, wait a minute. I'll tell you what I'll do. Tell your manager that if wants to come off your asking price two-hundred thousand dollars, I'll buy the DC-8, provided it's F.O.B. Chattanooga."

"Wow, David, that's going to be next to impossible."

"Tell him if he wants to deal, that's my offer." And then he lied to Ted. "Tell him that I found another plane that I'm going to see while I'm over here if he doesn't meet my price."

"Can I ask where it is?"

"It's in Amman, Jordan. It was also owned by a Sheik, and it sounds equally as nice and it may be a little cheaper. I'll probably make a deal on it if it's as nice as they say it is."

"When are you going to look at it, David?"

"Friday."

"Well, don't do anything until you hear from me. I'll call you in Munich by Thursday afternoon. Okay?"

Smiling, David said, "Okay, Ted, I'll wait 'til I hear from you, but I'm going to Amman Friday if we don't have a deal."

"I'll call you one way or the other."

"Bye, Ted."

David was having a hard time keeping his mind on his work for thinking about the DC-8. He was pretty sure he was going to buy it, but he wanted to dicker a little more. He knew he made a nearly impossible offer, but thought, *All they can do is say no, and then I can give in to their best deal.*

Liam was off to a fast start in the United Kingdom. The

warehouse and office looked great, and the new sales reps Urey hired were selling Shepherd goods like crazy. David was comfortable with the fact that he had things pretty well under control, so he wasn't afraid to leave, but now he had a new problem.

Business was good and getting better and the Shepherd manufacturing capacity was starting to worry him. Even though they had built a large, new plant, he wondered how much longer they could keep up with orders. They were running two full shifts, but he thought they might have to add a third. They never had very much luck with a third shift before, but it might be necessary to try it again. An additional new plant couldn't be ruled out; in fact, he may talk to his key people about that when he gets back to Chattanooga.

They took an airport limousine to the Lufthansa section the next morning and boarded a plane to Munich. It was a two and a half hour flight, and they were scheduled to land at twelve-forty-eight. This time David rented a car and let Thil drive since she knew the city. They stopped and got some lunch before she let David out at the office. He told her to be back at six o'clock and they would go to her place.

As she drove away, David made up his mind to have a telephone installed in the apartment. That would simplify many things when in Munich. As soon as he got inside the office, after he spoke to Marlene, he told her to call the telephone company and set it up.

Bruno had gone out to see a customer when David arrived, but Gerhard was there. They sat down in his office and talked about how things were running. He asked if Bruno was working on his English, and Gerhard said he was; in fact, he made a *make-believe* speech to him and Marlene in English the other day. He said it was pretty good.

"Gerhard, you may have already done this, but if you haven't, I want you to talk to all the guys about projections. Our manufacturing is almost to capacity, and I have to make some decisions. If volume continues to increase the way it has,

I may have to build an additional plant. We've already built one, but it's bursting at the seams, so I believe another one might be necessary. If you and your guys project additional growth within the next year, and you're able to get the Tel Aviv branch off the ground, a new plant will definitely be necessary. The only question will be how big to make it."

"Speaking of Tel Aviv, what do you hear about the situation over there?"

"I hear things are getting hot. Israel believes it's only a matter of time before Syria, Jordan, and Egypt coordinate a massive attack on them. Egypt is already concentrating military forces in the sensitive Suez region. It won't surprise me if Israel attacks first, and it could be any day now."

"That being the case, I guess we had better hold off going to Tel Aviv," David said.

"I think it would be a good idea."

"Gerhard, I had hoped we could go to a couple other countries on this trip, but it's going to have to wait until next time. I'm negotiating on getting a company airplane and if the broker accepts my offer, I may have to go back to London tomorrow or Saturday."

"Really? What kind of plane are you looking at?"

"A DC-8 and boy, is it a honey? It belonged to an Arab Sheik, and it's hard to describe how plush it is. The man is supposed to call me here around four o'clock to let me know whether or not we have a deal."

No sooner had he said that than the phone rang. "David, it's an overseas call for you."

"Thank you, Marlene. Hello, this is David Shepherd."

"Hello, David. Ted Mosier here."

"Hi, Ted. What's cooking?"

"Well, I hope you're getting ready to buy an airplane. David, I've been beating on my manager ever since I talked to you yesterday, and here's the best we can do. First of all, we will cut the asking price by two-hundred thousand dollars. Next, we will fly the plane to Chattanooga for you. We will pay for the flight crew, but you will have to pay for the fuel. How does that sound to you? David, this is a really good deal, and I'm confident you're not going to do any better in Amman."

"Ted, you did good. I'm going to buy the plane from you. What do we do first?"

"Your credit has already been approved, so if you will give me the name of your CFO, we can start the ball rolling."

"You can call Sam Armstrong at my office in Chattanooga. He can handle everything. When do you think you will be taking the plane to Chattanooga?"

"Maybe Monday or Tuesday."

"Look, Ted. As you know, my wife and I are in Munich right now. What if we fly back to London and catch a ride home on my new plane? Would that work?"

"I don't see why not. I'll call Leslie and tell him what you're going to do. Will you be at the Airport Hilton when you return to London?"

"Yes, I'll book a flight for Sunday, so he can reach me Sunday night. Ted, you said I'll have to buy the fuel. I don't have an account set up with anybody. How will I do that?"

"My company will fill the tanks, and you can reimburse us when you get home with the plane."

"When I get home, can you come to my office? I need to pick your brain. I have no idea how to go about finding pilots, someone to paint our name and logo on the plane, where to get it serviced and about a hundred other things. If you'll come the day after I get back, I'll appreciate it."

"Consider it done. Congratulations, David. You're going to love owning a DC-8."

Gerhard had left the office when David got the call and when he hung up, he walked to the outer office and said, "Well, I now own an airplane."

"Good. When do you get it?"

He explained that it was in London and he and Thil were going back there and would ride home in it. "Do you have

Andrea's phone number?"

"No, but maybe I can find it in the directory. Here it is," and he dialed the number and handed David the phone. David handed it back to him and said, "Ask for Thil. I can't speak German."

"Thil. I just bought the Sheik's airplane. We're going back to London, Sunday to get it, and ride home in it Monday or Tuesday."

"She squealed and said, "Really? Are we going to do what you said at thirty-thousand feet, going six-hundred miles an hour?"

"I don't know. Maybe. I'll tell you more when you pick me up. I just wanted to tell you about the plane. I'll see you in a little while."

"Marlene, what did the telephone company say about putting a phone in our apartment?"

"They said they could do it tomorrow if someone would be there."

"Good. Gerhard, could we go see a couple customers tomorrow?"

"Yes sir. In fact, we'll go see our largest account here in Munich."

At six o'clock on the dot, Thil drove up, and she and David headed home.

"Before I forget it, I ordered a telephone for the apartment, and they're going to be there to put it in tomorrow. Can you stay home and wait for them?"

"Of course I will. We need a telephone, don't we?"

That night, after they went out for dinner, they came back, put on their PJ's, and talked about their airplane while watching TV. Then, Thil began to get a little frisky, so they went to bed early.

**

Gerhard and Daniele came over Saturday night to spend

some time with them. Gerhard brought a bottle of some kind of German wine that was really good, and it didn't take long to finish the bottle. Daniele was learning to speak English and some of the things she said by mistake were so funny. They all laughed at her, but she was a good sport about it. Time passed too quickly and they had to go home. Daniele, it was nice to see you again. Gerhard, I'll be back in a month or so, and maybe you and I can go to Austria and Romania and some other places. You're doing a good job; keep it up." After they both kissed Thil on the cheek, they left and David and Thil put on their pajamas.

The next morning they drove to the airport and turned in the rental car. When the paperwork was completed, Thil and David headed toward the gate to catch their plane.

After checking into the Hilton, they kicked back and rested. After awhile, David got bored and decide to try to call Don. He asked the hotel operator to place the call and it went through surprisingly fast. "Hello, Don. What are you doing?"

"Where are you, Pop?"

"We're in London. I just thought I'd call and tell you what I've done."

"What do you mean?"

"Son you know how much I've been traveling; I've been gone a lot, but still needed to go other places. I've been spending much unproductive time in airports, so I decided to do something about it. Guess what? I bought an airplane."

"You're not serious."

"I'm serious as a heart attack. The reason Thil and I are back in London is to catch our plane and ride home in it. And guess what, son? The plane belonged to an Arab Sheik, so you can just imagine how plush it is."

"Son-of-a gun. I'm impressed, Pop."

"I'll have to call you back and let you know when we'll be home. It'll either be tomorrow or Tuesday, We just don't know yet. I'll let you go. I just wanted to tell you about the plane."

"Okay, Pop. I'm glad you called. I can't wait to see it.

Bye."

The rest of the day was lazy and uneventful and David could hardly wait to get on his airplane. He told Thil that even if they don't leave 'til Tuesday, he's going to the airport tomorrow and spend some time on the plane.

***

Leslie called Sunday night and said they would be leaving the next morning and asked if they would be ready. "Of course." David said they would be and Leslie said he would have a car at the Hilton to pick them up at eight-thirty.

The car took them right up to the plane and they went straight from the car to the steps leading up to the plane. The flight crew of four had already boarded. David was expecting a crew of three, but he wasn't expecting a stewardess. That was a little something extra that Leslie had come up with.

At exactly nine-thirty, they began to taxi. Getting clearance from the tower, the pilot gunned the four Pratt and Whitney engines, and they roared down the runway. When they were airborne, it felt as if they were floating on a cloud.

The stewardess couldn't do enough for them; in fact, she was so attentive, David felt a little self-conscience. He insisted she relax, so after a while, she sat with them and became like a passenger.

David spent quite a bit of time in the flight deck, talking to the crew and learning about his airplane.

At noon, the stewardess asked if they were hungry and then served lunch. They must have picked the food up at a deli. It was very good. They had a wide choice of drinks, and they both chose Cokes.

Later, David and Thil decided to take a nap and try out the bed. They were tempted to do what David had said they would do at thirty-thousand feet, but with the stewardess on board, he thought they might not have enough privacy, so they just went to sleep.

At three-thirty, Eastern time, they landed at Lovell Field in Chattanooga. Don was there to meet them and couldn't believe his eyes when he saw the beautiful DC-8 coming in.

***

Most of the first week, after they returned with the airplane, was taken up with getting David familiar with aeronautical procedures, interviewing pilots and showing off the plane to family, friends, and some employees. He would send it to Atlanta to have *SHEPHERD GLOBAL APPAREL GROUP* painted above the long row of windows on each side and the Shepherd's staff painted on each side of the tail.

Shepherd Apparel continued to grow, and as David had foreseen earlier, ground was broken on a new, 200,000 square foot plant. Going to the Mid-East was still in the fore of his mind, but with the likelihood of war, those plans would have to wait. Gerhard was doing a *bang up* job in Europe and in the three months since buying the plane, David was flying over there every four weeks. He took Thil with him each time, and they found that getting romantic at thirty-thousand feet, going six-hundred miles an hour was every bit as exciting as they thought it would be.

CHAPTER FOURTEEN

One day when David was up to his neck in work, he was in a meeting with his general contractor, Harold Sanders. Ruby knocked on his door, then opened it and said, "I'm sorry to interrupt, Mr. Shepherd, but your wife is on line two."

"Ask her if I can call her back in a few minutes."

"Mr. Shepherd, I think you should take her call."

"Oh, all right. Hello Thil, I'm really busy right now. Can I call you back?"

"Yes, but I've got something important to tell you, first."

"What is it?"

"Darling, I'm going to have a baby."

"You are? Wow!" Taking the phone away from his ear, he said to the contractor, "Harold, we're going to have a baby," and then resumed his conversation with Thil. "Honey, I'm thrilled, but let me call you back, okay? Love ya."

As soon as his meeting with Harold was finished, David called Thil. "Okay, tell me about the good news. I didn't even know you suspected anything."

"I wanted it to be a surprise."

"Well, it is. When is it due?"

"As near as Dr. Crane could tell, it's due December 19th."

David counted on his fingers and said, "Then you're three months right now, right?"

"Yes. We will have a nice Christmas present. I can hardly wait."

"Me either. Tell you what. In honor of the occasion, let's do something special. Let's go to the Read House for dinner tonight. Want to?"

"Oh yes. I love to go there."

There was still much work to be done when David walked out of his office, but he wasn't going to miss celebrating Thil's pregnancy. He didn't have to feel guilty about this baby because they had hoped she would conceive soon. He invited Don to go, but, as usual, he had other plans.

It was a wonderful evening. Not only did they have a delicious prime rib at the Read House, but they went to the Tivoli to see a live musical, and they thoroughly enjoyed it.

Sitting on the balcony after returning home, David asked, "Would you like a glass of wine?"

"Yes I would. That sounds good."

"Let's toast our new baby," and they clinked their glasses. Sitting close together on the loveseat, David asked, "I wonder what it's going to be?

Thil said, "I don't care, do you?"

"Not really. I would like to have a boy, but as long as it's healthy, I don't care."

They finished their wine and went to bed. Snuggling up, they melted into each other.

***

The next morning, David went out to get the paper, and when he unwrapped it, the headlines read in very large letters, *ISRAEL ATTACKS ARABS*. He rushed inside to turn on the television, and that's what they were reporting on all the networks.

The reports said Egypt had been concentrating military forces in the sensitive Suez zone. That was a highly provocative act and the Israelis only viewed it one way: that Egypt was preparing to attack. The Egyptians had also enforced a naval blockade which closed off the Gulf of Aqaba to Israeli shipping.

Rather than wait to be attacked, the Israelis launched a hugely successful military campaign against its perceived enemies. The air forces of Egypt, Jordan, Syria, and Iraq were all destroyed on June 5th.

According to the news reports, the war was continuing and it appeared the Israelis were running all over the Arabs.

David wasn't able to hear anything about what was happening in Tel Aviv and he hoped the city was able to escape being damaged too much. He had postponed opening a Shepherd branch there, and now he was glad he did, and he wondered what was going to happen next. He called Senator Powell to see what he had heard, but the Senator was out of town, so he would just have to keep listening to the radio and television. Business was going so well in Europe, he could hardly wait to get into the Mid-East, but this is throwing a *monkey wrench* into any kind of plans they might have. David thought, *Oh well, we'll just have to keep doing what we're doing over here and in Europe.*

Although Tom Ratcliff had taken a tremendous load off him, he was still so bogged down, he decided he needed additional help. With the success he had promoting Tom, he wanted to elevate his new assistant from within the company as well. He called Tom in and told him what he was going to do, and the two them put their *thinking caps* on and tried to come up with a suitable person.

They didn't want to try to come up with just a name from memory, so David had the payroll department-head bring him a roster of all the office and supervisory personnel. From that list, hopefully, they would come up with the right person. They spent as much time as they could without letting other important things go, so they decided to think about the people they had talked about and get together again the next morning.

The next morning David called Tom in. "Did you think about any of the people we talked about yesterday who might fit in well for the job?"

"Yes sir, and I think I may have come up with the right one."

"Don't tell me yet. I may have come up with the right one, too. Just for fun, I'll write my name down and you do the same; then, we'll at least, have the list narrowed down to two." They each wrote the name of the person they thought would make the best assistant; then, David said, "Okay, let me see who you wrote." Tom turned his paper over, and the name of *Chip Lowe* was on it.

"Wanna see who I wrote down?"

"Yes sir."

David turned his paper over and held his hand over it. "Do you want to guess who?"

"I don't have any idea."

David took his hand away, and the name on his paper was *Chip Lowe*. "Well, I guess that settles it, doesn't it?"

"It looks like it. That's amazing. When are you going to tell him?"

"I'll tell him this morning, but Tom, I want him to work for you. I'll call him in and tell him about his promotion. Then, I'll call you back in before I outline the duties. Actually, the extra duties will be put on you, but you'll have Chip to do the actual work. Does that sound okay to you?"

"That sounds fine. I'll be anxious to work with him."

The three of them spent the morning together and then went to lunch, continuing to talk about Chip's new duties and the future of Shepherd Global. David felt very comfortable with Chip moving into this new position. Now, he could travel abroad without fear of things in the office falling apart.

Another thing that had been bothering David was Don's future with the company. Now that Liam had things running smoothly in the United Kingdom and with Gerhard and Bruno in place in the rest of Europe, he felt that the business was getting to be a *well-oiled machine* and he wanted Don to be ready to move into it when he got out of college, so he called him into his office.

"Son, I know we've talked a little about your part in the company before, but we've never, really talked. Now that you're getting ready for college, I think it's time you thought about what you want to do and where you'd like to be in, say, ten years. Do you think you want to come into the company when you graduate or do you want to do something else? If you want to come here, we should get started with your training now."

"I want to come into the company."

"Good. What do you think you want to do here?"

"I'd like to learn the whole business, Pop."

"I was hoping you'd say that. It's going to be four years before you graduate, but if we start with your training now, it will make your transition into the company easier when the time comes. I know I've had you working in the cutting department for a while because it was not only an essential part of what we do, but it made it easy to keep track of where you were. But now, I think it's time for you to start learning something else."

"Before any garment can be cut, a pattern has to be made, and this is what I want you to do; I want you to learn to make patterns. Tomorrow, when you come in, report to Sam Evans in the pattern department. I'll talk to Sam, so he'll be expecting you. This is an important job, Son, so do your best. Shepherd Global has a reputation for selling well-fitting garments and all that starts with the pattern. At some point, we'll probably move you somewhere else, and at the end of your four-year college time, you should know quite a bit about the business. How does that sound?"

"It sounds great, Pop. Spreading cloth was getting to me. Sometimes, Bud would let me do some cutting, but the cutting department is borrr-ing. I'll be glad to get away from it."

"One more thing, Son. In the last two years, you've been into some things you shouldn't have been into. Do you think you're through with those kinds of things?"

"Yes sir. After that phone call to you, threatening to break my legs, and the murder of Johnny W., I've learned my lesson."

"Good. I hope so. Shepherd has a spotless reputation, and if anybody in a responsible position does something wrong, it reflects on the whole company, and I don't want that to happen. I hope you follow through on what you say."

"I will, Pop."

"One more thing, Son."

"What's that, Pop?"

"In December, you're going to have a little brother or sister."

"Are you serious? Pop, that's great. Boy, this has turned out to be a great day."

David was pleased and cautiously optimistic about Don after their talk, but he knew better than to turn him loose without close supervision. The last two years taught him that.

For the next few months, everyone was really busy. Business was good and David was traveling to Europe every four weeks. Thil was trying to get the nursery decorated the way she wanted it, but couldn't use blue or pink because she didn't know what the baby was going to be, so she used mainly yellow since it would be good for either a boy or a girl. She went to Germany with David three times during the next three months, but then the doctor thought it would be best if she didn't travel anymore until after the baby was born. That didn't sit well with Thil because she loved being with David so much, and she also hated to miss seeing Andrea and Daniele and her other friends in Munich.

On one of their trips, they took Don with them, but it was something he didn't want to repeat anytime soon. His first reaction was like that of a typical tourist, seeing world famous landmarks for the first time, but then the new wore off. He couldn't understand what anybody said, so he couldn't go anywhere because of the language barrier, and he was more than ready to go home after a couple of days.

Finally, it was mid-December and Thil was ready for it. To say she was miserable would be an understatement. She hadn't gained that much weight, but she stayed swollen much of the time. She had been having a few pains even though her due date was not until the nineteenth. On the nineteenth, as if on cue, she went into labor. David rushed home from the office, grabbed her and her suitcase and headed for the hospital. Thil had called Dr. Crane before David got home and he was at the hospital, waiting for them when they got there. The medical team took Thil away, and David went to the waiting room and waited with two other expectant fathers. In about an hour, Margaret and Don arrived to keep him company. Two hours later, the phone rang, and it was Dr. Crane. "Mr. Shepherd, you have a beautiful baby boy. If you will meet me in front of the nursery, you can see him."

Hospital rules wouldn't let any visitors get near the newborns, but David took Margaret and Don with him anyway, and went to meet the doctor. Although most newborns look pretty much alike, David thought he could see a Shepherd resemblance in his little boy. He spent maybe a minute talking to the doctor and looking at the baby: then, the nurse whisked the baby away and into the nursery where he would be cleaned up and examined.

As soon as they took the baby, David went into the men's room, closed himself in one of the stalls and said, "Father, thank you for giving this beautiful little baby to Thil and me. Father, I pray that you will let it be healthy, and I pray that you will let Thil recover okay. Lord, if you will bless our child, I promise that we will dedicate him to you and try to raise him in a manner that will be pleasing to you. Thank you again, Lord. In Jesus' name I pray. Amen."

When he left the rest room, he went back to the waiting room and talked for a minute to Margaret and Don and thanked them for coming. They talked about what a beautiful baby it was and they were both very happy for him. "I can't believe I've got a little brother," Don said.

"I know," said David. "You can help us raise him. Margaret, we've got a built-in baby sitter."

They all laughed and joked about it; then, David told them he was going to go up to Thil's room and wait for her to be brought in. While he waited on Thil to come, he thought, *Don sure acted happy about the baby. He seemed genuinely happy to have a new little brother. On the other hand, he thought, Margaret tried to act happy, but I wonder if she really is. Some of her looks and remarks make you kinda wonder. Since she doesn't have any children or a husband, there might be a little jealousy there. We'll just have to include her more in our activities. I wonder if she'd like to go to Germany or London sometime when Thil gets able to travel. I think I'll ask her.*

It might have been that David felt guilt when Thil's first baby was born, but with this one, he felt nothing but joy. They had picked out names; both girl's and boy's and had decided if it was a boy, they would name him *David Montgomery Shepherd* and call him *Monty.* Thil insisted they name him David because of the love she had for him and Montgomery was David's mother's maiden name.

After five days in the hospital, Thil and little Monty went home, just in time for Christmas. David had arranged for a nurse named Mrs. Pless, to come in and help out for a few days, and she fit in really well with the family. Mrs. Pless was all alone and agreed to stay even on Christmas. Not only did she help with the baby, she even prepared some of their meals. Thil told David she hated to see her leave.

Thil, with help from Margaret, had done the Christmas shopping before she went to the hospital and after they found out who was going to be staying with them, Margaret went out and bought Pless some presents. Margaret came over on Christmas morning to open presents with them, and Pless fit right in. It was a wonderful Christmas, and little Monty made it even more so.

Many manufacturing plants closed the week between Christmas and New Years, and that included Shepherd Global. They closed at the end of the day on December 23rd and everybody enjoyed a long holiday except for a skeleton crew needed to perform maintenance and a few other jobs that couldn't wait until the plant reopened on January 1st.

David hit the ground running when they reopened New

Years day. He had worked during the week they were closed and accomplished more than he would have had a full complement of people been around. Among the ideas he had before they went international, was to have their own truck line, and that was about to come to fruition. He had made some real progress during the week the plant was closed.

He reasoned that since they had gotten so large, by having their own trucks they could save a ton of money. They could deliver the Shepherd Staff goods to the freight forwarders and major customers. They could also pick up incoming goods and bring them to Chattanooga. In the event that any of the trucks would have to *dead head* back, he was pretty sure he could get other companies with goods coming in to the Chattanooga area to let Shepherd trucks haul them. Even if he didn't make much on the *dead head* shipments, they would, at least, pay the overhead costs of driving the trucks.

David was glad Don was going to come into the business when he got out of college and he was doing an adequate job in the pattern department, however, he wasn't showing as much initiative as David had hoped for. Since trucking was so different than apparel manufacturing, he thought Don might like that area better. He would keep that in mind.

One of the first things he had to do when they reopened in January was to get the truck line up and running. He had leased a vacant terminal previously used by a trucking company that had gone out of business, and he was able to buy ten of their trucks from the bankruptcy court. He had the trailers painted the same colors as the airplane, and the Staff logo was really eye-catching. The terminal manager for the bankrupt company was a fellow named *Homer Galloway,* and David was able to hire him. Getting set up with all the different states was going to be a tremendously hard job, but Homer knew how to do those things, and that made the job run much smoother. He also knew how to get in touch with most of the drivers who worked for the defunct truck line, and David hired some of them who were still unemployed. It looked as if everything was all set as soon as they got everything from the states, and hopefully that would only be a matter of days. The truck division would be called Shepherd Truck Line and David could hardly wait to see some of the trucks on the road.

***

The baby was now three weeks old and starting to grow some. He was eating well and sleeping good, and Thil was in seventh heaven. She doted over him and hated to let him out of her sight, but when David was home, she tried to devote as much time to him as she could.

It had been five weeks since David had been to Europe and he thought he needed to get over there as soon as possible. One of Bruno's men was on the verge of opening a very large account, and David wanted to go with him to show the customer how much he would value them as a customer. He had Ruby call Bruno and set it up. In a couple of hours, Bruno called back and told David when they would be seeing the account, so David planned to leave on Monday. They would be going to Austria for a meeting on Tuesday afternoon.

Thil cried when David left. He had been at home for five weeks and during that time, Monty was born, and she was getting used to his being there. "I won't be gone a minute longer than I have to, sweetheart. You know, it won't be long until I can take you and the baby with me. Would you like that?"

"Oh yes, David. I don't like being away from you, and I really want to show Monty off to my friends, too. When do you think I can go with you?"

"Let's see how the baby does. If he continues as he is now, maybe you can go next month. That reminds me of something. The next time you go with me, I want to buy a car. I'm there enough to justify owning one, and if we take the baby, we need to have a car seat."

"Let's do that next month, darling."

"Okay, it's a deal."

When Monty was three months old, David called Reverend Nathan Fowler, his pastor, and asked when they could dedicate him. David had promised God when Monty was only a few minutes old that he would dedicate him to Him, and he wanted to keep his promise. Nathan said Sunday after next would be good if that was good for Thil and David, so they set it up. Thil wasn't sure why they were doing it, but since David said they should do it, she was happy to go along with it.

After the service was over, David, Thil, the baby, and Nathan went out for an enjoyable lunch. They talked as they ate and at one point, Nathan told the couple, "David, when you talked to me before your first baby was born, I told you that someone would have to pay for the sin in that situation, and I was right. The baby paid."

"Now, I believe God has blessed this child, and he will have a glorious life. David, among other good things that will happen, I believe Monty will be the one to carry on your legacy at Shepherd Apparel. I know Don is the oldest, but I believe in my heart Monty will be the one."

"Thank you, Nathan. You may be right. We'll see, won't we?"

***

The next three and a half years went by like a flash. Shepherd Global continued to grow and David expanded the Shepherd Staff line to include jeans. If business continued to grow they might have to build yet another plant. The women's clothing was making all the plants operate at full capacity, and if David's goal to start a men's line came about, a plant with 1,000,000 square feet would not be out of the question.

Don graduated from U.C. in May and was now a full-time employee of the Shepherd Global Apparel Group. He had been working in different areas for the last few years, and David was uncomfortable about where he would be best suited. At the time he started the truck line, he thought that might be the best place for him, but now he's having second thoughts. *I know what I'll do. I'll put him in the sales department and give him some accounts to call on. He should like that. He has a good personality and should be able to do well with our customers. I'll tell him that's what we're going to do.*

"One night, when Thil, David, and Monty were out on the balcony, Don came out and said, "Pop, what would you say if I got my own place? I'm twenty two now, and I think it's time I moved out of my parent's house, don't you?"

"Where do you want to go?"

"I'm not sure. I hear there are some really nice apartments being built around the lake, and somebody said there are some being built at the foot of Signal Mountain that look nice. I don't know what they are going to rent for, but if I can afford one, I'd like to get out on my own. What do you think?"

"I think that will be fine if that's what you want to do. When do you plan to move?"

"Well, I thought I would try to get one of those at the lake and move when they get finished. They say they will be ready in a couple of weeks."

"Okay, but let's talk more about it when we get to the office tomorrow. I've been thinking some about moving you into sales, and there's a possibility that you will want to move somewhere else if we do that."

"What are you thinking, Pop?"

"It's still just a thought, but we'll explore it further tomorrow, all right?"

"Okay. Pop, I'm going to Richard's. I'll be back early." And he left.

Thil and David got Monty ready for bed. He always wanted his daddy to read him a bedtime story, so David read *Jack and The Beanstalk*. Monty was asleep before David finished reading, so he went back to the balcony and joined Thil. "You know what, Thil? The way time is flying, Monty's going to be grown before we turn around, and we'll wonder where his childhood went."

"I know," she said. "Maybe we should try to make a little brother for him to play with."

"Want to?"

"Yes. I think we owe it to him, don't you?"

"I've been thinking that. Do you think we should do it now?"

"As you Americans say, *there's no time like the present.*"

David said, "And I believe that."

They got up, locked the doors, turned off the lights and went to bed. They tried their very best to make a little brother or sister for Monty, but didn't think they were successful. They would probably have to try again and again. The doctors had told Thil it was unlikely she could have any more children, but they acted as though they didn't believe the doctors, so she and David decided to keep trying. Besides, trying was too much fun to let a doctor's opinion spoil it.

***

Twelve years later

For almost twelve years, Don had been a sales representative for Shepherd. He only had thirteen accounts to service, and with that small number of accounts, one would think a good salesman would build business up, but Don managed to keep their volume steady through the entire twelve years. David had heard, by way of the *grapevine*, that he was doing some heavy gambling, so he took his accounts away and brought him into the office.

Don was thirty-four years old now, and he had never married. This bothered David. *He dates women, so he must not be homosexual. He has an opportunity that very few men have and, with his abilities, he should be one of the most successful men in America. There's no reason for him to gamble. That's why he never has any money. With his income, he should be able to buy just about anything he wants, but he's always broke, and now, he's drinking on top of that. What's wrong with him, anyway?*

Since Jane Ward left customer service, I guess I'll give him a chance to see what he can do in there. With his personality, he should be a natural. I'll start him in there tomorrow. I had hoped he could, one day, take over Shepherd Apparel, but I don't know anymore.

On the other hand, Monty was growing into quite a young man. At sixteen years old, he was a strapping six feet, one inch tall and had a muscular body that his team mates envied. He had become a very good athlete and was equally as good in football and baseball. He started at wide receiver as a sophomore and could catch anything that was thrown to him, and he loved to hit. In baseball, he played in the outfield. He threw right and batted left and could hit the ball a mile.

David let him work at Shepherd when he wasn't in school or playing in a game, and he always wanted to know if there was anything else that needed to be done before he left. That was a sharp contrast to Don, who couldn't wait to leave work, even if his job wasn't finished.

When Don was sixteen, he gave up a possible athletic scholarship to run numbers. At sixteen, Monty was not only on track to get a scholarship, but he and a couple of fellow football players organized an informal prayer group that met before school on Monday mornings. Other athletes were starting to attend, and the group had grown to eleven. Those boys were very influential among the student body, and news of their meetings was getting around. Non-Christian kids were wondering if they weren't missing something, and a couple of them actually started going to Church as the result of the prayer group's influence.

Thil idolized Monty and he, Thil. David was extremely proud of him and encouraged him to surround himself with his friends. The ball teams looked on David and Thil as part of their families. It was really a healthy situation.

***

Don's transition from sales to customer service was relatively smooth, although he considered customer service boring. He liked the freedom he had when he was in sales, and now he was confined to an office all day, every day. He liked to be actively helping customers, but most of the time the agents in his department were taking care of the problems, leaving him with not much to do. That allowed him to spend more time to study the lines and betting odds of everything from football to horse racing. David had hoped by giving him a new job where he would be closer would help to manage him a little more, but it seemed to have the opposite effect.

Don was spending money like crazy on gambling and was losing much more than he was winning. He would win one bet and lose two. Alcohol was creeping into his life more and more as well, and David was worried sick about him. Over the years he had had him in nearly every department in the company. He still had hopes that even though Don was now in his mid-thirties, one day, he would mature enough to take over the reins of Shepherd Apparel, but it was looking more and more as if it might never happen.

Thil reminded David, "You know how the reputation of the company is going to require someone with integrity and good character to step in and operate it without missing a step when you retire. I think you're forgetting that Monty will someday be able to fill that role if you can only wait until he finishes college and gets a few years of training under his belt."

"I know, but what am I going to do with Don? He's my son, too, and his whole life, I've been planning to hand over the company to him, but the way things are with him now, there's no way he could operate a conglomerate like Shepherd Global. Monty may one day be the answer. Do you remember what Nathan Fowler said that time when we had lunch? It looks more and more like his prediction is going to be right. I'm still relatively young, so I don't have to be in a huge hurry. I'm just anxious to retire, so I can be with you all the time."

"That will be wonderful, but we're together a fair amount of time right now. I travel to Europe with you and, we're together. I go with you to the Mid-East, and we're together. We spend time together in Port Charlotte when we go to Florida, so really, David, there should not be a rush to retire. Do you think?"

"I guess not. What do you want to do for supper? It's Friday night, and all the restaurants will be full. If you want to go to the store and get some meat and buns, I'll grill some burgers."

"Can we have hot dogs, too?"

"Whatever your little heart desires. Pick up some wieners and buns, too, and we'll have a feast."

"Roger, Boss." She went to the bedroom and got ready to go to the store.

"Thil, while you're at the store, pick up some potato salad at the deli, will you?"

"I will. Do you want baked beans, too?"

"That's up to you. I think we'll have plenty without them, but if you want to, get some."

"I'll see."

While David was cooking the burgers and dogs, Thil called Margaret and invited her over. She jumped at the chance, and the three of them had a great Friday-night cookout on the patio.

CHAPTER FIFTEEN

All weekend, David thought about Don and his *lackadaisical* attitude toward the company, and he thought he would have a serious talk with him when they got to work, Monday. He rehearsed in his mind what he was going to say to him, and when he arrived at his office, he was ready. Everyone was supposed to be at work at eight o'clock, but Don wasn't there. Eight-thirty came; still, no Don. Nine o'clock; Don was still not there. David called his apartment, but got no answer. Most of Don's friends that David knew were now married and he didn't think he would be with them. He was beginning to get worried.

A little after nine, David went to the break-room to drink coffee with some of the office workers and a *Chattanooga Times* was on one of the vacant tables. None of the employees would be there until nine-thirty, so he picked up the paper to see what had happened over the weekend. He did a double-take when he turned to page three. Midway down the page, a medium-sized headline read "*Son of Prominent Chattanooga Businessman Arrested.*"

As he read down, the article began, "*Donald Alexander Shepherd,34, son of prominent Chattanooga businessman, David Shepherd was arrested Saturday night after a hit and run accident on Signal Mountain Boulevard. Witnesses said Shepherd had just left the Fifth Wheel night club when he hit the rear of a car owned by Robert Walker. Shepherd fled the scene and was later arrested at his home by Hamilton County Sheriff's deputies. At the time of his arrest, Shepherd registered an alcohol level of 1.7, nearly twice the legal limit. Anything over .08 is considered intoxicated, and Shepherd was placed in the Hamilton County jail under a twenty-five thousand dollar bond. He is charged with hit and run and driving while intoxicated. He remains in the Hamilton County jail at this time."*

David took the paper and went back to his office. He had to sit for a few minutes to try to figure out what to do. First, he thought jail was what Don needed, but then, he realized the charges against him were serious, so he called his lawyer for advice and had him go to the jail and bail him out. He gave instructions that Don was to come straight to his office.

Around eleven-thirty, Don came straggling into the Shepherd office as if nothing had happened. His clothes were wrinkled and his uncombed hair went perfectly with his two-day growth of beard. As he walked past Ruby's desk, he smiled big. "Whatta ya say, Rube? How's it going?"

"I'm just fine, Don. Your father is waiting for you. Good luck."

"Thanks, Rube."

"Hi Pop. You wanted to see me?"

"Sit your butt down before I kick it up around your neck. Now, before I fire you, I want to know what, in heaven's name, you were doing driving drunk, and why did you run away after you hit that car? Why were you at the Fifth Wheel in the first place? That place is a notorious honky-tonk and there's always bad stuff happening there."

"Pop, how about letting me answer your questions one at a time. You're asking so many, I can't remember all of them."

"Shut up. Don't you be a wise-ass with me. I want answers."

"Okay. First of all, I did have too much to drink and I'm sorry. We were just sitting there having a drink, and one thing led to two and it went from there."

"Who is *we*?"

"Casey Thornton, a girl I used to know in college."

"Is she your girlfriend?"

"No, sir. I just happened to run into her, and I asked her

out."

"What's the deal on hitting a car and then running away?"

"Pop, I honestly didn't know I hit it. The radio was playing loud, and I didn't hear anything."

" Bull crap!! How in the name of common sense could you not know you hit something? You knocked the man's bumper off and messed up the front of your car. A loud radio wouldn't cover that up. Witnesses said you stopped to look, then took off. What about that?"

"I don't know, but I didn't know I hit anything."

"What did you do with the girl you were with?"

"She went home with me, and when the police came, she called someone to come pick her up."

"Don, I don't know what's going to happen with this, but I'm sure the law is going to punish you in some way. I'm so put out with you right now, I don't much care what they do with you. My main concern is Shepherd Apparel."

"Your granddad and I have worked a long time building this business, and we have built it, based on integrity and our good names. Now, here you come acting like an out-of-control idiot doing something like this."

"You've been working here ever since you were a young boy and ever since you were a young boy, you've been in one scrape after another. Every time something happens, you come to me apologizing, promising that you're sorry, and it won't happen again. I feel sorry for you and overlook it. I can't do my job, effectively, for worrying about what you're going to do next. You've worked in cutting, patterns, engineering, sales, and now, customer service. The sad part is, none of those departments are any better for having had you working in them."

"I have been hoping ever since you were born to put you at the helm of the company, but you have disappointed me every time. Shepherd Apparel is not a small, local company anymore. It is an international conglomerate with over four thousand employees, and it takes a special person to be *head honcho*, and right now, Son, you are not that person. Let me ask you something: what do you think should happen here? You're not a kid anymore; you're thirty-five years old and should know better. What do you think I should do?"

"Pop, I know you're mad, and I'm sorry for what happened, but in fairness to me, I wasn't on company time. I was on my own time, so it shouldn't affect my job. You've blessed me out, and that hurt, and I have apologized, so can't we just forget this happened?"

"Are you serious, Don? I may never forget this. I think it will be best if you find a job somewhere else. I have too much to do to worry about what you're doing. You have enough experience to qualify for a job at many places and should do well if you apply yourself. I love you, Son, but I don't think we can use you here any longer."

"This really hurts, Pop. I don't know how I'll live 'til I can find something? Can I work at Shepherd while I look?"

"Son, you've been making a high, five-figure salary, and without a family, you should have been able to put back a lot. Use your savings to live on."

"I don't have any savings."

"What's happened to all your money? Did you gamble it away?"

" No, I didn't. I don't know what happened to it. It just got away."

"Well, I'm sorry, but from now on, our relationship will have to be only that of a loving father to his son."

"I'm sorry, too, Pop. Do you want me to leave now?"

"Go clean out your desk and then take off."

Don got a box and went to the customer service department, and to his office where he emptied his desk. He didn't say anything to anybody. As he was leaving, he stopped by Ruby's desk, and with a big smile and a wink, "See ya Rube. My old man just canned me."

"Really, What are you going to do, Don?"

"No sweat. I'll let him cool off for a while and I think he'll let me come back. He doesn't think so, but he needs me. In the meantime, I think I'll run down to Hot-lanta for a few days. There's a lot going on down there, and I need a break. See ya, Rube," and he left.

As soon as Don left, David knelt down in front of the sofa in his office. "Father, I hope I did the right thing. Please stay beside me and help me make the right decisions, not only in business, but show me what you would have me do when it comes to my family. You know how much I love Don, but Lord, I feel he must pay for his mistakes. Please help me do what is right and Lord, please help Don. I thank you for all your blessings, Father, and these things I've asked for, I ask in Jesus' name. Amen."

When he finished praying, he called Thil and told her what had happened. She hadn't seen the paper, yet, so it was a big surprise to her. She knew how David loved Don and knew it must have really hurt to fire him. She wanted to be supportive, but didn't know what to say. So she simply said, "I'm sorry, Darling, but I know you did the right thing."

"I will need to explain some things to Monty when I get home, so be sure he's there."

David had a hard time keeping his mind on his work, so he cleaned off his desk and left the office around four o'clock. When he got home, Thil and Monty were there to greet him. Thil went up and kissed him, warmly and then Monty gave him a hug. "Hi Dad."

"Hey, Kiddo. What are you getting ready to do?"

"Nothing. Mom said you wanted to talk to me."

"I do. I need to talk to you about your brother."

"I think I know what you're going to say. I heard some guys talking about him at school, today."

"What did they say?"

"They said the paper said Don was arrested for hit and run and was in jail."

"They're right. Don was arrested Saturday night. He was drunk, and he hit a car after coming out of a honky-tonk on

Signal Mountain Boulevard."

"Is he still in jail?"

"No. I had my lawyer bail him out and Monty, he's no longer at Shepherd Apparel. I fired him."

"You fired him?"

"Yes, and I should have done it a long time ago. He's been in trouble ever since he was your age. I just hope you don't turn out like that."

"Dad, Don's a good man, and he's smart. Maybe he just needs some help. Can't you give him another chance?"

"Nope. He's had all the chances he's gonna get from me. He's on his own, now."

"At least think about it, Dad, won't you?"

"Yeah, I'll think about it."

"Good. How would you like some good news, Dad?"

"Boy, I could use some. What is it?"

"Coach Springfield told me this morning that a coach from the University of Georgia called him, asking questions about me. He didn't make any commitments, but Coach Springfield thinks they might want to give me a scholarship in baseball. He said the coach asked a lot of questions, and he thinks they will call back."

"Well, don't get your hopes up yet. You still have two more years in high school and a lot can happen in that length of time."

"I won't, besides I think I would rather get a football scholarship than one in baseball, but any kind would help you, wouldn't it, Dad?"

"It sure would, but you won't have to have a scholarship. Your mother and I will see that you can go to college when that time comes."

"I know you will, Dad, but I want to help by doing what I can and a scholarship would help."

"Thil, have you fixed supper yet?"

"No, I was just getting ready to start it when you came home. Why?"

"I thought the three of us might go out and get something? Whatta ya think, Monty?"

"That sounds great."

"Where do you wanna go?"

"Shoney's sounds good to me. I could do a number on some of their strawberry pie."

"That does sound good," Thil said.

"Then Shoney's it is."

Just being around Monty always lifted David's spirits, and he needed that help after his session with Don earlier. He thought to himself, *I love Monty so much. I wish Don would be like him. I guess I'm at fault there. I should have done a better job raising him. Hopefully he'll change, and we can get things worked out sometime.*

Thil has been a lifesaver for me. How could she have given birth to such a perfect child? The three of us are almost a perfect family. Maybe Don will join us some day.

"What are you thinking about, Darling?"

"I'm just thinking how lucky I am to have you two. I love you both so much."

Thil and Monty both responded with, "I love you, too."

After dinner, they went home, and Monty went to his room to study. Thil and David turned out the lights and went up to their bedroom and sat in the sitting area off the bedroom. David offered and Thil accepted a glass of wine. After two glasses, amorous feelings were beginning to show up in Thil, and it wasn't long until she moved to David's lap and started kissing him the way she used to do before they were married. David responded feverishly, and they moved from the loveseat to the bed where Thil made him forget everything bad that had happened earlier in the day.

Don spent three days in Atlanta drinking and partying with friends he had down there. He almost managed to get his head knocked off one night when he hit on another guy's lady while at a club in Underground Atlanta. When the girl's boyfriend went to the rest room, Don moved in, and when the boyfriend returned, Don didn't want to leave. Words were exchanged, and the boyfriend invited Don to go outside with him, but Don's friends grabbed him by the arm and pulled him away. They apologized to the couple and explained that Don was drunk, and he was really a nice guy when he was sober. The couple accepted the apology, and Don and his friends left. They took him to his hotel and put him to bed to sober up.

He pretty much passed out when his buddies put him to bed the night before, and when he woke up the next morning, he had a king-sized headache. He phoned his friend, Doyle. "Hey, are you alive?"

"Yeah, I feel pretty good this morning. How about you?"

"I feel like death warmed over. I've got a headache you wouldn't believe, and I'm sick at my stomach. I think I'll go home."

"You're not going to stay the rest of the week like you said?"

"No. I just want to go home. I'm going to go try to work things out with my father. I'll talk to you later, okay?"

"Okay Pal. Be careful."

***

Soon after David got to his office Thursday morning, he got a call from Ted Mosier. "Hi David. I haven't talked to you in a long time."

"I know. How have you been?"

"I've been doing great, David, and I hope you have. Listen, the reason I'm calling is to tell you about a great plane that has just come on the market. Yours is getting some age on it now, and I thought you might want to update."

"What have you got, Ted?"

"It's a Boeing 707-320B. It's a fantastic airplane and like your DC-8, this plane once belonged to a Saudi Arabian Sheikh. As a point of interest, Frank Sinatra owns a 707."

"How does a 707 compare to a DC-8?"

"The standard 707 is pretty close to the size of the DC-8, but this is a 707-320B. It's called a *stretcher.* It's equally as nice as your DC-8 and it's bigger. Your DC-8 has a range of a little over four thousand miles, and the 320B has a range of over six thousand. This plane has been well cared for and has been in storage for the last eight months, Both Qantas and Braniff fly 707's, and they get very good service from them. I'd like for you to take a look at it, David."

"Where is it?"

"Kansas City."

"When do you want me to see it?"

"How about this weekend? We could fly you out Saturday morning if that would work for you."

"Can I bring my wife? I like her opinion on these things."

"Of course. How about we meet at the airport at nine o'clock Saturday morning and we'll fly you out there and back. Our plane is parked close to yours, so let's meet at your plane, and we can walk over to ours."

"Okay. See you then."

David called and told Thil about their upcoming trip, and she was very excited. She loved airplanes, and she loved to travel.

About an hour before lunch on Friday, Don went to see David. "Hi Pop."

"Hi Don. This is a pleasant surprise. What have you been doing?"

"Not much. I went down to Atlanta for a couple days to see my buddy, Doyle Watson, but that's about it. I've been thinking about my life and just wanted to come by to see you and tell you how sorry I am for the way I've behaved for the last *umpteen* years."

"I appreciate that, Son. It's way past time for you to grow up, and maybe this is a start. Thank you. Listen, I'm up to my neck in meetings today, and I'm not going to lunch. Ruby's going to bring me something when she comes back. Do you want her to bring you a sandwich or something?"

"No thanks, Pop. I ate breakfast late. I just came by, hoping to talk to you about maybe letting me come back to work."

"Don, you've only been off a week. I think you need to apply to some other places and see what's out there. Shepherd Apparel is the only company you've ever worked for, and apparently it wasn't what you wanted because of all the stuff you did while working here. You need to find something that will challenge you. You have so much ability and should be able to do good things for some company looking for a bright young man."

"I might have to go to Tel Aviv Tuesday and will be gone all week. When I get back, we'll have you over for burgers one night, okay? Son, I've got to get to work right now, so please excuse me."

"Okay, Pop. I'll see ya."

"I love you, Son."

"Yeah, right."

As Don left the Shepherd office, he thought to himself, *Well, that didn't go the way I hoped it would. He could have given me more time and consideration. He didn't even treat me like his son. I'm not going to get to see him again until, at least, week after next. I don't want to go around putting in applications. I've got to figure out some way to get back with Shepherd. Town and Country restaurant has just opened its new lounge. A drink sounds good.* He turned his car toward town and headed to North Chattanooga to get a drink.

Looking at a new airplane had not even crossed David's mind before Ted called, but now that he was going to see a 707-320B, he was getting excited. Thil was like a high school girl getting her first prom dress. They got to the airport early and in a few minutes, Ted got there. He was also a little early. They walked over to his plane which turned out to be a Gulfstream IV. In a few minutes the flight crew arrived and prepared for takeoff. The plane rode like a dream, and David wondered if maybe, he should consider one of these instead of the 707, but Ted convinced him he needed the larger plane with more range to handle the distances he had to travel.

The flight from Chattanooga to Kansas City took two hours. When they landed, the Gulfstream taxied to an area where private and corporate planes were parked, and David tried to pick out which one they were to see. He thought he spotted it, then, Ted said, "It's that long, sleek, white airplane with the navy stripe going along the windows from the nose to the tail. It's a beauty, isn't it?"

"Wow," David said.

"It's beautiful," Thil added. "I can't wait to see inside."

"Well, let's go look at it. David, if you like it, and want to, the crew that brought us out here is qualified to fly the 707, and we can take a ride," Ted said.

David, in awe, said, "I already like it. Let's see the interior, and if it looks as good as the exterior, I definitely want to ride in it."

The interior was magnificent. It was larger than their DC-8 and the bedroom was fancier. The cabin was a little more than one hundred eleven feet long and right at eleven and a half feet wide; however, it did not have gold plated faucets, but all in all, it was equally as nice, and maybe even nicer than their plane.

The tower cleared them for takeoff, and the bird shot up in the air like a graceful eagle. It was so quiet, the engines could hardly be heard, and the ride was like riding on a cloud. David had flown in the rock star's 707, several years ago, but this was larger and quieter. He had to have this airplane. They flew for about forty-five minutes and David spent most of that time in the flight deck, talking to the crew. Thil wanted him to sit with her, and he did part of the time, but he wanted to check out everything on the plane while they were in the air.

Thil asked, "Darling, did you notice the bedroom? It's fantastic. I'll bet we could fool around at thirty-thousand feet in this baby, don't you?"

"I know for sure we could. Do you think we ought to buy it?"

"Well, you're far wiser than I am, but if you're asking my opinion, I say yes, buy it."

David hated to land, but knew they had to. On the way back to Chattanooga, he and Ted talked money, trade-in, terms, and everything else that needed to be discussed when making such a huge transaction. He told Ted he would call him Monday and give him an answer. He said he was supposed to go to Tel Aviv on Tuesday, and if he got the plane, he would like to fly it over there, but didn't know if things could be worked out that fast or not.

They touched down at Lovell Field at five-twelve. It had been a full day, and they were both tired. Thil said, "David, do you think we could go somewhere and get something to eat? I'm awfully tired, and I hate to start cooking this late."

"Sure, we can. Let's find a phone and call Monty to go with us. He's probably at home, don't you think?"

"He should be."

David called and Monty was there. He said they were going to The Greystone and would like for him to meet them there. When they pulled in the restaurant's parking lot, they saw Monty was already there and waiting at the front door. They went in and talked about the plane and filled Monty in on their trip. They all seemed excited about it, and David said he thought he would call Ted on Monday and tell him he would take it.

When he called Ted, he was told that it would be Wednesday before they could have the plane ready for him, so he had a decision to make. He was supposed to leave Tuesday, and the Tel Aviv trip was an important one and didn't need to be delayed. If he waited until Thursday to leave, he wouldn't have enough time to do what he had to do before the Sabbath in Israel. On the other hand, if he could get in touch with Myron Hober and have him delay their appointment until the following week, it would really suit him better.

If he waited, the new plane could make it non-stop to Tel Aviv, but he would have to carry an extra crew because flying time between Chattanooga and Tel Aviv was thirteen hours and fourteen minutes. If he went ahead and made the trip on the DC-8, he would have to make it in two segments: fly to either London or Munich and spend the night to give the crew the required rest, and then go to Tel Aviv the next day. Even if he took the 707, he thought he would make the two segment trip in order not to have to take two crews, so either way, waiting for the 707 would only create a delay of one day. He decided to wait on the new plane, and go to Tel Aviv the following week, and maybe Thil could go with him.

Since he and Thil were the only ones that flew the DC-8, they kept some clothes and other things on the plane for their convenience. David had to be at the office all day on Monday, so Thil had to get most of their things off the plane by herself. David swung by on his way home and helped her finish up. They picked up Monty and went out to eat again. Thil loved that because she didn't have to cook.

While they were eating, Monty asked, "Dad, have you thought any about giving Don his job back?"

"He came by the office Friday and wanted to talk, but I was so busy, I didn't have much time for him. He said he wanted to talk about coming back, but I told him he needed to apply to some other companies, and that he would be better off somewhere else."

"I wish you would reconsider. He can help you a lot if y'all can get along. When I get out of school and come with Shepherd, it would be neat to have David Shepherd and sons working there together."

CHAPTER SIXTEEN

It was risky postponing the appointment in Tel Aviv, but the Shepherd Staff brand was in so much demand in Israel that David took the chance. How fitting it was to have a shepherd's Staff line of clothing in Israel, since King David was a shepherd before becoming king. King David was the most revered person in the nation of Israel, and Myron Hober, the manager of operations at the Tel Aviv office and warehouse was convinced that every Jew in Israel would own at least one piece of the Staff line.

David told Myron to try to set up their meeting for Tuesday, and if they needed more time or wanted to call on some satellite stores, there would be plenty of time.

Thil had arranged for David's dad to come over and spend the night with Monty each night, so she could go. They decided they would leave Sunday morning and spend the night in Munich.

David told her to go out and buy a new bathing suit because the beaches in Tel Aviv were supposed to be fantastic. Their hotel was on the waterfront, so she could spend time sunbathing while David worked. It sounded wonderful.

On Thursday, Thil and Margaret went shopping. They went to the usual department stores downtown and wound up at Eastgate Shopping Center before Thil found the bathing suit she wanted. She actually bought two suits plus cover-ups and some other beachwear. She was so excited to be going to the Mediterranean. She could hardly wait for Sunday to get there.

When they finished shopping, Thil took Margaret home and then went home to try on her new purchases. Before she did, though, she stopped downstairs and poured herself a Coke and went to the den to relax a few minutes. When she finished her Coke, she went upstairs to their bedroom to try on her new swimsuits. She tried on the first one and looked at herself from several angles in the dress-shop type mirror that she had. The suit was a tastefully made black bikini, and with her left-over Florida tan, she looked fantastic and very desirable. She was still thirsty, so before taking her suit off, she went back downstairs and poured another glass of Coke. While she was in the kitchen, she heard the outside door open and close, but thinking David must have come home early, she didn't think anything about it.

When she walked out of the kitchen, she was startled by Don standing next to the kitchen door. As soon as he saw her in her bathing suit, he let out a loud wolf-whistle and said, "Man, I must have the best-looking stepmom in the county. Wow! You look great, Thil."

Recovering from being so startled, she said, "Thank you, Don. What are you doing here?"

Sarcastically he said, "I was just messing around and thought I would come see what the upper-class is doing."

"Do you want a Coke or something?"

"I need something stronger than a Coke. Where's the *golden boy?* Not home from school yet?"

"If you're talking about Monty, no, he's not home yet. He had ball practice after school. Don, have you been drinking?"

"What makes you think that?"

"You act like you have been, and I smell it on your breath. What do you want, Don?"

With that, he walked over to her, grabbed her head tightly in both hands and kissed her. This was not an innocent kiss by a son kissing his stepmother; this was a very passionate kiss; tongue and all. He moved his left hand around to the back of her head and held her lips against his while sliding his right hand down to fondle her breast. She had a hard time pulling away from him, but when she finally got loose, she drew back and hit him squarely in the eye with her fist. "Du hurensohn!

Arschloch! Du bastard!" She not only called him those three names, but continued with about twenty seconds more rant in German. When she finished her rant she asked in English, "What do you think you're doing?"

"I've wanted to do that ever since I met you and I think you liked it, didn't you, beautiful?"

"Don, you're drunk. Go home before your Dad or Monty gets here. Either one will kick your butt if I tell them what you did."

"Pop's too old, and the *golden boy's* not man enough, so tell 'em whatever you want to. It's your word against mine."

"Who do you think they will believe, especially when they see your eye that's turning black?"

"All right. I'll leave. I enjoyed the kiss, Thil. We'll have to do it again."

"Don, don't come here again unless your father or brother are here. I mean it. Since you're drunk, I'm not going to tell them about this, but if you come back, I will, and if you hope to ever get back with the company, your chance will be shot after I tell your father what you did. Now, go."

Even in his semi-muddled mind, he realized he had crossed the line and knew he had better go while the going was good.

His eye was swelling, and he reached up to feel it as he walked to his car. He turned around and looked toward Thil. He smiled and blew her a kiss as he opened the car door.

The episode with Don got Thil out of the mood to try on anymore new clothes, so she put on a pair of jeans and went downstairs to try to decide what she would fix for dinner.

***

Monday afternoon, Ted Mosier called and told David he needed to pick up his plane and take it to Kansas City and wanted to know if he had everything out of it. When David said he did, Tom said they would get it Tuesday morning and be back with the 707 around noon, Wednesday. David told him he was anxious to get it and when they hung up, he called Thil and told her. She said she could hardly wait.

When it arrived, they thought it was even prettier than they had remembered. David bowed his head and said silently, *"Thank you, Lord, for this, another blessing."*

Thil and Margaret spent the next couple of days taking clothes, travel items, and some other things to add a little personal touch to the new plane. She made sure she took some of the wine she and David liked so well, and a couple of times, she and Margaret sat in some of the plush, easy-chairs and had a glass of the bubbly. This was an exciting time in her life, and she was enjoying it.

After the first couple of trips to Munich, David figured out what time he should leave Chattanooga in order to put him in Munich at the best time for a productive day. By leaving Lovell Field at six pm, eastern time and then allowing for time zone differences, they could be in Munich at ten the next morning, and that would allow him time to work all day with Gerhard.

Monty and Jesse took David and Thil to the airport around five o'clock Sunday afternoon. Monty saw the plane when it first got to Chattanooga, but David's dad hadn't seen it yet, so this gave him a few minutes to look it over, and he was very impressed. A catering vehicle soon arrived with their dinner and breakfast. Chuck Jacobs, the Pilot, had ordered meals for the two of them as well as the flight crew. They not only got their dinner, but they also got fruit and pastries for breakfast the next morning. David thought to himself, *Do I run a first-class outfit or what?*

In a few minutes the flight crew arrived and immediately began to check out the exterior and then boarded and started making preparations to take off. Thil kissed both Monty and Jesse goodbye, and they went down the steps so the door could be closed. They lifted off promptly at six o'clock while David and Thil sat in their seats, holding hands. "I can't wait 'til we get to thirty thousand feet," Thil said.

"Just cool it, sweetie. We'll be at that altitude all night, so there's no rush, is there?"

"I guess not. I'm just so excited. I can hardly wait to see how comfortable the bed is."

"I know. We'll turn in early, okay?"

"Okay."

After they leveled off and were flying over North Carolina, Thil went to the galley to start getting ready for dinner. She put on a pot of coffee, and David went to the flight deck to see if the crew was ready to eat. In a few minutes the coffee was ready, and the co-pilot and engineer came back and sat at the table and ate with David and Thil. When they finished, the pilot came back to eat, and David stayed at the table and visited with him while Thil cleaned the galley. The food was delicious, and they all agreed they could make it 'til breakfast, although they might have to have some more coffee. They complimented Thil on her good coffee. "Danke," she responded in German. The crew didn't say anything when she responded, but looked at each other with smiles on their faces.

In a little while Thil asked, "Would you like to have another cup of coffee, darling? If you want one, I'll get it for you."

"Yeah. That would be good. Thank you,"

She came back with a cup for each of them, and they sat there in silence enjoying their coffee, and in a little bit, Thil asked, "You're so quiet. Is something wrong?"

"Oh, no, I'm just thinking."

"A penny for your thoughts."

"I'm thinking about Don. I just can't seem to get my mind off of him."

"What are you thinking about him, darling?"

"Just the way he is. He's my son, and I love him, but he's such a loose cannon, you never know what he's going to do next. I wish I could bring him back to Shepherd Apparel, but I'm afraid he'll pull some sort of shenanigan again, and I'd have to fire him again. I don't know what to do. I hope he finds a job somewhere while we're gone. That would solve my problem."

"What if he can't find one, David?"

"If he looks hard enough, he can find one. I just don't know how hard he'll look, and I can't let him starve. He can draw unemployment, but I don't know how long that will last."

"If he can't find a job, and his unemployment runs out, do you think he will move in with us?"

"No! I'll put him to work at Shepherd before I let him come back home. He definitely won't be coming to live with us."

Thil breathed a sigh of relief when David said that.

Around nine o'clock, Chattanooga time, David went to the cockpit and told the crew he and his wife were tired and were going to turn in. He said, "Good night. I'll see you fellows in the morning."

Each of them said, "Good night, Mr. Shepherd," and as he was leaving the cockpit, the co-pilot turned around to the engineer and winked. The engineer smiled.

While Thil brushed her teeth, David turned the bed down. While David brushed his teeth, Thil undressed and got into bed and then David joined her when he finished brushing. For a long time, the couple just laid there, in each other's arms, looking out the window at the starry sky. In a few minutes, Thil turned to David and kissed him tenderly, and they soon found that fooling around in a 707 at thirty thousand feet was every bit as exciting as fooling around in a DC-8.

Business-wise, the trip was a huge success. David and Myron landed the largest retailer in the whole country of Israel and the volume with that one account could reach well over a million dollars a year. It was huge.

David spent Tuesday and Wednesday with Myron, working with three other accounts, then spent Thursday and Friday with Thil, mainly at the beach. Life was good for the Shepherds. That was also like a vacation for the flight crew. From Monday, when they arrived in Tel Aviv until Friday afternoon, when they left to return to Chattanooga, all they had to do was lie on the beach or anything else they wanted to do.

They enjoyed spending time on the beach, most of all, looking at Thil as she sunbathed.

On the trip back to Chattanooga, David's mood became serious. "What's bothering you, darling?"

"Nothing's bothering me; I'm just thinking about Don. I'm going to call him when we get home. I may bring him back to the company. I have an idea that might just be the ticket for Mr. Don."

"Can you tell me what it is?"

"I don't have all the details worked out in my mind yet, but as you know, in addition to the apparel end of the business, we own a truck line."

"Yes, I know. How would Don fit into that?"

"Well, I've been thinking about broadening the responsibilities of the truck line to include all the company vehicles, and here's the big one; the airplane. I'm going to put it under the umbrella of the transportation department. Right now, we're only using the plane on the average of one time a month, and there are several companies out there that need the use of an airplane but can't afford to own one. This is where Don comes in. He can head up what we will call the Transportation Division, and part of his duties will be to contact those companies and try to work out a trip-lease deal that would let them use our plane at a reasonable price."

"This could be a win-win situation for a lot of people. It would let us recover some of the costs of owning an expensive airplane like this, and it would give several companies a chance to use a plane as if it were theirs without owning one. If Don comes on board, it can be a big deal for him as well. I'm going to try and get this straight in my mind and then call him sometime after we get back."

"Darling, I think you're about the smartest man I ever saw."

"Thank you, sweetie. I don't know about that, but I do know I was smart when I married you; I do know that."

Thil went over and kissed him on the cheek.

When they arrived in Chattanooga, Monty was there to meet them. It was getting close to dinner time and they had to decide where they would eat. Thil and Monty said anywhere was fine with them, and David said he thought some Krystals sounded good, so they went to the Krystal and pigged out on hamburgers.

Monday was a busy day for David. The first thing he did was to arrange to have the company name painted on the plane and the Staff logo painted on the tail. Then, he went into the regular staff meeting. Afterwards he had meetings with Tom Ratcliff and Chip Lowe. Their meeting ran into lunchtime, so the three went to Oscars and finished their discussion.

Back at the office, David picked up the phone. The answering machine said "This is Don. I can't take your call right now, but if you'll leave your number and a brief message, I'll call you back."

"Don, this is your dad. Give me a call when you get this. Thanks."

As he was hanging up, Ruby came into his office. "David, could I talk to you, please?"

"You sure can, Ruby. What's up?"

"David, you know I've been working here nearly as long as Shepherd Apparel has been in business."

"I know you have. You're an important part of this company, Ruby."

"Well, I've been thinking and talking to my husband, and I think I want to retire. If you want me to, I'll stay until you get a replacement for me, and I'll train her if you would like for me to."

"Ruby, I surely do hate to lose you, but to be honest with you, I've been wondering how much longer you planned to work. I was thankful for every day that you didn't say you were leaving, but I know it's time, and I want you to enjoy some well-deserved leisure time."

"Do we have any ladies working for us now that you would recommend as your replacement?"

"Yes sir. I've been thinking about that. Do you know Connie Young, in accounting?"

"Yeah, I know Connie. Do you think she would be good?"

"I really do. She's been here quite a while, and she's good at her job. She never misses work and is always on time. I think she would make you a real good secretary."

"Okay, I'll talk to her."

"Thank you, David. Would you like for me to call her to come in?"

Smiling, David said, "Man, you had this thing planned out, didn't you, Ruby?"

Smiling back, she said, "Yes sir. I just don't want you to be without help when I leave. The company is getting so big, you really could use two people as secretaries. I know I have a hard time getting everything done without working many extra hours."

"I didn't realize that, Ruby. Why didn't you say something?"

"I just didn't."

"Don't call Connie right now. Let me think about what you just told me. You may have to call two people instead of just one."

The next morning, David called Connie Young and Mae Hampton to his office, one at a time, and promoted Connie to be his secretary and Mae, to be her assistant.

Don never returned his call, so David tried again to reach him. Aggravated that Don didn't call him back, he thought as the phone rang, *If I don't get him this time, and if he doesn't call me back, I'm just going to forget about offering him a job.* After three rings, Don answered, "Hello, this is Don>"

"Don, this is Dad. I've been trying to reach you. I left word yesterday, but you didn't call me back."

"I'm sorry. Whatta ya need, Pop?"

"If you're interested in coming back to Shepherd, I need you to come to see me."

"When?"

"How about this afternoon?"

Don asked, "Okay. How about we eat lunch together?"

"Sounds good. I'll see you at twelve o'clock."

When Don arrived, they decided to go to Tomlinson's restaurant. It was quiet there and they could talk. The interior of the restaurant was pretty dark, and Don kept his sunglasses on. "Why don't you take your sunglasses off, Son?"

"I'd rather keep them on."

"You look strange in this dark room, Take 'em off."

"Okay, Pop, but I don't know what the big deal is."

"It's no big deal, but if you're going to be a professional man, you need to look like one and not a thug. My gosh, what happened to your eye?"

"It's nothing. I got into a little scrap last week, but everything's all right now. I don't want to talk about it." He hoped David would let the subject die because he sure didn't want him to find out Thil was the one who hit him and why she did it.

"Okay. I see now why you were wearing sunglasses. Aren't you getting a little old to be getting into fights?

"Yeah, I guess I am. Let's drop it, Pop. Okay?"

"Okay, it's dropped."

After they ordered, Don asked, "What have you got in mind for me, Pop?"

"You know we've got a new plane, don't you?"

"Yeah, I heard."

"Well, Thil and I just got back from a trip to Tel Aviv, and while we were gone, a thought came to me about all our cars and trucks and the plane. I have decided to create a Transportation Division. The division will be comprised of two parts. The truck line will be one part, and the plane and vehicles will be the other."

"I don't want to mess with the truck line. Homer's doing a good job with it, and I want him left alone. We're getting ready to add some more tractors and trailers, and his job is really going to be demanding."

What I want to talk to you about is the other part. If you think you can behave and act like a professional, I would consider putting you in charge of that. There won't be much to do about the cars and vans; they pretty much take care of themselves. What I'm interested in is this."

"We own a multi-million dollar airplane that gets used about once a month. There are companies out there that need a plane but can't afford to own one. I believe we can structure a trip-lease plan that will let some of these companies lease our plane when we aren't using it, and this is where you come in. If you come back, I will want to put you in charge of the second part of the transportation division and have you go out and contact these companies. If we can get some of our costs back by leasing the plane once or twice a month, it will be a big help. Are you interested?"

"You bet I am."

"When do you want me to start?"

"Maybe Monday. I'll have to call you tomorrow. There's another thing, Son. If you come with us, what I have outlined isn't going to keep you very busy, so I will want you to work under Homer Galloway in the truck line, because when we get the additional trucks, he's going to need a lot of help. Is this agreeable to you?"

"Yes sir, and I won't let you down this time."

"I sure hope not."

***

The rest of the week was so hectic for David, he was unable to bring Don in on Monday. Before starting him in his new position, he wanted to *pick the brains* of some aviation savvy people so he could outline for Don how he wanted the trip-lease contracts to be structured. After he was satisfied that he knew what needed to be done, he called Don and told him to report to work Wednesday and to meet him at the truck line office.

To say Don was disappointed with his office would be a gross understatement. Since he was going to be head of a department, he assumed he would have one of the plush offices in the office complex of Shepherd Global. Instead, there was an extra office in the truck line terminal furnished with a metal desk, three straight metal chairs, a file cabinet, and a telephone. *How could someone in charge of millions of dollars-worth of equipment be relegated to a slum office like this,* he thought to himself.

David was amused when he saw the expression on Don's face, but didn't act as if he knew he was disappointed with his office. Instead he opened his briefcase and laid out several papers on the desk. He explained how the trip-leases would work and how to figure the cost of trips. He also gave him a list of possible customers to contact. When he mentioned dollar figures, Don was blown away. He couldn't imagine anyone paying that much to rent an airplane.

After a fairly-detailed explanation of airplane-leasing, David said he had to go to his own office and asked Don if he had any questions. "Just one, Pop."

"What is it?"

"Is there any way I could get a desk chair instead of one of these straight chairs?"

"We may have one at the warehouse. I'll have Eddie bring one over when he's out this way. Anything else?"

"No. I guess that'll do it. Oh, I'd like to have a desk calculator, too. Could you send one of those over?"

"Yeah, you'll need one of those. Tell you what. When you go to lunch, come by the office, and I'll have Connie round one up for you."

"Thanks, Pop."

When David left, Don sat down with a legal pad and pen and worked on learning how to figure operating costs for a 707-320B until lunch time. After the initial shock of seeing the astronomical figures, he thought to himself, *This thing can really work.*

While he was at the main office, he got the calculator and several other office supplies he needed. He found Eddie Randolph and told him his dad said to bring a desk chair to his office, so Eddie went to the warehouse immediately to get the chair and deliver it.

After lunch, Don spent the afternoon working on costs and dummy trips until he felt he had enough confidence to start calling on some customers.

The next morning, he took the list of prospects his dad had left with him and divided it into zones. He would concentrate on one zone at a time when calling on the companies until he completed all of them. The city of Cleveland was one complete zone, so he decided to start there. Cleveland had several very large manufacturing companies, and only one of them had their own airplane parked at Lovell field. He thought that meant only one Cleveland company had their own plane because any other airport would be too far away to hanger a plane. Knoxville was the next closest large airport, and it was seventy miles away, so he was comfortable thinking only one company had a plane, and that left the door open to explore all the others.

Since it was already Friday, Don thought he would wait until Monday to start calling on prospects. He would spend the day getting more familiar with the program and going to the airport to spend some time on the plane, itself. He felt if he were more knowledgeable about the actual plane, he could do a better selling job to the customer. He would hit the ground running Monday morning and try to do a good job for his dad.

CHAPTER SEVENTEEN

Six Years Later

May fifteenth was a Chamber of Commerce day in Cookeville. After four years of hard work, it was fitting that graduation be held on a beautiful day like that.

Monty was graduating Cum Laude with a degree in business administration. His college career was coming to an end after a very successful four years. His play on the football field was outstanding, and his grades were straight A's. His work with the Fellowship of Christian Athletes endeared him to many, and he was a very popular young man.

After all the speeches and then calling the graduates' names one at a time, it seemed that Monty's name would never get called. Finally, it was over, and after a reunion outside the auditorium for pictures, Monty, Thil, Margaret, David, and Don went out to eat, and then they went back to Chattanooga. Since Monty had his car in Cookeville, Don rode with him, leaving the other three to return in David's car.

Don enjoyed being with his *little* brother, and they had a good time talking on the way back home. Monty told him about their Dad inviting him to come to work at Shepherd Apparel, and Don thought that was awesome. "What are you going to be doing?"

"I don't have any idea."

"Well, whatever it is, I'm sure you'll do well."

"Thanks."

Ever since Monty was in Junior High School, he had dreamed of playing in the NFL, and his good play at Tech gave him hope that his dream would come true, but it didn't happen. He contacted an agent, but after the agent went through all the stuff agents do to make things happen, it looked as if he would probably be drafted, but wouldn't go until the tenth or eleventh round.

Monty, David, and the agent sat down and discussed it, finally deciding that earning a starting position on a team would be a long-shot because of being drafted that low. David encouraged him not to go through what would be an almost certain disappointment and come to work full-time at Shepherd Apparel, which he agreed to do.

After a week at Daytona Beach with some of his buddies, Monty returned to Chattanooga, ready to start work full-time at Shepherd Apparel. David had always made it a practice not to talk business at home, so there had not been much discussion about what he would be doing.

On his first day each drove his own car to work, and Monty had to park in one of the visitor's places. He reported to David when he arrived, and David immediately took him to the Human Resources Department where they did all the paperwork involved in getting him signed up as an employee. David told him to come back to his office when he finished up there. In a little while, Monty walked into David's office, smiling and said, "Okay, Mr. Shepherd, your newest employee is reporting for duty. Are you ready for me to take over the company or do you want me to learn a few things first?"

David smiled back. "I guess you had better learn a few things first. You know Tom Ratcliff, don't you?"

"Yes sir. I know him."

"I'm gonna turn you over to Tom who will probably turn you over to Chip Lowe to acquaint you with how we do things. Monty, I don't know how much you've paid attention to our company while you've been in school, but we've grown into a huge conglomerate. We're now one of the largest companies in the state, and we're in the top ten, worldwide, in apparel manufacturing. There are many opportunities for people who want to work hard, keep their nose clean, and advance up the ladder. Being my son really gives you an advantage, and I would like to see you and Don take over completely someday."

"I'd like to see you and Don have a little professional competition. Of course, Don is older and more experienced, but sometimes, Don keeps his mind on other things, and even though you're new and inexperienced, I think you can catch up to him. I have a lot of confidence in you, Son."

"After having his office in the truck terminal for a long time, I finally relented and gave Don an office over here. You know, he works on trying to lease our plane when we're not using it, and he's been able to lease it a few times. The job fits him pretty well because he has been just about everywhere in the company at one time or another. He's been in that job longer than most of the others, and I think he's actually taking an interest in the company for the first time. Okay. Are you ready to go to work?"

"I'm ready."

David pushed a button on the intercom and picked up the microphone. "Tom Ratcliff, come to David Shepherd's office, please."

In three or four minutes, Tom arrived at David's office. "Yes sir. Good morning. Good morning, Monty."

David and Monty both responded with, "Good morning."

"Tom, I want you to take Monty and familiarize him with the workings of the company. I want him to learn everything there is to know about Shepherd Apparel, and I think it would be good to start him in the pattern department, and then, go to cutting and on up the line until he reaches shipping. Spend a few months doing this, and then, I'm going to take him away from you and put him in sales and marketing. I may even let him go to Munich with me on the *big bird* sometime."

"Okay. I'll be glad to take him. Will it be all right if I let him work with Chip some?"

"Absolutely. Don't let his training hinder you in your job. Do what you have to do."

"Okay, Boss. It's good to have you with us, Monty."

"Thanks."

On the way to the pattern department, Tom said to Monty, "I'll bet you didn't know I went to Cookeville last fall to watch you play. In fact, my wife and I went to two games. You played really good in both games, Monty. I was very proud that I knew you."

"Thanks, Tom. I had no idea. That means a lot to me."

From that moment on, Tom was Monty's newest best friend."

About three months into Monty's training, Chip told Tom, "You know, in my opinion, Monty's talents are being wasted with this slow training. This kid picks up everything extremely fast. All you have to do is tell him something one time, and he knows it. Why don't you tell his dad he should go ahead and put him somewhere more advanced because I think he's ready?"

Tom took Chip's suggestion and talked to David. David thanked him and said he would be glad to move him up a little. The following Monday, Monty was given an office in the sales department and put under the capable wing of Charles Crawford, the sales manager.

***

"Your dad put you in sales just in time," Charles told Monty.

"What do you mean?"

"The New York Market starts next week, and David wants you to go. He wants me to give you the accounts that your brother once had to see what you can do with them. All of them are going to be at the show."

"Okay. Do you know the buyers?"

"Yeah. I know them."

"Do you have any tips for me about how I need to work with them?"

"Just be natural. They're all nice, but they know their business. Be sure you know the line, and when you show it to them, be ready to answer their questions, and there will be questions. They like to work with salesmen who know what they're doing. If you stammer and act unsure about the line, you will turn them off and have a hard time gaining their confidence, later. That was the trouble Don had with them. I hate to say anything about your brother, but he acted as if he didn't care if they bought from him or not, and that's why the accounts never developed. Monty, those accounts can be huge if you work them right, but if you do like Don did, they will never be important to Shepherd Apparel, so let me help you, and let's hit a home run with them in New York, okay?"

"Okay. Will you help me learn the line? I've been going over the samples, but don't know much about any of the styles as far as details are concerned."

"Yeah, I will. We'll go over them today; then, you can study them this afternoon or tonight and then pretend I'm a buyer tomorrow and present the line to me. That will be a little awkward for you, but it will help you quite a bit. I will ask questions just like the buyers probably will. We'll keep doing that until you're an expert on Shepherd Staff sportswear."

That same afternoon, David's phone rang. It was Thil." Hi Darling. Are you busy?"

"I'm always busy, but never too busy to talk to the prettiest woman in town. What can I do for you?"

"Well, a Catherine Smith from Miller Brothers just called and said they are getting ready to open a new department in all their stores and call it *The Mature Woman*. She asked me if I was over fifty, and I told her I was afraid I was, and she asked if I would be interested in modeling for them when they have some of their shows to promote the new department. I told her I wanted to talk to you first. What do you think?"

David, jokingly said, "Well, I think they will be sorry if they have you as a model. When you walk the runway, nobody will be able to take their eyes off you. They will be so taken with your beauty, they won't see what you're wearing. Do you think Catherine realizes that?"

"Silly. Do you think it will be all right?"

"Of course I do. Is it a paying job?"

"She said if I do it, then I can get my clothes at cost. Is that a good deal?"

"I guess so. Do what you want to do, honey. When you call Catherine back, tell her I said "Hello."

"Do you know her?"

"Yeah. She used to be the assistant buyer in sportswear."

"There's another thing, David."

"What?"

"Margaret called, and I think she has found a fellow. She wants to know if we would go out to eat with them tomorrow night."

"You're kidding. Who is this guy?"

"I forgot what she said his name was, but one of her friends in her circle introduced them. His wife died two years ago and they seemed to hit it off right away. What do you want me to tell her. I've got to call her back."

"That'll be fine. I'd like to see that dude."

On Tuesday evening, David and Thil met Margaret and her new friend, John, at the Town and Country restaurant and had a great time. John seemed to be a real nice guy and seemed to fit well with Margaret. David thought it was time for her to find someone to spend time with, and he was happy for her. The day had been tiring, so when they finished dinner, he didn't offer to go anywhere else. He just wanted to go home and get comfortable, so they said good-bye and agreed to do it again real soon.

**

In New York, Monty wowed his buyers. He carried himself like a seasoned veteran and knew the answers to all the questions. His incredible good-looks didn't hurt, either. With the exception of one account, he wrote the largest orders any of his accounts had ever given Shepherd. The other one placed a sizeable order with the promise of a large back-up order when she got back home. Charles Crawford was very complimentary of Monty when he called the office each day to report on the show, and David was exceedingly proud of him.

Later, Don and David were having coffee in the break-room and David mentioned they had a fantastic market. He was gushing with pride over the business Monty had written, and it didn't set very well with Don. After all, he had worked those accounts for several years and never did show much progress with any of them. He thought to himself, *It looks like the golden-boy strikes again.*

"It looks like your little brother may have found a home in the sales department. I know he's only been in it two weeks, but I think he's really going to be something after he has been in it for a while."

"Yeah, right," Don sarcastically answered.

"They'll be home this afternoon and I'm anxious to get a full report. I'm proud of the way Monty handled himself at his first market."

Again, Don sarcastically replied, "Yeah, maybe you can give him a promotion."

David didn't say anything for a minute. He just looked at Don. Then he said, "Well, I'll be doggone. You're jealous?"

"No. I'm not jealous. I just don't see that a good market is so great. It's not the first good market we've ever had. Monty just happened to be there. Why would I be jealous?"

"It looks like jealousy to me, but let's talk about something else. Do you have anybody wanting to use the plane?"

"The ones that have been leasing it are going to keep on using it, and there are a couple more that have shown an interest. I should know something in about a week from one of them."

"Don't forget that I've got to go to Munich week after next, so don't book it for that week. Gerhard has a really big deal

Bud Fussell

cooking, and I want to be there when he closes on it. I think I'll take Monty and let him see how the big-time works."

Total silence. Don didn't open his mouth.

When the beautiful, white and blue 707 was approaching the airport, David was filled with pride. *How could a simple boy from Hamilton County own something like that? God is truly good to me.* After it landed, David hurried to the area where it would taxi and waited for it to stop. The two salesmen with Charles and Monty were the first off the plane, then Monty and finally, Charles. They all shook hands with David and talked for a few minutes. David had Eddie bring the van, and all but David and Monty went back to Shepherd to get their cars. Monty and David got in David's car and went home. Thil was thrilled to see Monty and gave him a huge hug. "I've got your favorite meal fixed for you; meatloaf and pintos. Are you hungry?"

"Yes ma'am, I'm starved."

"Well, wash your hands and come on. It's ready."

They all had a delicious meal and afterwards, still sitting at the table, Monty filled David in on the market. Before they got up, David said, "I've got to go to Munich week after next, and I think I'll take you with me. Would you like to go?"

"Yes sir. I really would. Wow!"

"Thil, honey, would you like to go?"

"I always want to go to Munich, and it will be good to show Monty to some of my friends, too. They haven't seen him since he was small."

"Dad, what day will we be back?"

"We're scheduled to be back on Friday. Why?"

"When I was in the FCA at Tech, we had a meeting one time and had several ministers as our guests. I had to speak at that meeting, and afterwards, we had sort of a reception where we all got acquainted. Last week, one of those pastors called me and asked if I could come to his Church to speak at a youth rally on that Saturday night. I told him I would come, but if we won't be back, I can call him and cancel."

184

"Where is it, Son?"

"In Nashville. Actually, it's out in Madison. I forget the name of the Church, but I have the preacher's phone number."

"Don't call him. We'll be back in time; I'll make sure of it. I'm proud of you, Son. You're an outstanding young man."

"Thanks, Dad. God's been good to me, and I want to be good to Him."

For the next two years, Monty continued to grow his accounts and had done so well with them, Charles added three more to his portfolio. He was the hit at every show in New York, Atlanta, and Dallas, and the volume he was creating was amazing.

Jealousy of Monty was making Don a miserable man. He was stuck in the transportation department with no way out, and Monty's successes in sales were taking a toll on him. Also, for the last year or so, he had been diverting money from the company to his personal account and he was beginning to be afraid that it was going to be uncovered.

Don's extension was 201 and Monty's was 210 and people frequently dialed one, intending to dial the other. One day, Monty's phone rang and when he answered, a voice on the other end asked, "Is this Mr. Shepherd?"

"Yes it is."

"Mr. Shepherd, this is Mary Humphries. I'm Tom Shelley's secretary. Mr. Shelley wanted me to call and be sure the check for the airplane rental is to be made out to you instead of Shepherd Apparel."

"What is your company's name, Mary?"

"East Tennessee Reinforced Concrete."

"Mary, I'm afraid you've got the wrong Mr. Shepherd. I think you were calling my brother, Don, but I can answer your question. The check should be made out to Shepherd Apparel Company, Okay?"

"Thank you, sir. Good-bye."

Monty was shocked to think his big brother would do such a thing as steal from the family business. He didn't know whether to confront Don or just what to do. He would have to think about it, but before he had too much time to think, Don came into his office, fuming. "Did you just talk to Tom Shelly's secretary?"

"Yeah. Why?"

"Tom just called me and wanted to clear up some confusion. He said his secretary spoke to my brother and was told to make out a check to Shepherd Apparel rather than to me. That check is mine to pay for some work I did on my own for Tom's company. In the future, stay out of my business, okay?"

"What kind of work did you do for them?"

"That's none of your business."

"If you're stealing from the company, it's my business and don't forget that, big brother."

Don wanted to get physical with Monty, but he knew better. Monty would tear him apart. He wanted to say something else, but didn't know exactly what, so he stormed out of Monty's office and went back to his own.

Although Don explained the check deal, Monty couldn't help but be suspicious. *After all the lady did say it was for airplane rental.* He wished he knew how he could check up on some of Don's dealings. He loved Don and had always looked up to him, but if he was stealing from the company, something would have to be done to stop it.

He couldn't sleep that night for thinking about the chance that Don was stealing from the company. He decided he would go to the airport and talk to the airport manager. The next day, he went to work at the regular time, but left an hour early for lunch. He wanted to see the airport manager before he went to lunch.

"Mr. Tomlinson, hi. I'm Monty Shepherd, David's son. I know you're busy, so I won't keep you, but I hope you can help me. I'm trying to reconcile some records concerning our company airplane, and I wonder if you could give me the dates, destinations, and companies that rented our plane for the last five years? There probably aren't too many."

"That shouldn't be a problem, Ronnie."

"It's Monty."

"I'm sorry, Monty. That shouldn't be a problem. When do you need this?"

"Just as soon as I can get it."

"Would after lunch be okay? My secretary had to go to the dentist and took her lunch-time early, but I'll have her get everything together when she gets back. Can you come back around two?"

"I can, and thank you so much. Who should I ask for when I come back?"

"Joan Murray, She's a fine young lady."

"Okay. I'll be here at two and see Joan. Thank you, Mr. Tomlinson."

"You bet. Say hello to David for me."

Monty went by the Krystal and grabbed a sack-full of hamburgers and went back to his office to eat. They smelled so good, two or three people stuck their heads in the door just to get a whiff and said they wished they had done that for their lunch.

Charles Crawford was out of town, so Monty didn't have anything special to do. Not one to waste time, he decided to call some of his accounts to see if there was anything he could do for any of them. After a while, it was time to go back to the airport and get the records he wanted.

CHAPTER EIGHTEEN

The administrative offices at the airport were on the second floor, so Monty took the stairs. Opening the door to Mr. Tomlinson's office, he looked into a vaguely familiar face. The girl was a natural blond with her hair cut fairly short. She had dimples and big brown eyes. Her five foot seven inch frame had a figure that other women had to envy.

"Are you Joan?"

"Yes I am, and you're Monty Shepherd. I know who you are. You went to Tech and played football. I remember seeing you a lot."

"You went to Tech? When?"

"The same time you did. We even had one class together, but you never noticed me."

"I must be crazy not to have noticed anyone as good-looking as you."

"Why, thank you. I've got to tell you, I noticed you."

"Wow! Are you seeing anyone now?"

"No."

"Would you like to go out sometime?"

"Yes. I'd like that."

"Let me make a suggestion. Why don't we have dinner Friday night and discuss what we're going to do Saturday for our date?"

Smiling, "That's two dates."

"No, no, it's only one. Friday is the pre-date."

"Okay. Sounds like fun. Where do you want to go?"

"I don't know. What do you like to eat?"

"Just about everything."

"Do you like the Town and Country?"

"I love it."

"Great. That's where we'll go. Write down your address and I'll pick you up."

She handed it to Monty. "Where is this?"

Do you know where Meadow View Country Club is?"

"Yeah, I play out there sometimes."

"I live in that area. Our street turns off Hixson Pike. So you shouldn't have any trouble finding it."

"I'll find it."

"Okay, Monty. I'm looking forward to Friday."

"Me too. See ya. Oh, I just about forgot why I came. Do you have some papers for me?"

"I sure do. Here they are."

"Thanks. See ya Friday. I'll call you Friday afternoon just to be sure everything's still on go."

Monty took the papers and returned to his office. When he removed them from the folder, he found some interesting stuff. The plane had been leased a surprising number of times. More than he would have thought. It looked as if it was *on the go* more than it was at home. The report he had not only showed the dates, destinations, and companies but also the length of stay. He made mental notes and then returned it to the folder before putting it in the bottom drawer of his desk. Next, he needed to match up the individual leases with the bank deposits. As a Shepherd family member, getting the information from accounting would not be a problem. He just didn't want anyone to know why he was doing it.

He thought his buddy, Sheryl, was the one who made the bank deposits, so he would ask her for the information. When he asked her, he didn't tell her why he wanted to see the deposit records; he just said he was reconciling something and assured her he would take full responsibility for anything she gave him and asked her not to say anything about it.

In case his suspicions were wrong, Monty didn't want anybody to know that he was investigating his brother's activities with the company plane, so he was very careful to go over the figures only when he knew nobody would come into his office.

Going back five years, he laid out the trip leases on one side and the bank deposits for the corresponding flights on the other side. If there was a deposit for a trip, he would check it off. If there wasn't, then a separate row was used.

For the first year and a half after Don started leasing the plane, it looked as if all the trips and deposits matched, but then, things started to unravel. Roughly, one third of all the leases made after the first year and a half had no deposits associated with them. He needed to find out how much each lease was for in order to know how much money was missing, but he knew thousands and thousands of dollars were. He was in shock. He couldn't believe his brother would do something like this, but figures don't lie. He just hoped he could somehow come up with a logical explanation, and Don would be innocent.

He didn't know what to do. Even though this was a family member embezzling from the family business, the business was a corporation, operating in accordance with government regulations. Don could go to jail for a long time if this was exposed, so Monty decided to keep quiet until he could be sure his move would be the right one.

***

Turning off Hixson Pike onto Van Buren Street, Monty began looking for house numbers. Soon, he saw the number he wanted and turned into the driveway. He got out and went up to the door and had hardly knocked before Joan opened the door. "Hi, Monty. Come in."

Monty went into the living room and Joan introduced him to her parents. "Monty, I'd like for you to meet my Dad, Charles, and my Mom, Kathleen. Mom and Dad, this is Monty Shepherd. He's is one I was telling you about."

Both parents said, "It's nice to meet you, Monty."

Monty responded with, "It's nice to meet you, too. I'm going to take your little girl out and feed her a big meal. Would you care to join us?"

"No thanks," they said. Joan's dad said, "I don't think we've ever had any of Joan's dates invite us to come on a date with them. That's nice, Son, but you young people go on without us and have a good time."

"Okay. We won't be too late."

When they arrived at the restaurant, there was a line, so they had to wait for a table. While they were waiting, a couple walked up to them, and the man spoke to Monty. "Aren't you Monty Shepherd?" he asked.

"Yes I am."

"Hi, Monty, I'm Bob Watson. I remember watching you play in high school, and then at Tech. I was happy when you made All Conference up there. You really kicked butt."

"Thank you."

"Well, I just wanted to speak. Have a nice evening."

"Thank you, Mr. Watson."

Right after Bob Watson left Monty, another man came up to speak to him. Then, the hostess came out and led them to their table.

Joan said, "I'm impressed. I didn't realize I was with a celebrity. Can I have your autograph?"

"Stop it. Those kinds of things are flattering, but many people keep hanging on to college activities too long." Jokingly, he asked Joan, "What do you want me to write when I give you my autograph?"

At dinner, things could not have run smoother. They both felt like they had known each other for years, and the things they had in common were amazing. They both liked sports and pizza, and most importantly, they both liked fruit-cake. Both were Christians and were members of the same denomination. Each had an older brother and they were both in the same graduating class at Tech. How much more could a couple have in common?

Joan looked at Monty like she could eat him up, and he looked at her the same way. "I can't believe we had a class together and never met," Monty said.

"I know. I almost introduced myself to you two or three times, but you were always busy talking to some of your friends. Do you know I secretly had a crush on you? Each time we had class together, I would hope that would be the day you would notice me, but you never did"

"That just shows you what a dummy I am, but pretty lady, I'm noticing you now. I hope I can continue seeing you, that is, if you're not turned off by me."

"Monty, I'm certainly not turned off by you. I'm happy and comfortable just being with you and hope we can see more of each other. You know, you impressed my dad when you invited him and my mom to come eat with us. I could tell by the look on his face when we left."

"I think I would like them. Maybe sometime we can take them out to eat with us and get better acquainted."

"I'd like that and I know they would."

"Look, this is supposed to be our pre-date dinner to plan our date for tomorrow night. Do you still want to do something tomorrow night?"

"I do."

"Well, do you have any suggestions?"

"Not really. Do you?"

"Yeah, I do have one. Why don't we get dressed up and go to the Read House for dinner and then go to the Tivoli. There's supposed to be a good show on there."

"That sounds like fun. Let's do it."

"Okay, that takes care of tomorrow night. What about tonight? Do you like miniature golf? We could go up the mountain and play at Tom Thumb, if you would like to."

"I love Tom Thumb. Let's go up there, and I'll show you how it's done."

"Right. Tell you what. Let's make a bet. If I beat you, then you have to kiss me, and if you beat me, I'll have to kiss you."

"That sounds like my kind of bet. Let's go."

After two rounds, they came down the mountain and Monty took Joan home. Monty had won both rounds, so it was up to Joan to pay him off with kisses. She wasn't about to *welsh* on their bet and willingly paid her debt. In fact, she gave a couple extra kisses, just in case she lost the next time they played.

They said good-night and Monty went home. Neither of them could sleep for thinking about the other. As soon as Monty figured it was okay to call the next morning, he called and Joan answered, immediately. She said, "Good morning. I was hoping you would call."

"Good morning. Did you sleep well?"

"No, I'm afraid I didn't."

"Me neither. I couldn't sleep for thinking about you."

"That's why I didn't sleep. What are we going to do about this problem?"

"I guess we'll just have to keep seeing each other until the new wears off."

"I guess."

"Do you like picnics?"

"Yeah, why?"

Why don't you come to my house right now and we'll go on a picnic. I'll run to Kentucky Fry and pick up some chicken and stuff and we'll go down by the lake and eat lunch. Would you like to do that?"

"I don't know where you live."

"I can give you directions. It's easy to find."

"Okay. Are you sure?"

"I'm sure. I want you to meet my parents, too. Got a pencil?"

Monty gave her directions to his house, then went to the Kentucky Fry and picked up some fried chicken, potato salad, and all the trimmings. He was back home when Joan arrived and met her in the driveway when she pulled in.

"Come on in. I want you to meet my parents. Inside, Monty said, "Mom, Dad, this is Joan Murray. Joan, this is my dad,

David and my mom, Bathilda."

Bathilda said, "My friends call me Thil, so please call me Thil."

"Okay, Thil."

David said, "Don't you work for Bob Tomlinson?"

"Yes sir. I sure do."

"I thought I recognized you. Well, Joan, it's good to have you here. I understand you guys are picnicking for lunch."

"That's what I've been told. It beautiful out here and your house is beautiful, too."

Monty asked, "Are you hungry?"

"Starved. I didn't have breakfast."

"Then, let's go eat. Mom, where's that big blanket you use when you go to the beach?"

Thil said, "I'll get it for you."

Next to their house, there was a vacant piece of land that sloped gradually down to the lake, and Monty thought it would be a good place to spread the blanket and have their picnic. He remembered to take a radio, and they listened to good music while they ate and talked. They stayed until around two-thirty, when Joan said she needed to go home if she was going to have time to get ready for their date. Monty kissed her, and they picked up their stuff and went back to the house.

Joan said good-bye to Thil and David and left. After she was gone, Monty told Thil, "Mom, you just met the girl I'm going to marry."

"You're going to what?"

"I'm going to marry her. She doesn't know it yet, but just wait and see. She will be your daughter-in-law."

"Okay, if you say so."

Monty picked Joan up early, so they would have plenty of time to eat before the show. He ordered prime rib and baked potato for them both, and it was outstanding. Midway through the meal, Monty said, "Do you know what I told my mother after you left this afternoon?"

"What? That you were stuck with me tonight?"

"No. I told her I was going to marry you."

Turning white, she asked, "You told her what?"

"I said I was going to marry you. I told her you didn't know it yet, but one day you will be her daughter-in-law."

"When you get ready to do that, are you planning to tell me?"

"I don't know. I may."

They both laughed, but throughout the rest of dinner and through the whole show, Joan was more serious than she had been. The thought of marrying Monty, even said in jest, was something to be taken seriously. This was only their second time to be together, but she knew if he asked her to marry him, she would say "yes."

After the show, they went to Ellis' and had pie and coffee. They talked for a while and then they headed to Joan's house. Before kissing goodnight, they agreed to go to Church together the next morning. Joan wanted her friends to meet Monty, so they decided to go to her Church. They kissed and talked and talked and kissed and finally, Monty said he had to go. He gave her one more little peck on the forehead, and turned, and went to his car. Joan stood on the porch until he got in the car and drove off. It was easy to see that this couple had it bad.

Joan went to Sunday School with her parents the next morning, and Monty met her outside the sanctuary in time for the worship service. After Church, he and Joan went out to eat, and this time, Joan's parents accepted Monty's invitation to go with them. They went to a little neighborhood restaurant that was a favorite of theirs, but one that Monty had never been to. He enjoyed Joan's parents, and it was plain to see, they enjoyed him. It turned out that Charles was a big Tech fan and remembered seeing Monty play ball several times. After arguing over who was going to pay the check, Monty finally won. He paid at the cash register, and they all left.

Monty took Joan home to change clothes. Then, they went to Monty's where they spent the whole afternoon with David and Thil. It was a lazy Sunday afternoon, and after a while

David and Thil were both asleep, but Monty and Joan were wide awake. They teased and picked at each other, took a walk down by the lake, and just generally enjoyed being together. The day ended too soon for both of them. On the way to Joan's, they stopped by a drive-in and got a hamburger and milkshake, then, went on to Joan's house. Each of them said how they dreaded the upcoming week, not being able to be together all the time, but decided that maybe it wouldn't be too bad because they could see each other at night.

"Joanie, you made a big mistake going out with me because now, you're not going to be able to get rid of me. I'm crazy about you and want to be with you all the time."

"That's all right with me. I feel the same way. My college crush has become real. Will I get to see you tomorrow?"

"If nothing happens, you will. Is it all right to call you at work?"

"Yes, if it's not too often."

"Then I'll call you tomorrow. I've got to go. Give me a kiss."

They kissed and Monty left to go home. Thinking about work the next day had already started to depress him because he was going to have to deal with the situation with Don. While the thought of it was depressing, the thoughts of the weekend he'd had with Joan were uplifting. He thought, *I've only known her for three days, but I think I really love her.*

***

Monty finished reconciling the trip-leases with the deposits and now he had to come up with dollar figures to see how much shortage there was. He was racking his brain, trying to figure out how to come up with the costs when a thought hit him.

"Mr. Tomlinson's office."

"Hi Joanie, it's me."

"Hi. I was hoping you'd call. I miss you so much."

"I miss you, too, but this is a business call."

"Okay. How can I help?"

"Remember those papers I got from you last week? Well, I need to get somebody to show me how to figure trip costs for our company airplane. Do you know anybody that could help me with that?"

"There's an aviation company here at the airport that leases planes, and Tom can probably help you. Tell you what. Let me make some calls and call you back. There's a man named Tom Cook, who can probably help you. I'll call him and then I'll call you back."

"You're a jewel. I owe you a kiss for that."

"Just be sure you pay it. You don't want to owe anyone, anything. I'll call you."

"Thanks. I hope he can help me. I don't want to talk to anybody in the company about this just yet."

In about five minutes, Joan called back and said Tom Cook would be glad to help with figuring costs for the airplane flights. She gave Monty Tom's number and told him where to find him.

"Thanks, Sweetie. I'll give him a call. Can I see you tonight? Good, I'll see you then. Bye. I love you. Oops. Did I just say what I think I said? I think we need to talk about this, don't you? I'll see you tonight."

Joan wasn't much good after that. After her conversation with Monty, she was in dreamland and thankfully, Mr. Tomlinson was out of town and couldn't see the shape she was in.

Monty called Tom Cook, and Tom invited him to come to his office whenever he wanted to and Monty asked if he could come right then. He said he could, so Monty gathered up the trip-leases and went straight to the airport. Tom showed him how to figure everything from fuel cost to airport landing fees. When Monty left him, he was pretty much an expert on airplane lease costs.

The next thing he had to do was to try to find out where the money was and how Don got it there. He had graduated with a guy that went to work for his bank after he got out of school, and while he didn't expect him to give him any confidential information, he thought maybe he could help him with some scenarios.

Monty was right about his friend at the bank helping him. After spending about an hour with him, he was pretty sure he knew how Don diverted the money. All he had to do now was find out from some of their customers how they paid for the trip-leases. He didn't have to call East Tennessee Reinforced Concrete; he already knew how they paid for theirs.

When he got back to the office, he began calling some of the companies that had leased the plane within the last five years. His hunch was right. On the leases in question, he found that if the lease was for less than ten thousand dollars, the company would pay with a check made out simply to Shepherd and mailed to a post-office box owned by Don. If it was for more than ten thousand dollars, the lease payment would be made to Shepherd by wire transfer to a routing number and an account number. They thought they were paying Shepherd Apparel, but those numbers were also owned by Don and were at a bank in the Cayman Islands. These were verified by the CFO's of the companies he called. He thought, *Now, what do I do?*

He thought he would think about it overnight and do something tomorrow. In the meantime, he had a date to see a pretty girl. Maybe she could cheer him up. When he went home, after work, Thil said, "Bill, next door, has been transferred, and they're putting their house up for sale. I hate to see them move. Eleanor and I have become such good friends."

"I wonder what they're going to ask for it," Monty asked.

"I don't have any idea, but it's a nice house, and it has a great pool."

Monty had been thinking about getting an apartment, but now that the neighbor's house was going to be for sale, he began to wonder. *I sure would like to have the Martin's house and be close to Mom and Dad, and some day, when I get married, I would already have a place. I wonder what they're going to ask for it. I think I'll go see them tomorrow.*

When he went to Joan's a little later, he couldn't shake the thoughts about the plane leases and he wasn't as outgoing as usual. Joan picked up on it and wanted to know what was wrong, but Monty just said, "Nothing." They had both already eaten, but decided to go get an ice cream cone, just to be together away from the house. Again, Joan asked, "Monty, I can tell something is wrong. Have I done something you don't like?"

"Oh, Heavens no. Right now, you're the only one keeping me sane."

"Won't you tell me about it? It might help if you talk about it."

"Joan, Sweetie, I'm going to tell you something that cannot be told to anyone. I haven't told anyone else yet, so you're the only one who will know it. I'm not going to mention any names right now, but you'll probably guess."

"What would you do if you found out someone very close to you was committing a serious crime? It's not murder, so don't think that. It's something else. I'm the only one who knows about this, and it's extremely serious. If I tell about it, it will ruin the person's life and maybe even send the person to prison for a long time. If I don't tell about it, I will feel like I'm just as guilty for not exposing it. I know what I should do, but I don't know if I can or not. What would you do?"

"I don't see that you have any choice. If you know for sure that a crime is being committed, then you must report it. That's the law."

"I know. I guess I just needed to hear it from someone else. Thank you. Sweetheart, I'm sorry to put you through this. We haven't known each other long enough for you to have to be exposed to my problems. I'm sorry."

"Sorry for what? You told me today that you love me. Well, buddy-boy, I love you, too, and when you love someone, you share the bad as well as the good."

Right there in the ice cream store, Monty leaned over the table and kissed Joan. "Thank you."

After Monty's mood lightened up a little, he asked Joan, "Wanna know what I'm thinking about?"

"What?"

"Do you remember the house next door to where I live?"

She said, "Yes. It's beautiful, why?"

"It's going on the market and I'm thinking about seeing if I can buy it. I've already been thinking about an apartment, but that's a great house, and I'd rather have it than an apartment. I'm gonna try to see if the Martins will let me come over tomorrow and look at it. Would you like to go?"

"Yeah. That's exciting. They have a pool, don't they?"

"A really nice pool. You'd look good lying beside it in a bikini."

"I don't know about that. I feel self-conscience in a bikini. Maybe a one-piece."

"Whatever, but I think you'd look good in any kind. Joanie, would you mind if we cut our time a little short tonight? If I'm going to expose what I was talking about tomorrow, I want to go home and plan my strategy. We'll be together longer tomorrow night, okay?"

"That's okay, but before you go, don't we need to talk about something?"

"What?"

"Today, when you let *I love you* slip out, you said we would need to talk about it. I thought that was tonight, but if you don't want to, that's okay."

"I did say that, and I was prepared to apologize to you for saying it, but when you told me you loved me, I thought I wouldn't have to. I make no apology for loving you. I just didn't want to offend you. I've never told a girl I loved her before, and it's totally new to me, but now that you've said it, too, I guess you're not offended."

"Oh Monty, I would have told you at the Town and

Country on our first date if I hadn't been afraid I would drive you away. You can't imagine how much I love you and this isn't supposed to be, after only knowing each other for only a few days, but I love you."

"What do you suggest we do about it?"

"I don't know. What do you think?"

"I don't know either. I told my mother I was going to marry you, but this might be a little quick."

"Let me say this, David Montgomery Shepherd. It's quick, but whenever you decide to marry, if you decide you want to marry me, I'll be ready."

Monty drove Joan home and kissed her goodnight. On the way to his house, he was filled with mixed emotions. He loved Joan so much that when she told him she loved him, it made things so much better, but then, there was the Don thing. He still didn't know how he was going to go about exposing it and to whom.

He decided to pray about it and turn it over to God to handle.

CHAPTER NINETEEN

Shortly before lunch on Thursday morning, Monty heard Connie, frantically yelling for him to come up front. He ran out of his office and saw Connie and two or three other office employees standing in the doorway to David's office. When Monty went in, he saw David lying on the floor next to his desk. "Connie, call the operator and tell her we need an ambulance immediately. Then call Dr. John Strickland and let me talk to him. Hurry. While you're doing that, I'm going to call my mom."

Before he could call Thil, Connie said, "Monty, the ambulance should be on its way and Dr. Strickland is on line two."

"Thank you. Hello, Dr. Strickland. This is Monty Shepherd. Fine, thank you. Dr. Strickland; my dad is lying unconscious on his office floor right now, and I need your help. An ambulance is on the way, and I hope you can meet it at the hospital. I'm afraid he's had a heart attack. Can you go to the hospital right now? I'll tell the ambulance to go to Erlanger, is that okay? Thank you, Doctor. I'll see you there."

"Hi Mom. Listen, Dad has had some kind of spell and he's going to have to go to the hospital. He's going in just a few minutes, and I'm going to go, too. Can you meet us at Erlanger? . . . Okay. I'll see you there. Love you,"

The ambulance arrived in about ten minutes and the attendants didn't waste any time putting David in it for the ride to the hospital. They did the usual; checking blood pressure, listening to his heart and all the other things as they loaded him into the ambulance. Soon, it was on its way with the siren screaming.

"Connie, when Don gets back, tell him what's happened, and that we're at Erlanger," then Monty ran to his car and followed the ambulance.

Monty arrived at the hospital just as they were rolling David into the Emergency Room, and he couldn't tell if his dad was conscious or not. The hospital staff rolled him to a treatment area and told Monty he would have to wait in a nearby waiting room after he completed the necessary insurance paperwork. Monty didn't have David's insurance card, so he walked back to where his dad was and got his billfold out of his pocket. The ER doctor wasn't happy about his coming back there, but Monty didn't care. He would do whatever he had to do for his dad.

In a few minutes Thil arrived, and she was frantic. "What's wrong, Monty? Is David all right? What happened?"

"Take it easy, Mom. I haven't seen a doctor, yet, but I think he may have had a heart attack. I called Dr. Strickland, and he said he would come on, so I hope he's here. Somebody will probably come out and tell us something pretty soon. Don't worry. These people know what they're doing. They'll have him fixed up in no time."

"I hope you're right. Your father has been working so hard, I've been worried about him."

"Mom, will you excuse me for a minute? I want to call Joan. Do you have any change?"

Thil gave him two dimes, and he found a pay telephone down the hall. "Hey Joan. Whatta ya say? Listen, I'm gonna have to cancel tonight. My dad's in the hospital. He may have had a heart attack. Yeah, I'm here now at Erlanger. I'll probably be here all day. I'll call you later after I know something. Honey, pray for him because it doesn't look very good. Okay? I love you. Bye."

In a little while, Dr. Strickland came to the waiting room and told Thil and Monty, "David has suffered a serious myocardial infarction. In layman's terms, a heart attack. Monty, it was good that you got the ambulance there when you did. He is resting comfortably right now and is doing as well as can be expected. They will be taking him to the Cardiac Care Unit in just a few minutes where we can continually monitor him."

"Can we see him?" Thil asked.

"If they haven't already taken him upstairs, you can see him for just a minute. Come on. I'll walk with you."

David was still in the treatment room, so they got to visit with him for a couple of minutes. He looked at Thil. "Don't worry, honey. It'll take more than this to get me. Tell you what. When I get out of here, we'll go to Florida for a while. How does that sound?"

"It sounds wonderful, but don't try to talk. Just rest."

He looked at Monty. "Son, I hate to leave you guys with so much to do, but old John here, says I'll be out of commission for a while. You know enough to handle the company and I'm putting you in complete charge. You have two good helpers in Tom and Chip, so depend on their guidance and help. We've got a big deal about to happen in two weeks in Europe, and you will have to go over in my place and work with Gerhard. It'll be good experience for you."

Before he could tell Monty anything else, they came to get him to take him upstairs. Tearfully, Thil said, "Bye, darling. I'll see you in a little while."

Monty went to the desk to find out where David would be and the visiting hours. They wouldn't get to see him for three more hours, so they went home. Monty left his car there and would pick it up when he and Thil came back to see his dad.

While they were at home, Don called and Thil answered. "Hey, good-looking, this is Don. I'm at the hospital, and they said you guys left. Are you coming back?"

"Just a minute, Don. I'll let you talk to your brother." Things were still strained between Don and Thil, especially on the part of Thil. She didn't trust him and didn't want to talk to him.

"Hi, Don."

"Hey, little brother. I'm at the hospital. When are you guys coming back? I tried talking with some of these characters, but nobody would tell me anything except that Dad had a heart attack. What happened?"

Monty told him about David having the attack at the office and everything else he knew and told him when he and Thil would be back.

When they got back to the hospital, Joan was there to see how David was and to be with Monty. Monty introduced her to Don who really gave her the *once over,* looking her up and down. She appeared uncomfortable around him, so Monty took her hand and they walked away.

***

David responded well to the treatment and was allowed to go home on Friday, after ten days in Erlanger. Dr. Strickland told David to do very little for a couple weeks. David asked, "When can I go back to work?"

"Oh, let's not talk about going back to work just yet. I want you to stay off for an indefinite period of time. I understand you have two sons who can do your job, so let's let them do it for a while. I would like for you not to return to work for several months. If you would consider retiring, it would be even better. You have a big, comfortable airplane; why don't you and Thil go to your place in Florida for a couple of months." David didn't want to hear all that kind of talk, but he trusted Dr. Strickland and would do what he said.

Monty had filled in for his dad at the company and with Tom's and Chip's help, things were running smoothly. He would have to leave Monday for Munich to work with Gerhard and Bruno on landing a huge account in France on Wednesday.

With all that had been going on for the past ten days, Monty never did have a chance to look at the Martin's house next door. When they got home from the hospital Friday afternoon, he saw the Martins outside on the patio. He went over and talked with them, briefly, and then said he would like to see the house, inside, but wanted his girlfriend to see it, too. They said, "fine." Monty went in and called Joan. In about forty-five minutes, she arrived, and they accompanied the Martins through the house. It was lovely.

Monty and Mr. Martin talked about the price, and Mr. Martin told him he hadn't given it to a realtor yet, and that would make the price much cheaper than it would be if a realtor had it. Monty had grown up next door and was used to seeing it every day, but he never thought about it in terms of maybe, someday, owning it. He had been inside several times, over the years, but couldn't describe anything about the interior, except for the door opening out to the pool. He told Mr. Martin he would think and talk about it and get back to him, later.

As he walked back home, he told Joan, "If I can swing it, I think I'm going to buy that house. What do you think?"

"I think it's out of my class. I don't know why anyone wouldn't want a beautiful place like that. Do you really think you'll buy it?"

"Yeah, I really do. I'm going in and see if Dad feels like talking. I'd like to get his advice because he's a pretty wise feller."

David and Monty talked at length about the house and after a while, David gave his blessings. That's all Monty needed. He and Joan went back over to the Martins, and Monty told them he would buy the house. They shook on it, and Monty said he would be out of town the next week and asked Mr. Martin if he could bring the earnest money when he got back. Mr. Martin said he could. Then Monty said, "I have a better idea: I'll borrow the money from my dad and pay him back when I get home."

Mr. Martin said, "Any way you want to handle it, Monty, will be all right with us."

Monty wanted to be sure the house didn't get away while he was gone, so he borrowed the earnest money from David and sealed the deal with the Martins.

Friday night, Monty and Joan went out for a good meal to celebrate his buying the house. "I'm really going to miss you while you're gone," Joan told him.

"Not half as much as I'll miss you. I wish you could go with me, but I know you can't. If Mom was going, you could, or if we were married." His words trailed off. "There I go again." He just sat there and stared, smiling at Joan. He reached over and took her hand and kissed it. "Look, we've still got two days until I have to leave, so let's make the most of them, okay?"

"Okay."

By the time they finished dinner, it was late, so Monty took Joan home. "I have to go to the office for a while in the morning, so it might be around noon before I can call you. Be deciding what you would like to do tomorrow afternoon and tomorrow night and we'll do it."

"I already know what I want to do tomorrow night."

"What?"

"I'd like to go back to Tom Thumb and play golf."

"I don't know why. I beat you twice the last time we went. Why would you want to be humiliated again?"

"I'll do better next time. Besides, you liked collecting for your bet, didn't you?"

"Yes, I did. Why don't we double it this time?"

"Sounds good to me."

They kissed goodnight and Monty went home.

The rest of the weekend flew by and time for Monty to leave was getting closer. He wished his Dad was well, so he could go instead of him, but if he was going to someday take over the reins of Shepherd Global, he would have to get used to sacrificing his own desires, occasionally.

***

At six p.m. Monday, the 707 with Monty on board took off

from Lovell field on its way to Munich, Germany. Monty had been there before, but hadn't traveled on the company plane by himself. It was pretty lonesome sitting there alone. A few months ago, David had equipment installed that let them play movies on flights. One movie that Monty hadn't seen, but wanted to see was *The Dirty Dozen* and it happened to be one that was available, so he figured out how to play it and sat back and watched Lee Marvin whip those convicted prisoners into shape.

Dinner and breakfast had been catered for Monty and the crew, and the co-pilot came back and ate and watched the movie with him. Later, the pilot and flight engineer came back. When everybody had finished eating, Monty went up to the flight deck and spent quite a bit of time with the crew and enjoyed it thoroughly. Around ten o'clock, he went to bed and slept like a log. When he awoke, they were getting close to Munich. The engineer had made a pot of coffee, and Monty had that and a pastry for breakfast.

Meanwhile, back at the Shepherd office, things were getting ready to take a strange turn.

Connie noticed Don carrying things into David's office. These were not the normal things one would take into someone else's office. There were pictures, a desk set, and a solitaire board game. She asked, "Moving, Don?"

"Yep. I'm moving into Dad's office since he won't be coming back."

"I didn't know he wasn't coming back," Connie said.

"That's what the doctor said. He told Pop to retire."

Don called Tom and Chip into David's office and told them that he was the new head of Shepherd Global Apparel since his dad wouldn't be back, and hoped they would continue to work for him the way they did his dad. When he told them he was the new head man, they looked at each other, puzzled.

When Monty got to the office in Munich, it was four-thirty, Chattanooga time. He told Marlene to call the office and was shocked when Connie told him that Don had installed himself as the new head of Shepherd Apparel.

"Let me speak to Don, Connie."

"I can't, Monty. He has already gone for the day."

"Connie, call my mother and tell her I'm going to be calling her in the next few minutes and to be sure and be home when the call comes through."

The call home took a remarkably short time to go through. "Hello, Mom, how're you doing?. . .How's Dad?. . . Listen, Mom, I don't know if you want to tell Dad about this or not, but I just got the shock of my life. I called the office, and Connie told me that Don had moved into Dad's office and said he was the new head of Shepherd Apparel since Dad wouldn't be back. Is Dad not coming back, Mom?"

"Don had meetings with Tom and Chip and I don't know who else, and he told them all he was taking over the top spot in the company. I hope Dad feels well enough to hear this because I think he should know. Look, Mom, if you think he's okay to hear this, tell him and call me back. Also, Mom, would you please call Connie and tell her to have Don call me here, Thursday, at three o'clock, your time."

"I'll tell this to your Dad. He's feeling pretty good today, and I'll call Connie for you."

"Thanks, Mom. I'll talk to you later. Love you."

Due to the size of the airport in the small town where the potential customer was located, they couldn't fly the 707, so Bruno, Gerhard, and Monty piled into Bruno's car and headed for France. They had a six hour drive ahead of them. Monty wanted to talk to Joan, but didn't know how to call her from France unless Gerhard or Bruno knew how to do it. They reached their destination and checked into a nice little hotel. Monty, of course, couldn't speak a word of French. He was just glad one of his companions could. As it turned out, the hotel clerk spoke very good English and that made things easier for him. The next morning, he would have the hotel clerk place the call to Joan.

Monty had been used to seeing large orders, but nothing

like they wrote for that French customer. The customer not only put in the Shepherd Staff line, they placed orders for all two hundred-twenty stores in their chain. That was a gargantuan order. He couldn't wait to tell David.

Bruno and Gerhard credited Monty with clinching the deal for them. He had pointed out several facts to the buyer about the Staff line with which they weren't familiar, and that made the difference. They were certainly going to pass that on to David when they talked to him.

It was going to take most of the night to finish writing the orders, so it was necessary that they stay in France one more night. They checked back in the little hotel and immediately went to bed. Bruno and Gerhard shared a room, but Monty had his own. While he was lying there, thinking about their successful day, he looked at his watch and it was one a.m.. That was seven a.m. at home. He jumped up, put his clothes back on, and went to the front desk and asked the clerk if he would place an overseas call for him. The clerk was very helpful and in just a couple minutes, he heard on the other end, "Hello."

"Joanie. Hi honey. I was afraid you might have already left for work. I've been dying to talk to you."

"I have you, too. Are you having a good trip?"

"You wouldn't believe how much business we did today. I can't wait to tell Dad. How're you doing?"

"I'm fine. I'm going to see your Dad when I get off work this afternoon. I called yesterday and your Mom said he was feeling pretty good. She said he's getting ornery because he can't go to work, but she's working on him."

"Well, Sweetie, I won't keep you. I just wanted to hear your voice. Have a good day and I'll try to call again when I can. Listen, I'm going to tell our flight crew to be ready to take off at seven o'clock Friday morning, and that will put us in Chattanooga around ten, Friday night. Wanna meet me?"

"I'd love to meet you. I'll see you then."

"I love you."

"Love you, too. Bye."

Talking to Joan was just what Monty needed to top off a nearly perfect day. He went to bed and slept like a baby.

The next morning, they took the orders to the buyer for signatures and by the time they left, it was almost noon. They grabbed a quick bite and hit the road to go back to Munich. Gerhard and Bruno were already friends, but spending nearly two days in the car with them made Monty a friend as well. They both enjoyed him and hoped he would be back to work with them again soon.

They didn't arrive back in Munich until around six o'clock Thursday night, so if Don called, Monty missed him. Since he was leaving the next morning, he would just wait until he got home to talk to him, and he was loaded for bear. *Don will wish he had never seen his little brother.*

When Monty got back to the apartment, he called his pilot and told him to be ready to take off at seven o'clock. He wanted to get home in time to see his girl, tomorrow night. "Yes sir," the pilot said. "We'll leave earlier if you want to."

"Naw. I think seven is early enough."

The pilot immediately arranged to have food catered for the next morning and to have it there by six o'clock. They would need three meals for four people plus snacks and drinks.

At exactly seven o'clock, wheels were up, and Monty was on his way home. The flight engineer had made a pot of coffee prior to takeoff and as soon as they got to altitude, Monty poured himself a cup and sat back and enjoyed it. *This would be perfect if Joan was sitting here beside me,* he thought.

Almost exactly at ten o'clock they landed at Lovell field, and before they stopped taxiing, Monty saw Joan's car. He could hardly wait for them to open the door and let him out. When he finally did get out, he ran down the steps, grabbed Joan, and kissed her like he hadn't seen her in months instead of five days. He said, "I'm not leaving again without you. Is that clear?"

"That's clear."

They went to a drive-in and got a burger and Coke and talked for a while, then, Joan took him home.

"Are we going to see each other tomorrow?" he asked.

"I hope so. What do you want to do?"

"Be with you, mainly. I need to spend some time talking with Dad, but you can be there for that. Tomorrow night, we'll go to a movie or something; whatever you'd like to do. Tell you what. I just had an idea. Let's take your mother and daddy to the Town and Country. Do they like the Town and Country?"

"They love it. Are you sure you want to do that?"

"I'm sure, unless you don't want to."

"I want to. I think you're wonderful for wanting to."

"Okay then. It's a double date."

They kissed goodnight, and Joan went home.

Monty didn't realize how much fun Joan's parents were. They went to the Town and Country and had a ball. Charles was full of jokes and kept everyone at the table laughing all evening. Kathleen was fun, too. She wasn't as outgoing as Charles, but when she said something, it was usually something funny. They all had a good time and promised to do it again soon.

After dinner, Monty and Joan drove her parents' home, and for lack of something better to do, they stayed there and sat on the porch while Monty told Joan about his trip. They fit together like a hand in a glove, and Monty was convinced that Joan was meant to be his. He loved her so much, and she loved him.

In a little while, he said he needed to be going, so he kissed her goodbye and got up to go home. Before he left, he asked, "Who's Church are we going to in the morning?"

"Let's go to yours, want to?"

"I'll pick you up at ten-thirty. Night night"

On the way home, Monty began dreading Monday morning. He knew it was going to be unpleasant confronting Don, and he wasn't sure just how much to reveal to him about what he knew about the embezzling. On the other side of the coin, he could hardly wait to see Charles Crawford and tell him about the success they had in France. Monday was going to be an interesting day.

The Church service was very good the next morning, and afterwards, Rev. Nathan Fowler told them how happy he was to see them there. He asked Monty about his dad and asked if he could come by the office sometime to talk to him, Monty said, "Sure, anytime."

They left Church and went to Fehn's for lunch. While there, they saw several people they knew, and it took forever to get finished. From there, they went to Joan's, so she could change clothes, then, to Monty's for the afternoon. They took a blanket down to the water's edge and spread it out. They lay on the blanket for a long time talking about Monty's house, Joan's job and about a hundred other things.

When they got back to the house, Thil asked Monty if he would like to start a fire in the grill and cook some burgers for dinner. He and Joan both said that sounded good, so that's what they did. David ate as if he hadn't eaten in days, and his coloring was good. That encouraged Monty, and he was glad they did that for dinner.

CHAPTER TWENTY

Everyone was on edge when Monty arrived at the office Monday morning. He spoke to Connie when he passed her desk and told her to call everyone involved in the Monday staff meeting and postpone it until after lunch. He told her to call him when Don got in. He said he would probably be in Charles Crawford's office if he wasn't in his.

Even though Charles was Sales Manager, he didn't have anything to do with the overseas sales, but Monty liked him and felt comfortable with him and wanted to share his successful trip to France with him. They talked for a while and then went to the break-room to get coffee. While in the break-room, Monty was paged. He picked up the phone, and Connie said, "Monty, Don just came in."

"Thank you Connie. I'll be up there in a minute."

Monty told Charles he had to go do something and excused himself and went to his office to get some papers. When he had what he needed, he headed to his Dad's office, and as he passed by Connie's desk, he said, "Connie, I'll be with Don for a while. Please don't put any calls through unless it's an emergency, okay?" He walked into David's office and shut the door behind him.

"Hey, little brother. What brings you in here so early in the morning without knocking?"

"I would have knocked if Dad was here, since this is his office, but since he's not here, I didn't need to knock."

"What do you want?"

"I hear you've promoted yourself to head of the company."

"That's right. Since Dad won't be back, someone has to step up and take the reins, and since I'm about the oldest employee, in terms of service, it's only logical that I do it. Do you object to that?"

"You might say so."

"What's your objection?"

"Well, first of all, I'm wondering how you're going to run this huge company from a jail cell."

"Jail cell. What are you talking about?"

"You're still on probation from that hit and run thing, aren't you?"

"Yeah, but that doesn't have anything to do with running the company."

"No, but this does." Monty laid out some of the papers on the desk showing the discrepancies in the airplane trip-leases. "I don't have the exact totals, yet, but it looks like you've embezzled more than 300,000 dollars over the last five years."

As the color drained from Don's face, he asked, "Where did you come up with that?"

"Remember when that lady called me and thought she was talking to you about making out a check to you for plane rental instead of the company? That made me start thinking, so I did some checking and found that you have been stealing from our Dad all this time."

"I didn't just pull some figures out of the air. I reconciled bank deposits with trip-leases and even called some of the customers. I found out that you had set up a bank account in the Caymans and had the money wire-transferred down there. The wires went to Shepherd with your routing and account numbers, so the customers had no idea they were sending their money to your account. Occasionally, on charges of less than ten-thousand dollars, you would have them send a check to your post office box made out to simply *Shepherd.* You could cash those without the IRS getting involved. And oh yes, big brother. I almost forgot. About a year ago, while Mom and Dad were in Florida, you and a group of your friends took the plane to Cabo San Lucas for five days. Apparently, the company paid for everything; hotel, food, entertainment, everything. Don, that trip cost Shepherd Apparel over forty-thousand dollars and that's not even in the 300,000 dollar figure that I mentioned. How could you do that to your own father?

Don's hands were trembling and he asked, "Have you said anything to Dad?"

"No. Not yet"

"Little brother, please don't say anything to him. It'll kill him."

"I know. That's why I haven't told anybody yet, but this has got to be reported to somebody. If I don't report it, I can be charged as an accessory and I'm surely not going to let that happen. Do you still have the money?"

"A little bit."

"Where did it all get to?"

"Bookie's got most of it."

"You mean you gambled away more than a quarter of a million dollars?"

Don began to cry. "What are you going to do?"

"You're my brother, Don, and I love you, even though you are an arrogant, obnoxious sump hole. I have looked up to you ever since I was a baby. Can you possibly know in your warped mind how much this has hurt me? Well, big brother, it has hurt me bad, but I'm sure that doesn't matter to you."

"When Dad had his heart attack, he told me he was putting me in complete charge of the company and for me to work closely with Tom Ratcliff and Chip Lowe, and that's what I intend to do. Now, if I'm head of the company, I have the power to hire and fire and you need to be fired in the worst way. Dad's fired you before, but felt sorry for you and brought you back, but big brother, this time, things are different."

"So, here's what I think we'll do. To keep you out of prison, I'm going to let you pay back the money you stole. You can keep your job, leasing the plane, but there will be tight controls attached to it, and I'm going to have five hundred dollars per week deducted from your paycheck. You might not live long enough to pay it all back, but at least some of it will be returned. Now, you have a choice. Either accept my offer, and keep Dad from finding out about it or face the charges that will be filed when I turn it over to the police. I think I know what you'll choose, but it's your choice."

"Monty, I'll take you up on your offer, and thank you for not telling Dad. I appreciate that. I've already hurt him too many times."

"Now, to save you a little bit of embarrassment, wait until after everybody leaves this afternoon, then, move all this stuff back to your office."

"Monty, thank you so much." Don came around the desk and put his arms around him and sobbed for a long time.

"Now, Don. There's more. As I said earlier, this has got to be reported to somebody because a serious crime has been committed. I thought about this all the way to Europe and back, and this is what I'm going to do. Since Dad said he is putting me in complete charge of the company, I'm going to see if he will officially make me the CEO. As CEO I will have more power and leeway to do things. If he will do that, then I will report the crime to Sam, our CFO, and tell him I worked it out where you will pay the company back in exchange for our not pressing charges. He will see to it that the money is deducted from your check each week. That's the only way I can think of to handle the situation. Do you know of anything any better?"

"No, I can't think of anything better. I knew you were smart, but I guess I thought I was smarter. I see I was wrong."

"I'll talk to Dad tonight about the CEO thing and let you know what he says."

"Thanks again, Monty. Your loyalty to family is very impressive and much appreciated."

Monty left David's office and returned to his own. He felt as if a huge load had been lifted off his shoulders. He picked up the phone and called Joan. "Hi Sweetie. Can you talk?"

"Hi, good-looking. Yeah, I can talk for a minute."

"You know that problem I told you about? Well, I just exposed it, and I think everything is going to be worked out satisfactorily. I feel good about it and just wanted to call and tell you."

"We'll have to celebrate tonight."

"That sounds good. There's something I want to talk to you about, too."

"What are we going to do, so I'll know how to dress?"

"Let's go somewhere and eat and then drive out to the lake and watch the moon come up."

"What's your name, Roy Romantic?"

"You've got that right, and don't you forget it. I'll pick you up at six-thirty. Bye, smartie."

Laughing, Joan said, "Bye."

Monty was finding out that in a large business, it's really hard to wear several hats. Before today, he just wore the hat of a salesman, but now, he's wearing the hat of an executive in addition to that, and it's much harder than he thought it would be. In addition to the staff meeting, he had three other meetings after lunch; then, the day ended. Before he left, he went by Don's office, stuck his head in the door and asked, "Are you okay?"

Don said he was, so Monty left for home.

He got to Joan's at six-thirty and when Mrs. Murray came to the door, he smiled and said, "Tell Joan that Roy Romantic is here."

She smiled, and he could hear her tell that to Joan when she went to get her.

They decided to go to Shoney's on Highway 58 to eat as it was on the way to the lake. They talked as they ate and then went to a special place that Monty knew about up close to Harrison Bay. He had thought to bring the blanket they used for their picnic, and they spread it out to wait on the moon to rise. It was very relaxing, and in a few minutes, Joan said, "I thought you had something you wanted to talk to me about."

"I do, but I can't talk until the moon comes up. It'll be up soon. Then I'll tell you. It'll be a surprise. Oh, I forgot to tell you, I'm going to the bank and apply for the loan for the house, tomorrow."

"Really? How long will it take to get approved?"

"I'm not sure. I hope not long."

Monty brought a radio and turned on some easy listening music, and it was starting to get dark. In a few minutes, the moon began to make an appearance, and Monty turned the music down a little. Joan, what I wanted to talk to you about is us. I nearly went crazy last week without being with you, and I don't want to do that again. I love you with all my heart and want you to be my wife. Will you marry me, Joan? Please say yes, because I'll just jump in the lake and drown if you say no."

"Monty, do you remember our first date, when we went to the Town and Country? Well, if you had asked me to marry you that night, I would have said yes. I love you deeply, Monty and can't wait to be your wife."

They kissed and must have held it for a full minute. Man, what a kiss.

"Do you want to go tell your folks?"

"Let's do. They love you, too, Monty. The only thing they might say is something about how quick we've done this, but they'll be happy for us. I know they will."

When they got to Joan's house, they went in and told Charles and Kathleen they had something to tell them. Joan said, "You tell them."

Monty began with how the time frame was short, but knowing how much they had in common and how much they loved each other, they both thought it was only right that they get married. "So, tonight, I asked Joan to marry me and she said, "Yes."

"Yea! We're happy for you. Monty, we liked you the first time you came to pick up Joan. I told Kathleen, "Kathleen, that boy would make a good husband for our Joan. Like you said, the time frame has been short, but we have already grown to love you." He shook hands with Monty, and Kathleen gave him a big hug. "Kathleen, do you still have some of that brandy. If you do, get it and we'll toast the newly engaged couple."

She found the bottle with just a little bit in it. She poured maybe a sip in each glass and they drank a toast. Monty was sure he had found the right in-laws, too.

"Do you think it's too late to go tell your parents tonight?"

"I'm afraid it is. Dad goes to sleep really early since his heart attack. Tell you what. I won't say anything tonight, and we'll tell them tomorrow night. They're going to be so happy. You're all my mother talks about."

"I love her, too."

"Oh yeah, Kathleen and Charles, I'm buying a house, so I'll have a place for your little girl to live."

"It's beautiful, Mama. I can't wait for you to see it."

Charles said, "It looks like everything is falling into place for you two. I'm happy for you, and Monty, I'm going to be very proud to have you as my son-in-law."

"Thank you, Charles. I already love you guys. Well, I've already done as much damage to your family as I can do for one night, so I had better go home. I'll see you soon. Good night."

Joan walked him to his car. They kissed goodnight and told each other how much in love they were, and Monty left to go home.

As soon as David got up the next morning, Monty poured them both a cup of coffee and said he wanted to talk to him. David listened as Monty explained to him that if he was to be the acting head of Shepherd Apparel, he needed the title to go with it. Without it, his authority would be limited.

David immediately understood and said, "You're right, Son. You need the title and here's what I'll do. I'll make you President of Shepherd Global Apparel Group, but I'll retain the position of CEO. That way, you'll have all the authority you need, and I can step in sometimes, if I need to. How does that sound to you?"

"It sounds good, Dad. That's all I need. I think I'll call our key people together this morning and make the announcement."

"That's a good idea. I'll be interested in their reactions."

That move cleared the way for Monty to implement his plan with Don, and he would take Sam, their CFO, to lunch and go over it with him.

He called all the key people together soon after he got to work and told them that he was their new President. He got a standing round of applause. He had hoped they would accept him, but he had no idea they felt the way they did. He was humbled and promised to do the best job he knew how. As the meeting was breaking up, he caught Sam Armstrong and told him he wanted them to have lunch together. He had something he wanted to talk to him about.

In between the meeting and lunchtime, Monty ran to the mortgage lender to apply for a loan for his house. When he talked to the man, he was bowled over when he saw that Monty was President of Shepherd Apparel. He even asked him, "Do you think that will be enough?" When Monty asked how long it would take to get approval, the man said about a week.

Monty and Sam had lunch at Tomlinson's where it was quiet, and Monty went over the whole story about Don's indiscretions and told him his plan. Sam didn't like it, and thought Don should be reported to the police, but Monty was very persuasive, and Sam finally agreed that his plan might work. Monty swore him to secrecy, and when they finished eating, they went back to the office.

Monty called Don in and told him he thought he had things worked out and to relax. Don thanked him and apologized. Monty said, "Don, you're family and this is the way families work, but I've got to tell you something. If I get wind of you doing anything, anything wrong, I'm not only going to report the embezzlement, I'm going to kick your butt up so far, you'll be able to wear it for a hat. Do we understand each other?"

"I understand. Thank you again. I won't let you down."

When Don left, Monty called Joan. "Hi, sweet lady. I won't keep you. I was just wondering if you could drive over to the house after work. You know, we're going to tell my folks about our plans, and if we tell them early enough, maybe they'll go out to eat with us. Also, just in case you'd like to know, you're now engaged to the President of Shepherd Global Apparel Group. How impressive is that?"

"Ho-hum."

"Did you say ho-hum? Just wait till I get my hands on you. I'll teach you ho-hum."

"You know I was kidding. I think that's wonderful. We need to celebrate that as well as our engagement."

"I know. Hurry over when you get off. Love you."

Joan was so *at home* with Monty's folks she didn't have to knock; she just walked in. Thil was in the kitchen preparing something, and when she saw Joan, she spoke and talked for a minute; then, she said, "Monty's upstairs on the balcony. Go on up."

When she reached the balcony, she saw Monty and David. David saw her first and said, "Come on out, Sweetie."

Monty got up and went over to her and kissed her on the cheek. "Hi, pretty lady. How're you doing?"

"I'm fine and I know you are."

"Sit over here. Let me call Mom. Mom, can you come up here, please?"

Thil came out and asked, "What do you need, Monty?"

"Mom, sit down for a minute, will you? Joan and I want to tell you and Dad something. Joan, do you want to tell them?"

"No. You go ahead."

"Well, I got home too late to tell you last night, but last night I asked Joan to marry me and she said yes."

Thil gave out one of her *trademark* squeals and David almost yelled, "That's great."

Composing herself, Thil wanted to hear all about it as did David, so Joan related how Monty took her out to a very romantic spot on the lake, and proposed to soft music as the moon came up.

Thil said, "I can't believe my son is that romantic. That

sounds like something his father would do," then she walked over and gave David a kiss. She told Monty and Joan, "I'm very happy for you."

David said he was happy for them, too. Thil asked if they knew when the wedding would be, and they told her they hadn't had time to think about it, but they wanted to have it as soon as possible. Joan did say she wanted to have it at her Church, and have her preacher perform the ceremony.

After the initial celebration, things settled back down, and Thil said she was fixing a meatloaf and had plenty if they would like to stay and eat. Joan said she loved meatloaf, and told Monty she would like to stay.

She wondered if they ate meatloaf in Germany because this was really good. They had the best time sitting around the table talking while they ate. In a few minutes, David said he was wondering where they were going for their honeymoon. "I don't guess we've even thought about a honeymoon, Dad."

"Well, think about this. How would you like for your Mother and me to send you to Hawaii? You can take the company plane, and all expenses will be paid. That should make a pretty nice honeymoon."

"I'll say. Joanie, would you like to go to Hawaii?"

"All my life, I've dreamed of going over there, but never thought I would ever get to. Yes, yes, I would love to go. Thank you so much." She went over and hugged them both.

"Dad, I don't see how we could take the company plane on a personal trip like that without paying for it."

"That's one of the privileges of being a CEO. I can override the President if I want to."

"Well, thank you very much. That's going to be a wonderful honeymoon."

In a little bit, Monty yelled, "Man." Then he said, "You know what? I asked you to marry me and didn't even give you a ring. I can't believe I did that."

Joan said, "I don't need a ring. I've got you."

"Well, you're going to have a ring. Tell Mr. Tomlinson you

want to get off at three o'clock tomorrow. I'm going to pick you up, and we're going to buy you a ring. Man, what a dummy I am."

***

The happy couple thought if they set their wedding date for six months after they became engaged, there would be plenty of time to get everything done, but they were wrong. Just about the entire six months had been a madhouse. Monty had to spend a week overseas every month and Joan had three showers. Between picking out dishes, silver, and other things, planning the wedding, and working, it was time for the wedding.

The Church was decorated, but not overly so. Joan and Monty both liked simplicity rather than gaudy. Joan had four attendants and Monty had four groomsmen. Joan's sister-in-law acted as maid of honor and David was best man. The crowd was not huge because they didn't invite that many people, but the Church was almost full.

The ceremony was pretty traditional and the music was very pretty. After the ceremony, the wedding party gathered in the sanctuary for pictures, and then everyone went to the fellowship hall for the reception. Since Joan and Monty hadn't known each other very long, she didn't know many of his friends, and he didn't know many of hers, so it was a night with many introductions.

Around nine-thirty, the crowd thinned out, so Joan excused herself and went into the rest room to change out of her wedding gown. Monty had already decided he would wait and change on the plane. He had told the pilot to plan on *wheels up* at ten-thirty. Their luggage was already on the plane, so all they had to do was board and take off.

There was time to kill before they had to leave for the airport, so they stayed and visited with their parents. It was gratifying to see how much at ease both sets of parents were with each other. A little before ten, Charles and Kathleen kissed the newlyweds goodbye and left.

David and Thil drove them to the airport and pulled up right to the steps of the plane. They all hugged and kissed and wished the newlyweds a good trip and happy honeymoon. Joan and Monty climbed the stairs to the plane and turned around and waved to Thil and David. When they walked into the interior of the plane, Don had had three bouquets of red roses placed around the cabin along with a chilled bottle of French champagne. Monty thought, *Don, that old rascal. You just can't tell what he's going to do next.*

There was still fifteen minutes before takeoff, so Monty went into the bedroom and changed clothes. He came back out and showed Joan around the plane. She couldn't believe they were going on their honeymoon in something so lavish. The pilot announced they were preparing for takeoff, so the newlyweds sat down, buckled up, and got ready for the trip. It was going be the beginning of a fairy-tale life for a fairy-tale couple.

Also available from Second Wind Publishing
By Bud Fussell

In his first novel, Bud Fussell has penned an epic: a struggle between two very different brothers; a pioneer man of the early 19th century building a family and an empire; a troubled soul far from home encountering travel and grace. Jake is the Scoundrel, an unforgettable character living out a saga that remains in the reader's mind and heart long after the book is finished.